Looking for a City

By Jeffrey Lindgren

A work of fiction

inspired by actual events

LOOKING FOR A CITY:

A work of fiction inspired by actual events

CreateSpace

ISBN-13:
978-1722035099

ISBN-10:
1722035099

This book is dedicated to all those who strive to make the world a better place, not just for themselves, but for all.

LOOKING FOR A CITY: CHAPTER OUTLINE

Chapter 1

St. Louis; May, 1976

"Attention, please. Attention, everyone." The man shouted over the noisy crowd that filled the house. "Please, everyone. I wish to offer a toast to the memory of our dear friend, Rose Russo." Slowly, the noise quieted down, and people turned to look at Angelo DiMartini, a short, stocky man looking uncomfortable in an ill-fitting brown suit, his green tie awkwardly askew. He struggled to get out each word, but spoke with deep emotion.

"I want to say to the family of Rose Russo, that I would not be here today if it were not for that saintly woman. You know, people who didn't know her, all they saw was that woman who acted so hard and tough on the outside. But underneath she had a heart of gold," he said, tapping his left fist on his chest. "So many times my family had nothing to eat, and Rose," -- now he did tear up, so that it was hard for him to speak -- "Rose filled up bags of produce from her truck farm -- produce that she needed to sell to make a living for her own family -- and she gave it, (sob) gave it to the DiMartini family. And I know that we were not the only ones she helped. And Rose," he said as he looked up to the ceiling and raised his glass, "I thank God for you, Rose, and I know the good Lord has a special place for you, 'cause you've got a special place in my heart. To Rose."

Glasses of Asti Spumante or chianti, or bottles of beer were lifted up to toasts of "To mama" or "To grandma" or "To aunty" or "To Rose."

"Thank you, Angelo," said Lucia Russo, Rose's daughter-in-law and hostess of the gathering. "That was lovely. And now, *manga, manga*. You know grandma Rose would want you all to fill up your plates at least twice, not just pick at your food like birds." Lucia Russo looked out with love and pride at the crowd of neighbors and the vast extended family that filled her modest home in the St. Louis neighborhood commonly known as "The Hill." The Italian families that largely populated the community were justly proud of their numerous restaurants, gelato shops, sausage and pasta makers, and especially the fact that Yogi Berra and Joe Garagiola had grown up on the same block right there in their neighborhood. Extended family and neighbors had all come by after the funeral service at St. Anthony's for Lucia's mother-in-law, Rose Russo.

Lucia scanned the crowd as well as she could -- since they spilled over from the living and dining rooms onto the back porch, down into the basement, and out onto the small front and back yard lawns. She spied a young woman in her 20's -- long black hair and dark eyes that contrasted noticeably with her fair skin -- who was smiling broadly and talking animatedly (as much with her hands as her mouth) to a group of cousins gathered in a corner of the living room.

"Frances Marie, get over here," she called out. Franny, as she was more commonly called, told the others she'd be right back, and worked her way over to her Aunt Lucy. "Yeah, what is it Aunty?"

"Look at your cousin, Marco," she said, pointing to a young man who had commandeered a comfortable looking chair in the living room. "He's just sitting there by himself, no food or nothin', not talking to nobody. I know he loved his grandmother, but it ain't right. You're his favorite cousin. Why don't you do something to cheer him up?"

"Oh, he's probably just upset because the Eagles are having such a bad season," said Franny.

"The Eagles? Since when does he root for a Philadelphia team?"

"Not those Eagles, Aunt Lucy. Marco's a player-coach for that semi-pro team, the East Central Missouri Eagles, or something like that. You know he always loved football. But yeah, I don't get to see him much now that I'm up in Chicago. Help me get a plate of food together, and I'll bring it over to him."

After filling up a paper plate from the vast quantities of food that took up every inch of the dining room table, which had been extended by two extra leaves for the occasion, Franny worked her way over to Marco, and got his attention by waving the food right in front of his nose. "Hey Marco, you look like you need something to bring you back to the land of the living," she said.

Marco looked up with a big smile. "Hey, Franny, how's my favorite cousin? Come on, sit down here." He took the food from her as she sat next to him on the arm of the lounge chair. "I hear you're taking them by storm up in the Windy City. What do you call that school you're going to again?"

"University of Illinois, Chicago Circle Campus. One of the things I like about it is that it's right in this great Italian neighborhood. Makes me feel right at home. You should come up and visit sometime. I'll show you around town. But listen, Marco, what's with you? I thought you were glad to be over your hitch in the military. I know you'll miss grandma Rose, like everybody here, but I get the feeling that there's more going on with you than just that."

"Yeah. Well, you know, Fran, I was just thinking about how I always wanted to ask her about something she said to me once when I was just a little kid, and it's always bugged me. But now it's too late. You know, there are so many things about our family that are just a mystery to me, and

I'd really like to know more about it, but nobody ever talks about it. Know what I mean?"

"Well, Marco, you come to the right place. I've got everything you need to know about grandma Rose. I've got her recipes for lasagna, pasta *fagiole*, meatballs, toasted ravioli, spaghetti sauce, gnocchi, and my personal favorite, stuffed shells. What more could you ask for?" As Franny spoke, she picked a pepperoncini off of Marco's plate, stuffed it into her mouth, and began chewing it with relish.

Marco laughed and said, "All of them are priceless, I'm sure, but don't you ever wonder about some of our family history? Some things just don't make sense."

"Trust me, you don't want to know. Just be happy you've got such gorgeous and intelligent cousins."

"Oh, I am, Franny. Believe me, I am."

"But you know, if you really do want to know all that stuff, why don't you just ask Uncle John? He probably knows all of the sordid details."

"You know, that's a good idea. I think I will."

"By the way, Marco. I hear you're heading up to college in the Chicago area too. Never heard of the school though."

"Yeah, Trinity's just a small college, mostly for teachers. But they showed the great wisdom of offering me a football scholarship. Who could argue with that?"

"Not I, that's for sure," answered Franny. "But say, if you're planning to head up that way soon, I could sure use a ride. Trains and busses between the Lou and Chi Town ain't what they used to be."

"I'd love to, Franny. I'll be heading up there next week. We've got a lot of catching up to do."

"Great!" she answered. "I'll give you a call."

When Franny returned to the group in the corner, Marco got up with his still half full plate, and wandered around the crowd until he found his Uncle John sitting on the back porch with a fat, unlit cigar in his mouth. John motioned to an empty chair next to him and said, "Marco, Marco, come on over here and put a load on your brain while I pour you a glass of Spumante." John leaned over to reach the bottle on the table, and poured off a glass for each of them. He took the cigar out of his mouth and placed it on the table, then clinked his glass to Marco's, saying, "To my mother and your grandma Rose -- tough as nails on the outside, with a heart of gold underneath."

Marco replied, "To grandma Rose," and they both took a good swig of the clear, bubbly wine. Asti Spumante had always been too sweet for Marco's taste, but on this occasion it seemed the proper wine for a toast to his grandmother.

After a moment of silence, Marco said, "You know, Uncle John, I still remember something that happened one time when we went to visit my grandfather's grave at the cemetery. I was just 4 or 5 years old at the time, but I still remember it. We were just leaving the graveside and started walking back to the car, when grandma Rose came up to me, and she put her hands on my shoulders, and she looked me in the eye. She looked at me so hard and serious that I thought she was looking right into my brain, and I was afraid she was mad at me for something. She just stared at me real hard and then she said something that has puzzled me all of my life. I've never been able to make sense of it. She said, 'Marco, don't you ever let nobody tell you that's not your grandfather buried there.' I've never been able to figure out what that was all about, and it's bothered me my whole life, just like a lot of things about our family have never made sense to me. Uncle John, can you help me out here?"

John waved his hand in dismissal. "Who knows? Probably didn't mean a thing. You know, sometimes she just said stuff. Forget about it."

Marco looked hard at his uncle until John got uncomfortable and turned to look out of the window. Then he said.

"So if it didn't mean anything, explain this to me. Why is it that the tombstone over those two graves did not say 'Rose and Pietro Russo'? They said 'Rose and **Joseph** Russo'."

John put his Spumante back on the table, picked up his cigar, struck a match, lit up, took a big drag, and turned to blow the smoke thru the window screen behind him. "You sure you want to know?" he asked.

"I've wanted to know since I was 4 years old," said Marco.

"I'll tell you what," said John. "There's going to be a hell of a mess to clean up after this orgy we're having here today. Can you come back tomorrow to help out?"

"I've got football practice in the afternoon, but I could come by around 6 or so," said Marco.

"That should work fine. I'm sure there'll be leftovers you can have for dinner, but maybe you could pick up a six pack on the way over, just in case these barbarians don't leave any of the good stuff behind. Then I'll tell you what-ever you want to know, as much as I am able. I hope you realize it might be a lot more than you want to know."

"Thanks, Uncle John. I'll be there."

*   *   *

Marco stomped back and forth in frustration, then waved his clipboard around, pointed it at a big lineman named Kwame, and shouted, "He went thru you like rice thru a goose. How many times do I have to tell you? Keep your feet apart to give you a good base. Keep your knees bent. Keep your butt down. Use those elbows to keep him from getting around you. And when he moves right or left, you drive him into the turf."

Marco threw down the clipboard, got into the stance, and demonstrated for the linemen who were doing one-on-ones, hoping to improve their performance in the game coming up the following week. They groaned when he said, "Okay. Time for wind sprints," but they jogged over to the area where other players were gathering for the tradi-tional last exercise of the practice session.

Marco went up to another clipboard holder, head coach Billy Dobbs. "Billy, I've got to take off. Got to help my un-cle clean up after the funeral," he said.

"Okay," said Billy. "How are they doing?"

"Don't ask," said Marco, and jogged off the field to his car parked on the street. Semi-pro teams practice in city parks. They can't afford places that have lockers, shower facilities, and other such amenities.

As Marco drove by a Schnuck's Market on his way to his uncle's, he remembered he was supposed to bring a six pack with him, so he pulled into the parking lot and soon came out with a case of Bud Light. Not his favorite, but he knew his uncle still drank the piss. He had to park almost a block away from his uncle's house -- not an uncommon occurrence in a neighborhood where houses had single car garages, if any at all. The upside was that he got to walk down a street under the welcome shade of trees that were now fully leafed, past small but well-kept homes surrounded by the spring beauty of jonquils, azaleas, and dogwood trees. Spring was such a beautiful time of year in St. Louis, before the summer heat made everything way too hot and muggy for his taste. May in St. Louis was probably warmer than August in Wyoming, where he had spent most of his time in the military. Plus you have the added beauty of the flowers and trees all around you.

He stopped on the sidewalk in front of his uncle's house, took a deep breath, and got up the courage to walk up the steps to the front door. In the Russo family, you didn't ring the bell or even knock on the door. You assumed the door would be open, so you just turned the knob, stuck your head in, and announced yourself to the house.

"It's Marco! I'm here to help. And I remembered the beer."

"Marco, Marco," said Aunt Lucia as she came over to give him a big hug. She had been busy sweeping behind the living room sofa, but dropped the broom and opened her arms wide to give her nephew her always expansive welcome. "But you don't have to work," she said. "You're our guest, and there's lots of food left over. Pick up a plate, and join your uncle on the back porch. He'd love your company."

Marco loaded up on mostaccioli and meatballs, opened a couple of beers, and walked out on to the porch. Uncle John was in the same chair. It looked like he hadn't moved from the day before. He had an empty plate in front of him on the folding table that had been put up for the gathering, and a nearly empty glass of what looked like chianti.

"Can I get you some more food, Uncle John?" asked Marco.

"No way, Marco," he replied. "I'm already about to burst. But that cold beer sure looks good."

Marco pushed it across and said, "Thanks for being willing to talk to me, uncle. It means a lot to me."

"It's okay, Marco," he said. "I can understand how you'd have a lot of questions. And you deserve to know. It's your family after all. The question is, where do we start? You know, of course, that your grandfather, my father Pietro Russo, came over from Sicily in 1903. What you may not know is that it was not so easy to be an Italian in this country back then. We were not exactly welcomed with open arms in the good old USA. The people who had come over before us treated us pretty much like the nig -- I keep forgetting, we're not suppose to use that word any-more -- like the Afro-Americans or whatever the hell we're supposed to say. Say, you play football with a lot of them. What do you call them?"

"I call them by their names," said Marco.

"Oh," said John. "Well, anyway, people had to do whatever it took to get by, you understand? So, you know your grandfather, my father Pietro, was a prince of a man. What a shame he died so young in that railroad accident. But you know, he had an older brother, Joseph -- you probably know that your own father was named after him -- anyway, Joseph was already here in the US. He wrote a letter to his little brother that things were very good here and he should come too. Then he helped your grandpa get a job with the railroad. So Joseph looked out for his brother, but some of the things that Joseph did to survive were maybe not so legitimate, you know what I mean? . . ."

Chapter 2

Chicago; Labor Day, 1919

Patrol Sergeant William Byrne stepped out of the Orleans Hotel, licked his lips with the last of the fine pint of beer he had just finished, took a deep breath, and turned the corner from Chicago Avenue onto Orleans Street. Yes, there were lots of benefits to being a beat sergeant. He liked to plan his route so that he could space his stops between his favorite watering holes, where he was invariably offered a cool one on the house. As usual he was starting off in the part of this Near North community still populated by the last of the "old settlers," the Irish and Scandinavians who first moved in after the big fire. Then he would work his way over to the area that had been taken over by the growing numbers of Italians, mostly Sicilians, who were more recent arrivals. Chicago, now the second largest city in the country with over a million residents, was a city of immigrants. Over 80 percent of the residents were either new immigrants to the U.S. or the first generation born here. And they all seemed to settle in neighborhoods populated by people from the same areas of Europe.

Byrne crossed over Locust and continued north along Orleans. It was a pretty quiet day so far. Lots of folks had gone downtown for the big parade today. It would get more lively, he knew, when he made it to the Italian section. He was fine with patrolling in Little Sicily. That's what he called it anyway. Some of the guys called it "Little Hell."

That was a double *entendre,* referring both to the fact that all night long there were hot red fires burning in the gas refineries and heavy manufacturing factories nearby, and to the frequency of murders that occurred around the area when some poor slob refused to pay the protection money that was required by the underground criminal enterprise popularly known as the Black Hand. Byrne felt bad for them, but not much he could do about it. Seems when you tried to investigate, nobody ever saw anything or heard anything. So after awhile you just ignored it. They'd have to deal with it themselves.

Yes, he liked it here. Just over a month ago he -- along with just about every cop in the city -- had been called down to the Bridgeport area around the Stockyards, where all hell really did break loose. Race riots they called them. They went on for over a week, until Mayor Big Bill Thompson finally called out the National Guard. Sergeant Byrne lived down there, but he sure didn't want to police there. He had seen a gang of young Irish toughs from the Hamburg Athletic Club set off some fires in a Negro neighborhood. That Richie Daley kid was their ringleader, of course. Whenever Byrne thought of him, he just shook his head and said to himself, "Somebody should have used the strap on that kid years ago. Would have spared us all a lot of trouble."

Dealing with the trouble was another matter however. Some idiot of a lieutenant had ignorantly expected him to make arrests.   As if he could actually arrest some Irish boys for torching a nigger's house and expect to keep living there in his own neighborhood.   Let that smart ass Lieutenant try to do it himself. He was glad to be back up here in Little Italy.

Byrne turned left onto Oak Street, and started walking west towards Sedgwick. He really wanted to walk on the north side of the street, but not until he had passed St. Matthew's Methodist Church, which was located on the northwest corner. He grasped the St. Patrick's medal that he wore on a chain under his shirt, as he glanced furtively across the street. "Jesus, Mary, and Joseph," he said almost out loud to himself, and barely resisted the impulse to make the sign of the cross.   "Those Brits certainly love their heresies," he thought. "What with the Piscopales and all the other strange things, there's hardly a real Christian left among 'em. The Scandahoovians are almost as bad, what with worshipping that German fella and all. At least the Italians are real Catholics."

Once he passed Hudson Street, the foot traffic started to pick up on the sidewalk, and cars competed with horse-drawn wagons for space in the street. Byrne tipped his hat to a young woman passing by. He enjoyed doing that. Some of those Italian girls looked mighty fine to him. Made his patrol a lot more enjoyable. Most of them avoided eye contact with him, but sometimes he would see a smile trying to come thru as she looked away. The friendliest were the old women, of course. They made efforts to

18

tell him something in broken English. He was never quite sure of what they were saying, but they usually laughed and smiled, so he nodded and smiled back. He always hoped one of them would have a pretty young daughter he'd get to meet someday. With a wife and five kids at home, though, he didn't know what he'd be able to do about it. Especially on his meager salary.

By the time he came to the corner of Oak and Sedgwick, the foot traffic was thick on the sidewalk, and peddlers' carts were now competing with cars, trucks, and horse-drawn wagons in the street. Byrne wove his way thru the traffic to cross over to the north side of the street, then headed west again past Flynn's Drug store. Now he was truly in the neighborhood known as "Little Sicily." Three story wood frame buildings lined the street on either side, with small shops on the ground floor and crowded tene-ment apartments in the two floors above. Narrow gang-ways separated the buildings, leading to more tenement apartments in the rear, with postage stamp sized court-yards in between. Fences separated one property from another.

Byrne hated it when he had to go back thru the courtyards. You never knew quite what you would run into. They were dark, smelly, dingy places filled with dilapidated outhouses, garbage dumps, even sheep, goats and chickens. Chil-dren played there while their mothers did the laundry and hung it up to dry on lines stretched across between the two

buildings. If there was an alley back behind the rear building, the garbage was put there, but only infrequently removed. If there was no alley, the garbage and manure just
stayed there in the courtyard indefinitely.

In spite of these sad conditions, those Sicilians loved to
have a good time. Benches or chairs were lined up along
the fences, and families gathered there to socialize almost
every evening. Sometimes you could hear music played
by guitars, mandolins or concertinas, with a lot of singing
and dancing.

The sergeant passed Vicari the tailor and Terminisi's bar-
ber shop. Mr. Giamatto was out in front of his produce
store, as usual, trying to get customers for the fruits and
vegetables he had placed in baskets on top of tables on
the sidewalk in front of the store. Giamotto just smiled and
nodded as Byrne picked out a nice ripe apple, polished it
on the front of his uniform coat, and raised it to his mouth.
Just as he was taking a bite, swift movement across the
street attracted his attention. A man in the next block was
running in his direction, headed east down Oak Street.
The man turned south on Townsend Street and kept running with a determined look on his face. Byrne tossed the
apple into the street, spit his first bite after it, and started
running after the man.

The officer crossed kitty-corner from the northeast to
southwest corner of Oak and Townsend, slowed down by

Sergeant Byrne got a firm grip on the man's arm, pushed his revolver into his back, and started leading him thru the crowd towards Oak Street. Several times he shouted, "Make way. Make way. I have him in custody." The crowd reluctantly, but not quietly, opened up a small path, and Byrne led him back to Oak Street and then back down Oak to Flynn's Drug Store, as people shouted angry threats the whole way.

Patrick Flynn had come out to the front of his store, and was not pleased when Sergeant Byrne pushed the man past him, reached around to open the door, and propelled him inside, keeping the gun to the man's back as he followed him into the store. Flynn had to hustle to make it in himself, and he quickly shut and locked the door as the huge crowd outside continued to yell threats in a language that neither of them understood.

"What's going on, sergeant?" he asked, following Byrne as he pushed his prisoner towards the wall telephone at the rear of the store. "I don't know what this man has done, but you can't keep him here. They're going to tear my place down."

The officer ignored the grocer as he picked up the phone and made his urgent call in to the station. Then he turned towards the man.

"Don't worry, Paddy. There'll be a wagon here soon to pick him up. He shot some poor bloke over on Townsend. Saw it myself. Caught him red handed."

"That may be," said Flynn, "But that's no reason for us to die with him. Oh, no!" he cried, as two men pushed themselves to the front of the crowd and tried to get in thru the locked door.

"Let them in," said Byrne. "Those are my two new recruits. Never thought I'd be happy to see them, but we could sure use the help."

Flynn unlocked the door, opening it just enough for the two men to slip in sideways. They helped him shut and lock it again to keep out the others who wanted to come thru as well.

Byrne introduced them as Timothy O'Connell and John Hanrahan, two rookies so new to the force that they had not yet been issued uniforms. Ordinarily Byrne hated supervising new, inexperienced recruits, but he was glad to have them now. After filling them in on the basics of the situation, he sent them back out to open a bit of space in front of the door before the crowd bashed it in.

Soon two police vehicles worked their way slowly thru the loud, angry crowd. The ambulance went past, turning onto Townsend to pick up the wounded man. And a patrol wagon stopped in front of the drug store. Flynn happily un-locked the door, the sergeant pushed the man out, the two rookies and two other cops from the patrol wagon pushed the crowd back, Byrne and the shooter shoved their way into the wagon, and the wagon began to work its way slow-ly thru the crowd on its way to the police station.

Patrick Flynn locked the door, put up the "CLOSED" sign, pulled down the shades, sat down in a chair, put his head in his hands, and breathed a sigh of relief.

Meanwhile, around the corner on Townsend Street, the ambulance started off towards Passavant Hospital. It was not very far away, but Frank Ciccia would not make it there alive. As the crowd slowly dispersed from the scene of the murder, two young men approached the scene, clipped their fingers in the blood that was pooled there on the sidewalk, and swore to avenge his death.

Chapter 3

Law and Gospel: Chicago, 1919

The patrol wagon pulled up in front of police headquarters, and Sergeant Byrne jumped out, even before the vehicle had come to a complete stop. As he hurried into the building, his rookie assistants each grabbed an arm of their prisoner, hauled him out the back of the wagon, and pushed him inside the building. They muscled him over to the desk sergeant, who was standing in front of the long counter where officers checked in and out, and where citizens occasionally made complaints or sought information.

"Where's Byrne?" asked Hanrahan. "Where do we take the perp?"

Several other officers gathered around to get a look at the prisoner. Word was starting to get out about another shooting in Little Sicily.

"He's talkin' to the captain," said the desk sergeant, a short, round-faced man named Kelly. He stepped close and looked the prisoner up and down, his gaze finally settling on the man's face. "Take him to the grilling room. I think he'll be pretty popular there for awhile." He turned to the other cops and shouted, "Give these guys some room. Get your butts out of the way, and get back to what you're supposed to be doing. Anybody who's got time to waste around here, see me, 'cause I've got plenty for you to do."

As the prisoner was roughly hauled down the hallway to a small room on the right, Sergeant Byrne came quickly down the stairs with another uniformed officer whom the other cops would have identified as Lieutenant Edward Grady, a man legendary on the force as a hard -nosed interrogator. Byrne looked at Kelly, who nodded towards the hallway where the prisoner had been taken, and he and the detective continued that way without breaking stride. When they entered the interrogation room, Byrne looked at the two rookies and motioned with his head towards the door. They left reluctantly.

The prisoner was sitting on a bench on the other side of a wooden table that took up most of the small room. The walls were bare. There was one electric light hanging down above the table on a cord from the ceiling, and casting shadows behind each of the men in the room. Byrne sat down on a bench across from the prisoner and looked him in the eye without saying anything. Grady sat down and looked at a pad of paper he set on the table. He took out a pencil and started to write on the pad. He wrote in silence for several minutes, during which Byrne continued to stare as the prisoner looked nervously around the room.

Finally Grady spoke without looking up from the paper. "Do you speak English?" he asked.

"I speak some," answered the prisoner.

"What is your name?" asked Grady.

"Joseph Russo."

"Joseph or Giuseppi?" asked Grady, making a poor attempt to sound Italian as he pronounced the name.

"Joseph. I American now."

"Last name."

"Russo."

"Spell it."

"R - u - s - s - o."

"Where do you live," pause, "Jo - seph?" asked Grady, with a derisive emphasis of each syllable.

Continuing his questioning without ever looking up from the paper, though Byrne never relaxed his intense glare, Grady obtained all the basic information on their man. Russo claimed to be employed as a section foreman with a railroad based in Grand Rapids, Michigan. He had only been in Chicago for two days. He had emigrated from an island off the coast of Sicily in 1902, and settled first there in Chicago before beginning with the railroad two years previously.

Suddenly Lieut. Grady dropped his pencil, placed both palms on the table, leaned over it, looked up and glowered across at Russo, his eyes pinched tightly and his whole face in a scowl. "Why did you shoot him?" he asked. The action was so sudden and surprising that it broke Sergeant Byrnes' stare, and he turned to look at the detective, inadvertently sliding slightly away from him on the bench.

Grady held his position as the prisoner swallowed deeply and looked down for a second before answering, "He stole me $200 eight years ago."

Byrne jumped up, angry and agitated. "That's bull crap, and you know it. You told me you were doing your job, just like I was doing mine." Byrne pounded on the table. "Who hired you for the hit? How much did they pay you?" The sergeant could barely restrain himself, and the prisoner leaned back on the bench, nearly overturning it.

Grady put both hands on Byrne, and stuck his face in front of the man to get his attention. When Byrne calmed down slightly, Grady turned his attention back to Russo, who at first fidgeted with his eyes down and to the side, then looked up defiantly at the Lieutenant.

"Eight years ago," said Grady. He paused, looking daggers at the man, then said, "We will be back soon. In the meantime, you'd better think carefully about how you want to answer our questions. We don't take kindly to liars around here."

With a last hard look at the prisoner, Grady got up and left the interrogation room, taking Byrne with him. He led the way back down the corridor towards the front desk. On the way, they were accosted by several reporters from the many Chicago newspapers. The two men ignored their shouts and pushed their way thru to get behind the front desk. Kelly quieted the crowd and assured them that they would be given information as soon as possible, but if they didn't control themselves, they would all be thrown out of the building, or into a cell, if that was what they preferred. When things quieted down a bit, he joined the two men who were conferring in a corner out of sight of the reporters.

The lieutenant reached towards a phone that was affixed to the wall beside them. It was a wooden rectangular box with a black metal speaking horn in the center, and a black metal listening horn sitting in a metal bracket on the side of the box, connected to the box with a thick wire. He put the listening horn to his ear and began to speak into the box, but put his hand down to break the connection when he was interrupted by an angry Sergeant Byrne.

"Why were you so easy on the guy?" demanded Byrne. The sergeant's face had turned beet red. He banged his fist on a grey metal file cabinet. "He's lying thru his teeth. We know this was a Black Hand hit. Couldn't be plainer. First time we actually caught one of them in the act. Finally. We've got him dead to rights. We should have beaten the crap out of him. Got him to tell who his bosses are."

Grady had an intense look on his face and held up his hand to calm down the sergeant. "Let's think about this, please, Billy. I agree that this is the break we've been waiting for to finally nail one of these bastards. That's exactly why we need to be careful so we don't blow it. **You** know it was a gang hit. I know it was a gang hit. Now we've got to make sure we do everything just right so we can finally get a conviction on one of the scumbags. That's why I want to get somebody from the State's Attorney's office over here before we question him any more. This is going to be a big one. You did good, Byrne."

Grady took his hand off of the phone hook to speak. "Operator, get me the office of the District Attorney, Central 6, 1000. That's right. Make it fast." He held the phone slightly away from his ear, as all three men heard the phone ringing. He moved it back to his ear as a woman's voice came on the line. "Office of the District Attorney. How can I connect you."

"Daisy, this is Grady, over at Northside. I need to talk to Gorski right away. He needs to get over here real quick. We've got a live one here."

"I'll ring him, Lieutenant," she said.

As Kelly went back to the desk to answer more questions from the reporters, Byrne paced back and forth, hitting his right hand into his left palm.

A voice came on the line, "Gorski here."

"Ed Grady here, over at Northside. We've got a guy here caught red handed making a hit. We need you over here right away to observe the interrogation. I don't want to lose this one."

"I'll head right over," said Gorski. "Let's get him this time."

Grady hung up the phone, looked at Byrne and said, "He's on the way."

"He'd better hurry," said Byrne.

"I think he will," said Grady. "He wants to get one of the bastards even more than we do."

The two rookie cops, O'Connell and Hanrahan, joined them behind the counter. Byrne asked what they had found out.

O'Connell answered, "The guy he shot was Frank Ciccia. He was a candy maker. Had four kids. Lived right around the corner at 902 Cambridge. He was probably on his way home."

Hanrahan added, "He must have died on the way to the hospital. They declared him dead on arrival. Why in the world would somebody want to kill this guy?"

Byrne looked at Sergeant Kelly and said, "Babes in the woods. Babes in the woods. Saints preserve us. Would you please do a bit of educating these young men while we return to our work?"

"It would be my great pleasure," answered Kelly, giving a bow, as Byrne and Gorski headed back to the interrogation room.

Russo was still sitting on the bench. It looked like he hadn't moved in the time they were gone. The two cops resumed the places they had held before.

Grady led off. "I hope you're ready to start leveling with us," he said. "It will go a lot easier for you if you do. So I'm going to ask you again, nicely. Why did you shoot the man?"

Russo looked up over their heads to the top of the wall behind them and said, "He stole me $200 eight years ago."

"Oh, really?" asked the Lieutenant. "Just how did this come about? I want to hear this story. I bet it'll be a doozy."

Russo just kept looking at the same spot on the wall and said again, "He stole me $200 eight years ago."

Byrne broke in with, "You were doin' your job, you told me. Out with it. We know what the truth is, so out with it."

But Grady put a restraining hand on Byrne's arm and said, "No, that's okay. I want to hear this. This should be a good one. Let's let him hang himself." He looked back at the prisoner and said, "Go ahead, Jo - seph. I'm in the mood for a good one. Just how did it come about that that nice, quiet man -- who did you say he was, sergeant?"

"Frank Ciccia."

"Yes, Frank Ciccia. Now how did you happen to know this man?" asked the lieutenant?

"He stole me $200 eight years ago," was the reply.

"Just where did this theft occur?"

"He stole me $200 eight years ago."

"Oh, really? And how did he take this money from you?"

"He stole me $200 eight years ago."

Byrne grew more and more agitated, and was starting to stand to speak, when there was a knock at the door. The two men looked at each other, as the door opened slightly and Sgt. Kelly motioned for the Lieutenant to join him in the hallway.

When Grady joined him, the Sgt. said, "He's got a lawyer here."

"What? How the blazes?" asked Grady.

"Word gets around awful fast in Little Hell."

"Now I know how it got the name."

"Should I stall him?"

Grady thought for a second, then said, "No, send him back. We've probably got a hundred witnesses. I'd like to see him get their man out of this one."

Grady opened the door and motioned for Byrne to join them in the hallway. The Sgt. was not happy with the news. Kelly went back out front and returned with a thin man wearing a brown suit and a fedora hat. He introduced him as Attorney Nicolo Grasso. Grasso nodded at the two cops and went in to speak with his client.

Byrne continued to steam. "How does a guy like that get a fancy lawyer?" he asked. "I'd like to take that lid of his and stuff it down his throat."

"Nothin' fancy about Grasso," said Kelly. "He handles a lot of the low level stuff. Burglaries, street muggings, book makers, ambulance chasing, that kind of stuff. I'd better get back to the desk."

A few minutes later, Assistant State's Attorney Martin Gorski came walking briskly down the hall to where Grady and Byrne were waiting. After the three men conferred briefly, Gorski asked Byrne to wait there in the hall, while he and Grady entered the interrogation room. The lawyer was now sitting next to Russo on the bench across the table. Grady introduced Gorski, and the lieutenant resumed questioning.

"Getting back to where we were, Russo, we still need to know why you shot that man."

Russo looked at his lawyer, who nodded at him, then he replied. "I no shoot the man."

"What?" said Grady. He was stunned. "You already admitted to it. It's just a matter of why. The sergeant saw you. A street full of people saw you. What are you trying to pull?"

The lawyer said, "My client has told you that he is innocent. There must be some mistake." Grasso sat calmly, with a smile on his face, twirling a toothpick around in his mouth.

Grady turned his head and shouted towards the door, "Byrne, get in here."

When Sgt. Byrne entered the room, the lieutenant told him that Russo was now denying that he had shot Ciccio.

"What the crap is this?" Byrne asked. "I saw you kill the man. 50 people probably saw you kill the man. First you tell me you were only doing your job. Next you tell us he stole 200 bucks from you. And now you try to tell us you didn't do it? Do you think this is some kind of a game?"

Grady got Byrne to calm down, then spoke to the lawyer. "You may think this is funny, getting your client to perjure himself, but let me tell you, Grasso, things will go a lot better for your client if he cooperates."

"He **is** cooperating, lieutenant," said the lawyer. "He told you he did not kill the man. Maybe your out-of-control sergeant accidentally did it himself, and is just looking for a poor immigrant to use as a patsy."

*　　*　　*

Father Luigi Bastioni bumped into a large man who was entering Passavant Hospital just as the priest was on his way out. He apologized and stepped to the side to let the man pass. He hadn't even noticed him coming. His mind was still with the grieving wife and mother he had left in the emergency room.

Four children. So sad. And for what? Frank Ciccia was a kind and gentle man. Wouldn't hurt a fly. He lived for his family. What would they do now? Far too many times he had to deal with situations like this. There seemed so little he could do. He gave last rites. He prayed with the family and assured them of salvation, and that they would see their loved one again. He would say a funeral mass fitting for such a good, faithful man. The parish's Holy Name Society would help the family as much as they could. The sisters whom he had induced to come from Italy to run his new kindergarten and day nursery would help out, especially with the youngest children. The neighbors would be

a big support, he was sure.   That was one of the best things about the poor people who lived in Little Sicily.
But the senseless killings. How long would they go on?

The priest got on a streetcar headed back towards his parish, and took a seat next to an elderly woman with two missing front teeth.   They smiled cordially, but did not speak.   His eyes looked out the window at the passing storefronts, but he didn't really see them.   Instead, his mind kept going back to the scene in the emergency room, as Ciccia's family began arriving to grieve with the new widow. Two men whom he did not know especially stood out in his mind.   They had been introduced as Nick and Charles Conzello, cousins of the slain man, who lived just down the block from the Ciccias.   The two men always stood on the outside of the family circle.   They did not break out in weeping as did the others. Instead they stood very stiffly, with hard, grim faces. looking glassy-eyed off into a distance that only they could see. Father Luigi shivered at the thought.

Suddenly he realized that he had come to his stop at Oak and Larrabee, and quickly jumped up just in time to leave the car. As he began the two block walk east towards his church, his heart lightened somewhat as he saw the large brick building rising up above other structures in the area. He smiled as he remembered the dedication service for their new church building on August 23, the feast day of their patron saint, Philip Benizi, less than two weeks ago.

The sanctuary had been full. The words of Archbishop Quigley had been so encouraging. Several colleagues among the Servite Fathers had attended, along with some of the local priests. It had been such a proud, happy moment. But there was so much more to do.

Father Luigi stopped across the street from the new building and looked across to the three arched doorways that made up the main entrance leading to the sanctuary. The triple doorways accomplished their purpose, inspiring him to make the sign of the cross on his body in the name of the Father, the Son, and the Holy Ghost. Then he turned around to look at the vacant lot behind him. It would not be vacant long. By this time next year the new parish school would be nearing completion on this spot, right across from the church, and Dominican sisters would be arriving from Wisconsin to assume teaching and administrative duties. He tried to remember the architect's drawings so that he could visualize what the school would look like, when right on cue he heard several small voices calling out his name.

"Father Luigi! Father Luigi!" they called out. The priest turned to see four children running towards him. Three of them he recognized as Lombardo children, roughly seven, eight, and ten years old. They were from one of the first families he had recruited for the parish Sunday School. The fourth child he did not know.

"Father, we want you to meet our cousin, Sophia. She just moved here from Sicily, and her family is staying with us until they can find their own place. We're going to bring her to Sunday School with us!" The oldest girl, Lucille Lombardo, made the introduction, and pushed a shy little girl forward towards the priest. She looked to be about six or seven years old. Her dress was brown and had seen better days. Her hair was the same color. He couldn't see her eyes, because they were looking at the ground in front of her.

The priest hunched down on his haunches to get onto the girl's level, took her hand in both of his, and said, "Welcome to Chicago, Sophia. And welcome to St. Philip's Church. I am so happy to meet you." The girl's hand was limp, and she continued to stare at the ground.

"Oh, she doesn't speak English, father. Just Italian," said Lucille.

"Well," said the priest. Then we'll just have to speak to her in Italian." As he did so, the little girl slowly and carefully began to look up at him, and almost began to smile. Her eyes were the same brown color as her hair.

The priest then shared with the children his vision for the new school that was being built for them, right on that spot. He led them on a walking tour of the vacant lot, drawing verbal pictures of which rooms would be in which spots, what they would look like, and what wonderful activities would go on in each spot. Soon the children were jumping up and down and clapping, and asking, "When can we go? When can we go?"

Chapter 4

Past, Present, Future: St. Louis, 1976

Marco looked at his bottle of beer and spun it around on the table. "So you're telling me that my great uncle Joseph was a hit man for the Mafia, is that it?"

"No, not at all. That's not the way things were. For one thing, this was before there was something like the Mafia as it became later, during the Prohibition Era. But like I said before, Marco, it was tough making a go of it as an Italian immigrant in those days. My father and my uncle came over here because there was nothing for them in the old country. But what were they supposed to do once they got here? Neither of them had any formal education what-soever. No such thing as public school back on Porjareali. They couldn't read or write in Italian, much less English. The only English they knew was what somebody taught them on the boat on the way over here. And the people who had come earlier -- like the Irish and the Scandina-vians -- they were not exactly happy to see us coming. They looked on us as competition for the jobs. They called us dumb dagos and a lot worse. So you had to do what-ever you had to do to make some money and feed your family.

"You know that Uncle Joe helped your grandfather get his job with the railroad, right? Well, those were premium jobs in those days. Not easy to get. In fact, being hired probably entailed owing somebody some big favors, know what I mean? There was nothing like the organization of the Mafia. That came later. But there was a lot of what people called Black Hand activity going on. "

"What do you mean, Black Hand activity?" asked Marco.

"Well, like maybe you've got a little shop over there on Oak Street. One day a tough lookin' guy comes in, looks around, and compliments you on what a good thing you have going. Then he says, 'You know, it would be a shame if something happened to it. My friends and I can provide some protection, to make sure nobody messes with you.' But you don't want anything to do with it, so you give him a piece of your mind and chase him out of the store. Then a few days later, just when you're starting to forget about it, something happens. Maybe you have some windows broken. Maybe some merchandise is stolen. Maybe somebody sets a fire. So you call the police, and somebody comes and writes up a report, and then nothing happens. Maybe a week or so later the guy comes back again, and this time you decide it might be a good idea to pay for protection after all."

"But Uncle Joe didn't have a store or anything," said Marco.

"No, but somehow he got a job that you never would think he could have gotten. He wouldn't even have been able to fill out an application form. Maybe that job came with some stipulations attached, like, 'You owe me big time now.' It might even be that Uncle Joe asked somebody to give his little brother Pietro a job, and he was told, 'Sure, but first there's a little something I need you to do for me.' "

"My head is spinning, Uncle John," said Marco. "There's a lot more I'd like to ask you about, but I'm late to meet up with some friends tonight. Can we talk some more soon? I've got to go to Chicago for a couple of days, but then I'll be back until August."

"Any time, Marco. Anytime."

Marco got in his car, a black Chevy Camarro he had purchased when he got out of the Air Force the previous month, and drove to an area known as Dogtown, popular with young singles. Parking was tight, but after driving around several side streets, he found a spot. On his two block walk to Seamus McDaniel's Pub, he heard music coming from the open doors of some other taverns, and saw lots of couples and groups of young adults laughing and joking as they walked down the street. Some were clearly experiencing balance issues.

He stepped into the pub and scanned the room, looking for his friend Danny. He spotted him at the end of the long bar on his right that spanned the length of the room. Danny was deep in conversation with a bartender, and waving a bottle of Budweiser as he talked. Marco worked his way around knots of people towards the rear. When he got close, Danny noticed him out of the corner of his eye, turned towards him with a big smile, opened his arms wide, and said, "Marco! Marco! Welcome home, Buddy. Come over here. What're you having? This one's on me."

Marco was glad to see his old friend. During the four years he was in the Air Force, Danny had been in the Army, and there were very few times they had been able to get together. They exchanged an awkward man hug. Then Marco looked at the bartender and asked for whatever they had on tap.

"So ain't it great to be civilians again?" asked Danny, without waiting for an answer. "Back in the old neighborhood. Wearing whatever we want." (Danny was wearing a green knit shirt with thin horizontal stripes and washed out blue jeans.) He tipped up his bottle of Bud and slurped down what looked to be the last drop.

Marco said simply, "You bet," and took his own long drink of beer.

"So how long you got before you start college?" Danny asked. "You still heading off to that school in Chicago? What's it called again?"

"Trinity College. Yeah. They're giving me a football scholarship. That's what I like about it. I'll never make the pros, but I can at least have a good time working my way thru school. Got quite a few credits while I was in service, so I should be able to do it in three years. Maybe less."

"Yeah, sounds good, Marco. But you know, you've got an awfully serious look on your face. Something bugging you?"

"Not really. I just had a long talk with my Uncle John about some family stuff. Still on my mind, I guess."

"You know," said Danny, as he ordered another beer, "there's something I always wondered about. Your family is **SO** Eye-talian, man." As he spoke, he spread his arms wide, bumping the person on his left with the hand that held his bottle of beer. Some beer spilled out, and Danny hastily turned towards the bar to put down his bottle, and the man to his left jumped back out of the way and tried to wipe off the few drops of beer that had landed on his sleeve.

"Sorry man," said Danny. "Gee. I'm sorry. Look, can I buy you one, man?"

The man avoided eye contact, but got a disgusted look on his face and waved Danny off, saying, "It's all right. All right." He picked up his own glass of beer and pointed towards a booth that had opened up in the corner. He and his companion walked off in that direction.

"Well, that was weird," said Danny. Looking back at Marco he said, "Anyway, as I was saying before we were interrupted, your family is so Italian. I mean if I had met you on the street instead of in class, I would have figured you for a catlick for sure. You know, that's the way it was in our neighborhood. Two kinds of kids. Catlicks and publics. My family, no question. No way my father would ever pay good money to have the penguins teach us, know what I mean? I mean, he had all these stories about how tough and mean those old nuns were that he had in catlick school. Our mom wouldn't dare bring up the issue with him. He'd go on and on about how catlick school was worse than being in the army. How boring all the religious stuff was. How the nuns would rap you with a ruler. And my old man, I'll bet he sported a pair of red, raw knuckles just about all the time. And just between you, me and the lamppost" -- he looked around as if to be sure no one was listening -- "the real reason was probably that we barely had a pot to piss in, much less money to pay for catlick school. Besides, we didn't need nuns to knock us around. We got plenty of that from him.

"So with us, never an issue. We were publics. But I came to your house when you had a few of your family gatherings. All those people. All that food. It was impressive, man. Almost all of them were Eye-talian. And some of them were even priests and nuns! So I would've figured you for a catlick for sure. But you and I met way back in 4th grade at dear old Roe Public School. Then we were at

Southwest High together. And I don't think it was money that kept you out of St. Ant-ny's. Your dad, I know, went to mass every week when he was still living. Never missed it. So what was that about, Marco? I'm happy that you didn't go catlick. I never would have met you. But I always wondered about it."

"Yeah," said Marco. "That was my mother. She's not Italian, you know. She's English."

"You gotta be kidding me," said Danny. "The way she cooks lasagna? All that other stuff I can't even pronounce? How could she not be Eye-talian?"

"Learned it all from Grandma Rose. Self-preservation, Danny. Self-preservation. Anyway, she agreed for me to be baptized at St. Tony's, but she wasn't about to send me to school there. She took me to that Methodist church down the block for Sunday School. And to tell you the truth, I think that part of my dad was just as glad to keep me out of there. They had a few fights about it, but it always seemed like my father gave in a lot easier than I would have expected. Not that I wanted him to win that battle, you understand."

"So what's with that?" asked Danny.

"That's what I'm trying to figure out," answered Marco. "We always took part in family stuff with his side of the family, but there was always a little distance there, know what I mean? And my mom always went along like it was this chore that she had to do, but would much rather not. Her family background is English and some other stuff, not Italian, but I think there was more involved than that. She won't talk about it. But I'm starting to figure it out."

Danny looked at Marco, seemed to think for a minute, then said, "You know what you need, Marco? You need to find a good woman to get your mind off of all that stuff. I've got an idea. You're coming to Gary's wedding, aren't you?"

"I've been thinking about it. Say, I thought he was going to be here tonight."

"He is." Danny turned around and pointed to a couple dancing in a corner of the bar, next to a jukebox that was playing an old Elvis tune.

As Elvis sang, "Treat me like a fool, treat me mean and cruel, but love me," the two were swaying very slowly, barely moving their feet, and moving their hands all over each other.

"Is that Angelika he's dancing with?" asked Marco, looking puzzled.

"Nah. That's just one of the regulars here. Sandra, I think her name is. Or Suzy or something. He's just blowin' off some steam the last few days as a free man. Know what I mean? Don't mean nothin'. He's really into his Polish mama, Angelika. And I must admit, she has some very, very fine attributes. So come on over to St. Stan's for the wedding. Or at least make the reception afterward. They're having it right afterward in the church courtyard. You can eat some kielbasa or something. But here's the thing. We've got a cousin coming up from Texas I want to introduce you to. Just what you need, Marco. She's young and sassy. Got these flirty, big brown eyes. A lot of fun. Real good time girl. Her name's Melissa. If she wasn't my cousin, I'd be interested. So what do you say?"

"I'll think about it."

"What's there to think about? Afraid you'll have to dance a polka?"

"Okay. I'll come. I don't have a suit that fits anymore, though. And I'm not about to wear my uniform."

"Why not? The ladies love it."

"Not gonna happen, Danny. But I guess I can find some-thing appropriate. What time on Saturday?"

"Wedding's at 4. Reception starts around 5. I'm in the wedding party, so I've got to wear a monkey suit. Say, looks like we're ready for another round."

Chapter 5

Road Trip to Chicago, 1976

Marco woke to the sound of loud voices in the parking lot outside his house. The house was one of two large but plain two story houses that occupied space on several acres of land on Manchester Road, across the street from a steel foundry. A sign leading into the property said "Russo Plumbing Supplies." A similar sign stood over the door of a large, barn-like building on the other side of the parking lot. To the west of both was a garden, much larger than an ordinary family garden would be, but nowhere near farm sized. A beat up old panel truck had the name "Russo's Produce" painted on the door.

Marco got out of bed in his second floor room and spread two blinds on the window to look out. He was surprised to see an unfamiliar white panel truck parked there, easily twice the size of the Russo truck, surrounded by three police cars. Two of his cousins were standing there, talking animatedly to two of the cops. They took turns pointing at the van and arguing about it, while three other officers leaned back on their squad cars to enjoy the show. He quickly threw on some clothes and hurried down to see what was going on.

As Marco went out the front door, his cousin Vince waved his hand disgustedly at the cops, and walked off in frustration, while Tony kept up the argument. He went up to Vince and asked what was going on.

"Those imbeciles," he said. "They're always lookin' for a way to get to us. Always after the Russo's. You'd think they'd get a special medal for bringin' us in or something."

"So what's with the truck?" asked Marco.

"I don't know. We don't know. Not our truck. This morning we came out here early, found it sitting there. So Tony calls the police about it. Turns out it's a stolen truck from out west, California or someplace, and it's packed full of stolen alcohol. Worth a ton of money. So these clowns come out here and try to get us for stealing it, when we're the ones who called them up to report it. I ask you, what kind of shit they got for brains? It's like talking to a constipated monkey."

Marco wandered over to the officers and introduced himself. He showed them his identification, and verified that though his cousins did not live there, they indeed worked in the family businesses. He confirmed that it was not their truck, they did not know who owned it, and it had just appeared there sometime during the night. Marco was relieved that he did not find himself in the same kind of contentious conversation as his cousins. He wondered if it was because of the way he spoke with them, or his recent discharge papers from the Air Force, or the fact that, in contrast to his cousins, he had never had previous run-ins with the police. At any rate, he was glad that they did not wish to keep him any longer, and gave him permission to leave. He packed up a few days worth of clothes, threw the suitcase into the trunk of his Camaro, and left for his trip to Chicago.

Marco picked up his cousin Frances at her house on Edwards Street on the Hill. They found the entrance to Interstate 55, eastbound, and took it onto the Poplar Street Bridge, which would carry it over the Mississippi River into Illinois. Traffic was light, which was a good thing, because the bridge could get all backed up during rush hour. Marco looked out his side window at the Gateway Arch, always an impressive sight to people going and coming across the river. He asked, "Do you remember when the Arch went up?"

Franny answered, "Not really. I was too young. I remember the first time my family took me there though. We parked at the lot there on the north end and walked down that path with the row of ash trees on both sides. Then we came out into the plaza and there was the arch. Knocked my socks off. I stopped dead in my tracks. Just wowed. Then standing underneath and looking up to the top. It was awesome. Of course, then we went down the steps to eat at the MacDonald's riverboat, and I instantly became more fascinated with my Happy Meal."

"The thing I remember," said Marco, "was how so many people were saying that it wouldn't work. Even a lot of scientists and engineers said it couldn't be done. So everybody was fixated on when that last piece, the keystone, was going to be put on. And taking bets on whether the whole thing was just going to fall apart. Even my kindergarten teacher was putting up pictures for us to look at. She tried to make a model of it for us using blocks, but we could never keep it from falling over. But there's still something about it that, I don't know, inspires me or something."

"Me too," said Franny, as she reached out to turn on the car radio. Some garbled sounds came out as she turned the dial looking for the station she wanted. Then she started bouncing around in her seat and singing along with Elton John and Kiki Dee on "Don't Go Breaking My Heart." "This inspires me too," she said. She poked Marco in the arm and said, "Come on, Marco, get with it." At first he just laughed, but gradually he started singing along, and wiggling a bit in his car seat.

When Barry Manilow came on with "I Write the Songs," Franny groaned and started spinning the dial again until she settled on "Afternoon Delight" by the Starlight Vocal Band. Marco finally started getting his mind off of the events of the early morning, and his mood lightened up. Once they passed the industrial cities on the east side of the river, there was not much to see except the rich Illinois farmland, but the music kept their attention. Soon though, the sound began to break up on the radio as the car passed the long stretches of corn and soybean fields that covered most of the ground between St. Louis and Chicago. Franny gave up trying to find a good channel, and turned off the radio. As they settled quietly into the five hour ride to Chicago, she put her head back in the car seat and began to sleep.

Franny didn't wake up until Marco slowed down to pull off of the highway at one of the exits towards Bloomington, Illinois, roughly the half-way spot on the trip. She wiped her eyes, stretched, and asked where they were.

"Time to gas up, relieve ourselves, and get a bite to fortify ourselves for the rest of the trip," he said.

Franny went into the building while he filled the tank. Then he moved the car to a spot near the entrance to the store and restaurant. After a trip to the men's room, he found her looking into the very uninteresting but convenient restaurant. "Gives me the shivers," she said, "but it proba-bly beats an old, stale sandwich to go."

After they were seated and she had ordered a salad with grilled chicken, he a cheeseburger and fries, she said, "Say, Marco. Your mind was a million miles away when you picked me up this morning. What's up?"

After he told her about the early morning surprise in the parking lot, she said, "Dumb cops. Sometimes I wonder how they ever manage to get the bad guys."

"Yeah," said Marco. "But what I wonder about is why somebody parked that truck in our lot."

"Who knows? Maybe they ran out of gas and it was the first likely spot they passed by."

"Maybe," said Marco. "But I keep thinking maybe somebody knew about the place because of past business dealings -- know what I mean -- and that's why they headed there."

"What do you mean?"

"Well, you know the plumbing recycling business went down the tubes a long time ago. So lately Uncle Charlie's boys, Vince and Tony, have been using the building for recycling auto parts from old wrecks. Only I've looked into the building, and some of those cars ain't so old, and they sure don't look like wrecks to me."

Franny looked at him for a moment and said, "Are you telling me they're running a chop shop out of that place?"

"Let's just say I'm suspicious," he said.

She cocked her head and looked out the window, then said, "I guess I wouldn't put it past them. I always wondered where they got their money. Don't seem to ever have a regular job that lasts more than a couple of months.

I'd hate to see your mom have the house confiscated though."

"You & me both."

Conversation slowed down for a bit when their food arrived. Then Fran said, "On another topic, how come you're playing with the Eagles if you've got a football scholarship at college?"

"I don't have to report to pre-season camp until August," he said. "In the meantime, the Eagles' head coach wants me to work with this big lineman they've got named Kwame Williams. He's a big guy with lots strength, lots of power, but definitely lacking in technique. He's another one of these young guys with dreams of someday making it to the NFL. Never happen, but he can do a lot of good for the Eagles. I figure I can get in a couple of games, have some fun, and get myself in shape for when I report to camp at Trinity."

"Yeah," she said, "assuming you don't break a collar bone in the meantime."

"Well, there is that," he answered.
"You ever think about the pros, Marco?"

He got a sick smile on his face and looked off to the side for a few seconds before he looked back at her and answered. "Only in my dreams. 5'10", 248 pounds for a lineman is barely enough to make it on a small college team, one that a pro scout would never dream of visiting. It just helps to pay for tuition so I can finish the degree I started working on in the military."

"So why are you headed up there now?" she asked.

"Just have to finish some paper work, get a dorm assignment, meet the coaches, that kind of thing. Two or three days. But, you know, there's something I'd really like to do while I'm up there."

"What's that?" she asked.

"You know our family lived in Chicago when they first came over from Sicily. I had a talk with Uncle John, like you suggested I do, and he told me some things about our grandfather and his brother Joseph that really got me thinking. I'd very much like to go to the old Italian neighborhood where this stuff happened, just to see what it looks like. They called it Little Sicily or even Little Hell in those days. Is that the neighborhood where your school is?"

"Marco," she said, "there are probably half a dozen Italian neighborhoods in Chicago. It's a city of immigrants. People always say that Chicago has more Italians than Rome, more Poles than Warsaw, more Swedes than Stockholm, more Greeks than Athens, and more Germans than Berlin. I don't know if it's true, but I wouldn't be surprised. You can take a trip around the world without ever leaving the city if you know where all the ethnic neighborhoods are. But the Little Italy I'm in is off of Taylor Street on the south side. It's the biggest one. I'm pretty sure that our family was on the Near North Side. Do you know any of the streets?"

"Oak Street. Townsend. Orleans," he said.

"Townsend I don't know," she said. But Oak Street for sure is Near North Side. There's a great beach there. The 'in' place to see and be seen. And Orleans I think I know. Just west of downtown. Not hard to find out. I'd be happy to help you find it. There are some issues, though, that you should be aware of."

"Like what?" he asked.

"Like it's not an Italian neighborhood anymore. Let's get going. We want to make it to Chicago before rush hour, or this will be a lot longer trip than you figured on. I'll tell you more on the way."

They paid the tab, walked to the car, and got back on I-55. "So, Near North around Oak and Orleans," said Franny, when they were back on cruise control. "A long time ago they started tearing down the old wooden buildings and putting up public housing near there. First they built these two or three story, row house kind of things. Then they put

59

up this big housing project, Cabrini-Green. It's notorious. You've probably heard about it. They started out with some units for whites, some for blacks. Now it's almost 100% blacks."

"Sounds vaguely familiar," he answered. "Something like Pruitt-Igoe in St. Louis?"

"You've got it. But bigger and badder. I'm not sure just how close it is to where you want to go, but it's definitely in the area. Not someplace I'd ever go on my own, even during the day, but with a 5'10" lineman for a body guard I might venture over there for a peek. In the middle of the day, mind you."

"It's a deal," he answered. "By the way, how come you're going back so early? Taking summer classes?"

"Not classes exactly," she answered. "I've got an internship with this group called NCO, the Northwest Community Organization. The director is a guy named Bob Lynn, who's been an organizer for like, forever. He's sort of the dean of the old time organizers in the city. He runs NCO, has a few organizers under him, and takes on trainees like me. I work with him at NCO. Others come from all over the area. Doesn't pay much, but I'm learning a hell of a lot. And I really like it. Let's me get out my tough broad side."

"Heaven help us," he said. "So what do you do there? Is it political? Or more like social work? I thought you were majoring in political science."

"Definitely not social work. Yes, it's political, but not so much about elections as about actually getting stuff done. The politicians are usually the people we have to get out of the way."

"What do you mean? he asked.

"You ever hear about a guy named Saul Alinsky?" she asked. When Marco frowned and looked totally clueless, she said, "Well he's a University of Chicago professor who started this community organizing movement. It's caught on all over the country, but Chicago is where it's strongest, and the best place to learn how to do it. The basic idea is that our elected officials don't primarily work for the majority of their constituents. They work for the people to whom they are beholden for getting into office, and the people who can do something for them in return. Therefore, if the people want to get something done, they have to come together as a group and **force** the politicians to make it happen."

"Sounds pretty radical," he said.

"Yep," she answered. "Just like the Constitution."

Marco laughed.

"I tell you what," Franny said. "Why don't you stick around a couple of extra days. After we tour the old neighborhood you can go with me to a staff meeting on Tuesday night. Bob Lynn is the guy who runs it, and he's a tough old organizer. He's the best. Been around a long time. Then on Wednesday we've got an action planned that you could go along on, so you see what it's like."

Marco laughed again. "I'm not so sure."

"Come on," she said, hitting him on the arm again. "We're not going to start a riot or go to jail or anything. All very legal and out in the open. It's the way democracy is supposed to work. Besides, you're a big bad lineman. What are you worried about? I'm going to show you around Little Hell, aren't I?"

"I'll think about it," he said, as they drove by a large sign at the side of the road. It said,

Welcome to Chicago.
Richard J. Daley, Mayor.

Chapter 6

Struggles, Old & New: Chicago, 1976

Marco drove slowly down S. Halsted Street, looking for the student center, when he saw Franny waving to him from the curb. He pulled over and she climbed into the car. "Okay," he said. "You're the navigator."

"Just go around the block and head back the other way on Halsted Street," she said. "It's not all that far, and we'll make better time by avoiding Downtown."

Marco noted the large, modern buildings on the campus, which looked more like a corporate headquarters than what he envisioned as a college campus. "This is a far cry from Trinity College," he said. "I was expecting a grassy quadrangle, not a bunch of highrise buildings. And it's huge."

"Yep," she said. "It's an urban university. I think we're up to 25,000 students now. But keep your eyes on the road. The traffic can get pretty hairy. I'll give you a tour around here later if you're interested. Turn left here. That's it. We'll just go north on Halsted for a couple of miles to Chicago Avenue."

The volume of traffic took some getting used to for Marco. Trucks and cars filled the streets. They weaved in and out between lanes of traffic, sometimes blew their horns at him, and were always in a hurry. After a near miss with a car that cut in front of them, causing Marco to jerk to an abrupt halt and cuss, Franny laughed and said, "The pace of everything in Chicago is about twice what it is in St. Louis. Actually, I've gotten to love it. When I come to Chicago, my heart starts to beat faster. I feel more alive. Okay, we're coming up to Chicago Avenue. Turn right at the light."

Soon after the turn, they came to a bridge over a grimy looking waterway that Franny identified as the North Branch of the Chicago River. Passing a few blocks with small factories, taverns, and a greasy spoon or two on either side of the road, they came to Orleans Street, where Franny told him to make a left turn. He came to the corner and waited for an opportunity to turn, but the oncoming traffic was steady, so he stayed where he was as the light changed to red.

The driver behind him honked his horn several times. Franny laughed as Marco looked in his rear view mirror and complained, "What's the matter with that guy? No way I could have made that turn."

Franny poked him painfully on the arm and said, "Marco, you drive like a St. Louisan. Keep that up and we'll be here all day. That is, unless the guy behind comes up and shoots us."

Marco was becoming angry. "What are you talking about? No way I could have made that turn."

"Time to learn the Chicago way," she said. "When the light changes, don't just sit here. Pull out into the intersection."

"But I'll be blocking the street," he said.

"Now you're getting smarter," she laughed. "You sit there until the light changes. Then when the oncoming traffic stops for the light, you make your turn. Move fast, because the guy behind you will be right on your tail so that he can make the turn too, and the traffic on Orleans will now have a green light, so they'll be coming at you from both sides, and they won't take kindly to somebody who slows them down."

Marco followed her instructions, but beads of sweat broke out on his forehead as he quickly turned left onto Orleans St. As Franny had predicted, the car turning behind them was less than two feet off of his rear bumper, and the southbound cars on Orleans looked like they were ready to ram into his rear end. Laughing thru it all, Franny reached out to pat Marco's arm like a puppy and said, "Welcome to Chicago, Marco."

"Shit," he said.

"Okay," she said. "We're coming up to Oak St. Make a left at the next corner. Where the Methodist Church is."

He turned onto Oak Street and drove slowly. It was obviously a side street. There were a few small factories, a few dilapidated two or three story homes on either side, and several vacant lots. They passed Sedgwick St. and Franny suggested they park the car. There were not many cars there, nor was there any foot traffic. Walking west on Oak St., they passed more of the same until they came to Hudson St. Looking to his right, Marco saw a number of high rise buildings to the north. "Cabrini-Green," said Franny, after Marco pointed them out. "Home of the Gangster Disciples. They pretty much run the place. But look over there."

She pointed across Oak St. and west of Hudson to a 10 foot tall cyclone fence. There were some buildings behind it that were partially obscured by weeds and scrub trees. "Let's check it out," she said.

They crossed Oak Street and Hudson and walked over to the fence. A sign on the fence warned that anyone attempting to enter would be subject to prosecution, but it was not clear why anyone would want to. Thru the fence they looked down at several blocks of what at one time would have been a city street. On either side of the street were two story buildings that reminded Marco of some low end motels. There were stairs at regular intervals leading up to a balcony on the second floor. Doors at ground level and on the second floor indicated that there were separate apartments on both levels. Most of the windows had been broken out, and there was graffiti on most of the exterior walls. Many doors were missing as well. The degree of vandalism and neglect indicated that the buildings had been vacant for years.

"I think we found Townsend Street," said Franny. "From what I found out, these would have been built during the 40's. They tore down the old frame buildings to put up these lovely homes. The Frances Cabrini row houses. I am especially proud that these lovely homes and I were named after the same person."

"What?" asked Marco. "I thought you were named after St. Francis."

"Only second hand, unfortunately," she said. "I was named after Mother Frances Cabrini, a nun who helped other Italian immigrants, and ended up the first canonized Italian-American. **She** was named after the guy from Assisi. Anyhow, this is the place, but obviously it didn't look at all like this. They tore down the old neighborhood to create this utopia. At first there were mostly Italian residents, but gradually blacks moved in and us dagos moved out. Now most of the Italians live in the suburbs and the blacks live in the high rises over there."

They noticed an elderly African-American man at the western end of the fence and decided to speak with him. As they approached, they noticed that there was a vacant lot at the end of the fence, and the man was watching two young children playing there. They looked to be under three years old.

They introduced themselves, told him why they were interested in the area, and asked if he lived nearby.

"Yes, maam," he said. He pointed at a two story brick home across the street with similar buildings on either side. His home looked neat and well cared for, but the others were boarded up.

"How do you like living here?" asked Franny.

"It's hard," he said. "Gang bangers always coming thru at night. Gunfire. Have to keep a close watch on the grandkids. No good place for them to play around here. I'd like to move, but we can't afford it. We could get into one of them senior buildings, but we wouldn't be able to take the grand kids with us."

"Have you been here long?" asked Marco.

"Thirty three years," he said. "Used to be real nice around here. All of them apartments down there were full of families. Then they built all of them high risers. Gangs ruined everything. Good folks moved out. Two of my grandkids got killed. Two more are in prison." He shook his head and said, "Uh uh. Uh uh."

After Marco brought Franny back to the campus, he returned to his own, where he brought a few boxes up to his dorm room, ate some bland food in the cafeteria, and rested for a few hours before returning to pick Franny up again.

*　　*　　*

"11 o'clock is a pretty strange time to start a staff meeting," he said, as they drove towards the office of the Northwest Community Organization.   "What do you have in the sack?"

"Two six packs. My turn to provide. Meetings have to start late, because earlier on everybody's on the phone, or knocking on doors, or meeting with a neighborhood leader, or at an action. You'll hear about it tonight."

Once again they headed north on Halsted Street, but this time when they came to Chicago Avenue, they made a left turn and drove west.   When they passed Damen Ave., Franny told Marco to start looking for a parking place. He found one a block further down, where he demonstrated his parallel parking skills.   There were parking meters all along Chicago Ave., but Franny assured him they didn't need to be fed at that time of night.   He noted that there were small storefronts on both sides of the street, with what looked like apartments on the second and third floors above them.   He noted neon lights from at least three taverns on the block, along with a barbershop, a shoe repair, a pizza place, and a small grocery. All of the stores except the taverns were closed for the night.

They walked to a storefront with the letters NCO highlighted on the window. Underneath it said, "Northwest Community Organization," along with a phone number. There were lights on inside, and the door was open when they entered.

"Finally," said a voice. "I've been working up a powerful thirst." The speaker was a young man who looked to be in his late twenties or maybe early thirties. He had a shock of brown hair parted on the left side and flowing rather haphazardly from there in three directions.

As she handed over the sack of beer, Franny introduced him as Petrusiac, the resident clown of the staff. However, he was, she conceded, a pretty good organizer.

Taking a six pack out of the bag, ripping one from the plastic ring, and popping it open, Petrusiac decided to live up to his name. "So Marco," he said. "Do you know why Mayor Daley always gets a big majority of women's votes?" After Marco confessed that he did not know, Petrusiac replied, "Because they just love their Dick Daley."

Pleased with the level of groans elicited by his joke, Petrusiac put one six pack on the far side of the table, the other on the near side.   Marco noted that there were two long folding tables set next to each other in the center of the one room storefront, surrounded by eight chairs.   There were four desks in the long, narrow room, two on each side, each one with a telephone.   One desk looked very neat and organized.   The other three had papers and books scattered around the desktops.   There was another folding table in the front near the door, with various brochures and notices in piles placed on top.   Two more folding tables in the rear were covered with various kinds of paper and other supplies.   A copy machine stood in the corner beside them.   An open door next to the machine showed a small hallway leading to a back door.   To the right of the door was a small refrigerator.   There were a few posters on the walls, which seemed to be the nearest thing to an attempt at decoration.   The whole place was very basic and Spartan.

The door opened and another young man entered.   He was tall and thin, and looked to be in his early 20's.   Franny introduced him as Blake, who was in a social work program at a local community college and had been placed with NCO as a fieldwork assignment.   He was excited because he would have something to present to the group for the first time.

Two other young men entered and were introduced as Jim and Bill.   Almost everyone was sipping on a beer and talking, but one went to the refrigerator and took out a Coke.

At about 11:20, a middle-aged man entered. As soon as everyone noticed who it was, they looked for a place at the tables and sat down, while continuing their conversations.

Bob Lynn was of average height, slightly overweight, and had thinning brown hair. He wore a long sleeved sport shirt and khakis. Franny introduced her cousin and got permission for him to sit in on the meeting. Bob went to the refrigerator for a coke, sat down at the tables, and began by simply saying, "Okay, tell me what you got."

Blake immediately jumped in eagerly. "I just had a long conversation with a group of young adults in Blue Island," he said, referring to a suburban area south of the city. "So here it is," he said. He got an intense look in his eyes and held out his hands as though presenting the group with a valuable gift.

"Prairie," he said, and paused as if he expected the group to be awed by his extraordinary insight. After a moment of silence, during which most of the others tried to avoid looking at one another, he continued. "One of them had been reading about how prairie land has been disappearing in Illinois, and what a loss that is to our entire ecosystem. I actually know a lot about that. I wrote a paper on it once. So we were talking about it, and they all agreed it would be neat to get people together and set aside some land to restore to natural prairie."

At this point, Bob Lynn, who had been looking at Blake with no expression on his face, put up a hand to stop him. He looked at the others and said, "What do you want to ask him?"

Bill asked, "You said it was a group of young adults. How many exactly?"

"Three," he answered, "but they've got lots of friends."

Franny asked, "Where was this, and how did it happen?"

"I was going around knocking on doors, out in Blue Island where I live, asking people what the community concerns are, when this nice guy named Jack answered. He invited me in. His two friends were already there -- Jean and Ken -- and we all started talking."

Franny continued, "Was this Jack's house?"

"Yes," Blake answered, "It's his parents' house and he lives there. He's going to junior college and working at a gas station."

"One more question," said Franny. "Were you passing a joint around while you had this discussion?"

The others laughed, and Blake turned red. Bob Lynn did not laugh, but instead said, "Blake, first I commend you for getting out into the community to find out what people are talking about. Everything we do starts with that. So you made a good first start. Let's everybody lift our beer or whatever and make a toast." He lifted his can of coke as the others raised theirs. "Here's to Blake," he said. "Welcome to the club of community organizers."

They all toasted, and several slapped Blake on the back. He began to look a little better.

Lynn said, "So the first step in being an organizer is to find out what the people are thinking, what **their** issues are. This might be a good time to remind ourselves about the purpose of what we do. Petrusiac, you're our resident scholar. What does Alinsky say organizing is all about?"

He pulled out a book from a backpack on the floor next to his seat and opened it. "Here's what he says in his intro to Rules for Radicals," he said. "What follows is for those who want to change the world from what it is to what they believe it should be. The Prince was written by Machiavelli for the haves on how to hold power. This book is written for the have-nots on how to take it away."

"So Blake's dream of prairie," said Lynn. "Isn't that about changing the world to the way it should be? What's wrong with it?"

"First of all," said Bill, "it's not a real issue. These were just a few young people shooting the bull. It's just a pipe dream, so there won't be the kind of energy behind it that

74

you need to really change anything. You probably couldn't find a dozen other people there who care about it.

"Okay," said Lynn. "What else?"

Jim jumped in. "They don't have a real stake in it or even in the community. They don't own their houses or property. They're probably just looking forward to getting out of their parents' house, maybe go off to join a hippie commune." That got a few laughs.

"Let's hear what Frances has been working on," said Lynn. "I suspect that may help enlighten us about what a good issue looks like." He turned towards her and pursed his lips.

"Yeah, well," she said. "Tonight I met with a small group at Maryska Boyko's house right over there on Rice St., just this side of Leavitt. She's this big Ukranian woman, real active in her church . . ."

"St. Vol's or St. Nick"s?" interrupted Petrusiac.

"St. Nick's," she said. "Anyway, she's this big, imposing, pushy broad who won't take shit from anybody. My kind of woman. So Jan Zaleski was there, the Polish guy who's got that great deli over on Damen, and two women who live in the neighborhood, both Ukranian, and a guy named Vito who just bought the pizza place at Chicago and Western." Franny grew more and more animated and excited as she spoke. Her eyes lit up, and her hands went into action.

"And all of them," she said, "are up in arms about that junk yard that just got put in on Chicago Ave where the old department store used to be. I mean, they're going on and on about what a blight it is on the neighborhood, and why didn't the zoning laws stop it, and how their property values are going to go into the tank, and on and on. I thought they were getting ready to form a lynch mob and go after somebody. So then, who should show up but Emilio Torres?"

"Is he the guy who opened up the Mexican Restaurant on Hoyne?" asked Bill.

"You got it," said Franny. "A couple of years ago, everybody there would have been calling out the cavalry to keep anyone or anything Mexican or Puerto Rican out of the neighborhood. But now he's just one of them. They're all out for blood. Ready to assassinate the alderman and blow up the junkyard."

"So, said Lynn, "why is this a good issue?"

"It's got energy. Buy in," said Petrusiac.

"Right," said Lynn. "Change is hard. If you want the commitment it takes to really change something, there has to be a lot of energy behind it, and it has to be sustained over a considerable length of time, because real change never comes easy. Most of the time the energy you need is going to come from anger over what's going down. That's what you look for in your community leaders. A nice guy attitude of 'I want to make the world a better place' will never stand up against the kind of resistance you're going to run into when you want to make real change.

"One time a few years back a guy came in here who was so mad he couldn't even talk. He just stomped around the room going, 'Ugh! Ugh!' and banging his fist on the table. He turned so red I thought he was going to pop a vein in his forehead. It took a half hour to calm him down enough to even tell me what he was so mad about. I ended up hiring him, and in a month he had 120 people blocking the entrance to Commonwealth Edison. That's what it takes to make things happen. He's still an organizer, down at SCC."

"What's SCC?" asked Blake.

"Southwest Community Congress," answered Petrusiac. "One of our sister organizations."

"So," said Lynn. "She's got energy, buy in. What else?"

"There's a clear objective," said Bill. "And it passes the KISS principle." He looked at Blake and explained, "Keep It Simple Stupid."

"Or Keep It Simple Shit-head," put in Jim. "How are you phrasing the issue, Franny?"

"No junk yard in **my** neighborhood," she answered.
"So there's a clear objective, and it's got energy," said Lynn. "What else?"

"Is it winnable?" asked Petrusiac.

"You bet," said Franny. "Should never have been put there in the first place. Alderman O'Malley got them a variance with the zoning board. O'Malley can just as easy get it lifted, and get the junk yard booted out."

"But will he do it?" asked Bill.

"If he wants to hang on to his alderman job he will," she answered.

As the others were running their issues by the group, the office door opened and a tall African-American man entered the storefront. He had a short, rather tame version of an Afro, and wore a knit shirt and jeans.

Lynn looked his way and called out, "Richard, what are you doing on the north side of town? You out slumming? Sit down here and have a beer with us." As the man walked over and joined them at the table, Lynn introduced him, as he slid him a beer across the table.

"This is Richard Parker," he said, "out of West Englewood on the South Side. To what do we owe the honor of this visit?"

"Wanted to bend your ear about the best way to get to Hiz-zoner. You had that sit-in down at city hall last year. Got you a lot of publicity, but a lot of trouble too. I wonder if that tactic was worth it. We've got a situation with over-crowding in the schools. The Board of Ed has picked out the property for a new school, but they can't get the owner to sell to them. I've started to think the Boss Man is the only one who can make it happen."

"What have you tried?" asked Lynn.

"Well, after getting nothing but the run around from the owner -- he refused to meet with us, and his office just says he's not in or not available -- we got ahold of his home address and sent a team out to visit him there, five car loads," he said.

"I'll bet he loved that," said Lynn.

"Oh, yeah," said Parker. "When he came to the door I said, 'Since you're disrupting our community, we thought we'd come out and disrupt yours." This drew a big whoop from all around the table.

"So he started yelling at us, told us we had no idea what we were doing. There were a couple of clerics in our group, and he started yelling at the 'backwards collars', cussing them out. Only a few of us went to the door. The rest were marching up and down the street with signs, hoping the neighbors would see us. He still hasn't budged, though, and we can't do that trick again."

"Why not?" asked Jim.

"He called the cops, and he lives out in Oak Lawn. They showed up in a hurry, and ten of us got hauled into the station. Took a couple of hours to get our lawyer out there to get us out. Hell, that's Oak Lawn. Two of our cars got stopped on their way **out there**, before we had even done anything. In Oak Lawn it's apparently against the law for black folks to drive thru town after dark. So anyway, I figure the next step is to go to King Richard. If he wants the man to sell, he'll sell."

"Richard," said Lynn. "We've been talking about what it takes to make a good organizer. You used to be a teacher. What got you into organizing?"

"Yeah, I was a high school science teacher for ten years," he said. "But I just got too frustrated. It's pretty damn hard to teach science when you don't have textbooks for the class, you can't buy the supplies you need to run experiments, there aren't enough desks in your classroom, half of the kids can't concentrate because they either haven't had enough to eat, or they didn't sleep the night before or both, half of them have been passed into high school even though they can't read, most of the boys are thinking either about being in the gang activities happening that night or how to avoid them, most of the girls are trying to look good for the boys -- and yes, I realize that the math doesn't add up. That's my point."

"Richard," said Lynn, "you sound like an angry man."

"You bet I'm angry, "he said. "We've got to make big changes to the whole system, and it's got to start with the early grades. But they can't do the job there with 32 six year olds in the classroom, no books or supplies, and nowhere near the support those families need."

*   *   *

It was 3:30 am when Marco and Franny finally left. Driving her back to her apartment he said, "I was watching you the whole time in there. You really love that stuff, don't you? Going after the aldermen, the school board, even the mayor."

"You bet," she answered. "It feels so good when you actually get one of those bastards to do what the people want them to do."

"But they need the people's votes to get elected," said Marco. "Why wouldn't they just do what their constituents want?"

"So the alderman in the ward around NCO, where I'm working, is Billy O'Malley. He's in real tight with the mayor. Has a nice, simple bungalow in the ward, but a mini-mansion over in Grand Haven, Michigan, right next to Mayor Daley's. Spends a lot more time there than in the ward. Has a law practice where he puts in a day or two here and there, along with his part-time salary as an alderman. I'll bet he got a nice contribution for making a phone call to the zoning commission about one minor variance from the zoning code. I'm sure he would have told them that the neighbors didn't mind. So you're going to come along for the action tomorrow -- I mean tonight -- aren't you?"

"Wouldn't miss it," he answered.

*   *   *

That night the NCO office was packed. Since it was a small storefront, that did not take a huge crowd, but it still looked impressive. Marco estimated there were somewhere around 40 people there. One or two looked like young radicals, but most appeared to be ordinary neighborhood folks. Two women sat behind a table set up at the door, and were getting people to sign in with their names, addresses, and phone numbers as they entered. Franny stood behind them to supervise, keep an eye on the street, and survey the crowd. Marco sat on the display area in the front window and observed.

At about 7:15 pm, Franny gave a signal to Maryska Boyko, who stood up on a chair at the far end of the storefront. It took a minute to get everybody's attention. Then she thanked them all for coming out and asked, "Who here thinks we ought to have a junkyard in the middle of our main street?"

"No! No! No!" yelled 50 voices. "Not here!" "No Way!" "Not in MY neighborhood!" "Let's tear it down!" "Let's blow it up!"

She quieted them back down and asked her next question. "Who wants to tell Alderman O'Malley how we feel about it?" After more raucous responses she said, "All right. Let's go!" She stepped down from the chair and worked her way thru the crowd and out the front door. The crowd followed as she walked down the street to the corner. Jan Valeski and Vito Milano worked to keep the group some-what orderly, occasionally calling out for them to stay on the sidewalk. They walked to the corner, then crossed the street, and proceeded on the other side.

Another block and a half further they came to a storefront with four men standing in front of the door. When they saw the group coming, one of the men opened the door and hurried inside. The other three blocked the entrance to the storefront. One of them held up his hand and asked them to stop, saying there was not enough room for them all. Marco looked thru the storefront window and noted that

83

there was a desk at the far end of the room, with two men sitting behind it and two chairs in front of it, with a man and a woman sitting in them. There were several rows of chairs between there and the storefront, almost all of which were occupied. The window in front of the storefront said:

21st Ward, City of Chicago
William H. O'Malley, Alderman

Jan Valeski stepped forward and informed the man they were all voting members of this ward and had come to speak with the alderman about a very important matter. They were asked to be patient. As they could see, there were many people there ahead of them. As the crowd complained about this, the man who had gone inside returned and whispered in the ear of the man who had stopped them. Then he asked, "Who speaks for this group?"

"We do," said Maryska, as she stepped forward with Vito and Valeski. "We have come to speak with him about the junk yard which has been put in the middle of our business district."

"Please be patient," he said. "I will speak to the alderman."

He reentered the building, and thru the window Marco could see him whispering into the alderman's ear. O'Malley looked out towards the crowd outside the window, then spoke briefly to the man and returned his attention to the couple before him as the man returned to the front door.

"Since the office is full and there are so many ahead of you," said the man, "we ask if you could return next week instead."

Immediately angry cries rose from the crowd, loud enough that the alderman looked up from his desk. "Boo! Boo!" said the crowd. "No way!" "We're here now! We'll talk now!" "He works for us!" "We're the people!"

Then someone started chanting, "Hey, hey, ho, ho, junkyard, junkyard's got to go!" Others joined in, and soon the whole group was chanting, "Hey, hey, ho, ho, junkyard, junkyard's got to go!"

The man who had asked them to go became very agitated and went back inside again to speak with the alderman. This time they spoke longer, as the chanting continued, growing even louder. Finally the man came out again.

"Alderman O'Malley has agreed to meet with three representatives," he said.

Some in the crowd responded, "Yeah! Yeah!" while others wanted to insist that he speak with all of them. Mariska quieted the group, and there was a general agreement reached that tonight she would meet with the alderman along with Vito and Valeski. If the results were not satisfactory to everyone, they would have to come back again and again until they got what they wanted. A consensus was reached, although some were not happy with it. The

85

three accompanied the man inside. He led them into a smaller office in the rear of the storefront, where the alderman had preceded them, to angry looks and grumbling from the people who were still sitting and awaiting their chance to speak with the alderman. The rest of the crowd milled about impatiently on the sidewalk.

After about fifteen minutes the three leaders came out to report to the group. Mariska said, "Alderman O'Malley denies that he had anything to do with the zoning change." This statement evoked an outburst of angry words from the crowd, to which she continually nodded her head in agreement, before quieting them down to continue.

"We all know that's nothing but a crock. But he did commit to investigate the matter and to meet with us here next week. He's probably hoping that if he stalls us for a while this will all just go away. What do you think? Are we all going to just go away?"

At this the crowd erupted with shouts of "No way", "Never", "We'll show that son-of-a-bitch," and the like. She let them vent for a few minutes, and then asked, "So who's going to be here next week?" After everyone shouted they would be there, she asked, "And who"s going to bring friends and relatives along with you?" Most of them shouted that they would. Then she said, "Remember, we are the ones who voted for this guy. He works for us. He's supposed to do the things we want him to do. And do we want a junkyard on Chicago Avenue?"

"No way!" they shouted. "Hey, hey, ho, ho, junkyard, junk-yard's got to go!"

*　　*　　*

Driving Franny back to her apartment later, Marco said, "Well, that was interesting."

"Interesting?" she answered. "I thought it was pretty damn awesome!"

"Do you think they'll win?" he asked.

She shrugged and said, "Who knows? He clearly doesn't want to do it. So it all boils down to this: can they become such a pain in the ass that whatever kickback he got for the variance is no longer worth it to him? That means the people have to stay engaged over time, and maybe even escalate their tactics, and that's where the problem lies. They're all basically nice people who don't want to cause trouble, and there are lots of other things they'd rather be doing with their time. So we'll see. If O'Malley had any real opposition in the ward, he could make a big deal about doing what his constituency wanted him to do, come out of it as their champion, and get a few more folks to vote for him or even work in his campaign. But he's so secure he could care less."

"So why are you working so hard on it?" he asked. "What's in it for you?"

"Well," she answered. "First of all, we hopefully can show people that it is possible to actually make the government work for you, that if people get together they can make things happen. They begin to see the value in an organization like NCO. Maybe their church becomes a member organization, like St. Nick's is. You get a few small victories like this one, and you start to build some power, and then you get more publicity and more people pay attention to you, and you can take on bigger issues. Another thing is you start to develop leadership. If you ask me, that Mariska Boyko is pretty damn awesome. You agree?"

"I agree," he answered.

"Never been involved with anything like this before. The most she ever did was chair the mothers' group at the parish school. Now she's getting a taste of how she can really make things happen in her community. Wouldn't surprise me if she beat out O'Malley for alderman some day. And here's the real kicker, Marco. You ready for this? "Yeah, what?"

"When you come right down to it, I think I'm actually stupid enough to believe that government of the people, by the people, for the people shit. Who would have thunk it?"

Chapter 7

A 1919 Trial

"So how was Chi-Town?" asked Uncle John. "You all ready to start classes?"

"Oh, yeah," answered Marco. "That's no big deal. Just a few details. Mostly connecting with the football coaches. I go back in August for summer camp. It's kind of odd, though."

"How so?" asked John.

"Everybody else is so much younger. I think that's one of the reasons they gave me such a good offer. I'll be almost like an assistant coach, like I am with the Eagles. I think they expect me to be a little more mature than the other guys, show some leadership."

"Who? You?" asked John, feigning incredulity.

"Yeah, pretty funny. Anyway, the other really odd thing will be living in a dorm room again. I thought that after years of barracks life, it wouldn't be such a big deal for me, but now I'm not so sure. Those dorm rooms are awfully small, and I have to share with a roommate. All I can say is, he'd better be willing to take the top bunk."

"Yeah," snickered John, "and he'd better be willing to put up with your snoring."

"That too for sure," said Marco. "But anyway, I'd like to hear more about the epic tales and sagas of the Russo family. If my great-uncle got caught red-handed doing a hit job, how come he got away with it?

"Well, he actually did a little bit of jail time," said John. He was convicted once and got fourteen years, but that was thrown out in a second trial."

"What?" asked Marco. "How did that happen?"

"It's a pretty convoluted story," said John. "Here's what I've been able to piece together . . ."

Chicago, 1919 - The First Trial

Father Luigi Bastioni walked east down Hubbard Street towards a large, seven story Romanesque building between State and Dearborn Streets. The Cook County Criminal Court Building had been constructed in 1893 on the same site as its predecessor, best known as the location of the Haymarket Massacre trials in 1886. For several reasons he had decided to walk instead of taking a streetcar. It was not much further than a mile from St. Philip's, and he needed the exercise. Besides, he always learned something about the city and his flock as he walked thru

90

the neighborhoods. Another reason was that he just wanted a few moments to himself to think.   Unfortunately he had not anticipated that there would be such a large crowd blocking the door. "Luigi, Luigi," he told himself. "You saw the size of the crowd in the street on the day of the shooting. What were you thinking?" He hated to use the privilege of his office. Too many fellow priests forgot they were supposed to be servants, and took advantage of special treatment whenever they got the opportunity. But Mrs. Ciccia had especially pleaded that he be there to support her today. He didn't want to let her down.

The crowd was noisy. Several were waving signs with slogans such as: Cut Off the Black Hand; No More Murders; or Give Us Justice. He heard several chants go up. "Justice, justice, we want justice!" "String 'm up. String 'm up." "Death to the Killer." He squeezed between several knots of people, all jockeying to get to the door of the courthouse. A man wearing worker's overalls and a peaked cap grabbed him by the shoulder and spun him around.

"Hey!" the man shouted. "Think you're gonna butt in, do you?" His large right fist was pulled back, ready to strike out, when he saw that he was about to hit a priest. He immediately got a shocked look on his face and pulled his hand down. "Oh, sorry Father," he said. "I didn't know it was you."

The priest put up his hands, as if to say "No harm done," and resumed his effort to wade thru the crowd. Now the man took it upon himself to help, calling out, "Make way for the Father. Make way for the Father," as he helped to move others out of the way.

When Luigi finally got to the door, there were four officers blocking the entrance. They had their billy clubs out, and used them as a barrier to keep people back. They kept repeating, "Stand back. No more room. Stand back. No more room."

The priest pled his case to the officer who seemed to be in charge. "Excuse me, officer, but the family of the victim is expecting me in the courtroom. May I please enter?"

"Of course, Father," said the officer, speaking right into the priest's ear so that he could hear over the din. "They're in Courtroom 5 on the second floor. You could take the elevator, but it's probably quicker to walk up the stairs to the right."

"Thank you and God bless you," said Fa. Luigi as the officer held the door open for him and he entered the building. He stepped onto a landing leading to a wide marble stairway with black metal railings in the center and at either side. On both sides of this stairway were smaller stairs going down to a lower floor. He stepped up a dozen stairs to a landing with two glass doors leading into a long, wide hallway. Stepping inside, there was a noisy crowd in the hallway as well, but it was not as crowded as it had been outside. He saw the stairs on his right and walked towards them, noting that there were two more officers on guard at that location. After a similar explanation, he was allowed to pass and go up the stairs to the second floor.

While there were fewer people here than the first floor, there were still quite a few speaking softly, almost conspir- atorially, in several small groups or pairs. And once again there were two policemen barring the wooden doors lead- ing into the courtroom. After another repetition of his need to enter, one of the officers opened a door and led Fa. Lui- gi down the center aisle of the packed courtroom to the first row of benches on the right, just behind a wooden rail separating the trial participants from the spectators. Mrs. Lucia Ciccia, a small, plain looking woman with eyes puffy from crying, but with a determined look on her face, turned in his direction, smiled, and stood up to face him, with her arms opened wide.

"Father Bastioni," she said. "I knew you would come. I told them you would come." She waved her hands to indi- cate that he should come to sit next to her on the bench. She motioned with her hands to make family members scrunch in closer and move down the bench to make room for him. As he sat next to her on the aisle, he tried to look apologetically to the two men sitting on her other side. They did not look pleased. He now recognized them as the men to whom he had been introduced at the hospital. What were their names again? Conzello. That was it. Cousins. Nick and Charles. Was that it? He had no idea which was which. Mrs. Ciccia beamed at him as she held up a carved wooden crucifix in both hands before her. He wrapped his hands around hers and the crucifix, bowed his head for a moment in silent prayer, then released her hands, opened his eyes, and turned to face the court.

Front and center and dominating the room was the large raised bench of the judge. It was made of a dark wood, which the priest thought was probably oak. A bronze nameplate sitting on the desk said Hon. James Q. Murphy. On the left side, connected to the judge's bench but somewhat lower down, was the witness box. To the left of the witness box, against the courtroom wall was the jury box, with chairs facing the center of the room. To the right of the judge's bench was a wooden table where a man he assumed must be the court reporter sat writing in a binder. A man sat next to him, looking through another thick binder of records. In front of where the priest sat in the first row of spectators, on the other side of the rail separating the spectators from the participants, was a table for the prose-cutor. Asst. States Attorney Martin Gorski sat closest to the center aisle. On his right were two other attorneys. Both looked younger, and while Gorski seemed very quiet and composed, they seemed to be hard pressed to control their excitement. They continually looked around the room and whispered comments to each other.

At a similar table on the other side of the aisle sat Attorney Nicolo Grasso, a cocky, confidant look on his face, twirling a toothpick around in his mouth as he had done in the police station. He leaned back in his chair and smiled as he looked around the room. To his left sat the accused, Joseph Russo. He sat looking straight ahead with an expressionless face. In the spectator row right behind him sat his brother, Pietro, and his sister, Sophia. They sat quietly, looking slightly downward either in deep in thought or in prayer.

The one hundred or so spectators included several reporters writing in notebooks, but most people looked to be Italians from Little Sicily. The priest recognized several of them. A few looked at him and smiled as he entered. They were pleased to see the popular priest there to support the family.

Two police officers were stationed at the door to the rear, and several others surrounded the room in the rear and at the sides. They kept a close watch over the crowd, looking for anything suspicious. There was a low buzz of conversation in the room, but when it occasionally grew louder, a sergeant in the rear announced, "Quiet in the court," and the talking grew softer.

What the priest was able to glean from what he heard was that most of the crowd was out for blood. They were very angry about the growing mob activity in their community, and pleased that finally someone was being held to account.

After a time, a door opened to the right of and behind the court reporter. Two men entered the room, and as they did so, everyone in the room stood. The first man was short, with a barrel chest poorly restrained in his dark grey suit. His white shirt was slightly rumpled, and a green tie hung somewhat to the left of center. He strode directly to the center of the room before the bench, and announced that the 21st Circuit Court of the State of Illinois was now in session, the Honorable James Q. Murphy presiding. From now on there would be no talking allowed unless asked to speak by the judge. Anyone not showing proper respect for the judge or the proceedings would be immediately ejected from the courtroom and the building. Then he proceeded to the table on the right and opened a folder there.

As the bailiff was speaking, Judge Murphy, wearing a long black robe, climbed the stairs to his chair behind the bench. He scanned the crowd as the bailiff brought the folder from the recorder's table and placed it before him. The two men conversed silently for a moment, as Murphy opened the folder and scanned a few pages. Then the judge nodded and the bailiff turned back to the crowd to announce, "The people versus Joseph Russo."

Father Luigi had attended a few trials before as moral support for families whose loved one had been accused of a crime, and once to give moral courage to a man who claimed to have been falsely accused. He had never encountered a crowd even remotely like this one. He was not always convinced of the fairness of these proceedings, any more than he had been in the old country. Nevertheless, he found the legal system far more desirable than settling differences by murder in the streets. He noticed that the two men sitting on the right, Cuccia's cousins, were staring constantly towards the defendant with looks that were seeking to achieve a fatal result right there in the courtroom.

Something else got his attention after the jury had been seated. Two of the jury members, in addition to paying attention to the judge and the attorneys for the state and for the defendant, stole frequent glances towards the left rear of the courtroom. The priest finally let his curiosity get the best of him, and nonchalantly turned around to scan the room behind him, as if there was someone he was looking for. His eyes went back and forth until he noticed a large man wearing a shiny blue suit with wide pin stripes. He looked like he could be newly off the boat from the old country. His gaze was intensely focused on the same two particular jurors. The man seemed to sense Fa. Luigi looking at him, and their eyes met. The priest quickly went back to scanning the room, as though it had been a mere coincidence. Then he turned back towards the trial, but he could not help to think there was something ominous in what he had seen.

Martin Gorski, the prosecuting attorney, charged the defendant with first degree murder. Russo stood with his attorney to say, "I no do it," which was followed by his attorney, who had finally taken the toothpick out of his mouth, saying, "The defendant pleads 'not guilty,' your honor." He returned the toothpick to his mouth as the two men sat down. Gorski's opening statement laid out the basics of the case, emphasizing that in addition to the police officer, there were 36 witnesses to the arrest, including 10 who would testify to having seen the actual killing. Grasso claimed that Russo was an upstanding citizen, gainfully employed by the railroad, and that the witnesses had confused him with someone else. To the priest, the lawyer seemed oddly nonchalant about making his case.

Gorski's first witness was Sergeant Byrne. The entire courtroom seemed transfixed by his graphic account of the chase down Townsend Street, the killer pulling out a revolver and shooting the victim behind the left ear, the confrontation, and the arrest. Byrne became especially dramatic when he described the moment when the two men stood face to face with their guns drawn, and a feeling of deep suspense filled the room. Several people leaned forward in their seats and turned their heads to hear as clearly as possible. Their attention never wavered as he recounted the gathering crowd, the march to the drug store, and the wait for the paddy wagon.

Gorski dwelled over the words that the defendant had said to him when first apprehended. "Could you please repeat for the jury, Sergeant, the exact words spoken by the defendant at that time?"

"Sure." (Byrne turned towards the jury.) "He said, 'You got me. You good man. You do your duty, just like I done mine just now.'"

"So," said Gorski, "he admitted the killing, is that right?"

Before Byrne could answer, Grasso jumped to his feet. "Your honor, I object," he said. "Mr. Russo did no such thing. He was acknowledging that the sergeant was just doing his job, and like a good citizen, it was Mr. Russo's job to obey the command of a police officer."

The judge, with a disgusted look on his face, said, "Objection sustained. Please redirect, counselor."

"Sergeant, did you take his statement as an admission of guilt?" asked Gorski.

"I sure did," he answered. "I saw him do it. He never left my sight from the moment he did it. He dropped the gun he used to do it, and I picked it up. It was still warm from being fired. And when he said I was just doing **my** job, I most certainly was, because my job was to apprehend and arrest the murderer, and that's just what I did."

The crowd thought this most amusing, making it necessary for the judge to strike his gavel several times to restore order.

"One more question," asked Gorski. "Do you see the person who committed the murder of Mr. Ciccia here in this courtroom?"

"Yes, I do.," he answered, pointing to the defendant. "It was that man right there."

Once again a loud murmur rose in the crowd, causing the judge to gavel for silence. Gorski returned to his seat, leaving the witness to be examined by the defense, but Grasso remained in his chair, leaning back with the toothpick still in his mouth. "Sergeant Byrne, how long have you been policing in that part of town?" he asked.

"About six months," he answered.
"You're Irish, aren't you?" asked the defense attorney.

"I object," said the prosecutor. "That has no relevance whatsoever."

"Objection sustained," said the judge. "The defense must refrain from making such ethnically charged remarks."

"Sergeant Byrne," asked Grasso, still swirling the toothpick. "Do all Italians look alike to you?"

Gorski jumped to his feet, shouting, "Your honor, this is an outrage," as more shouts were raised from the crowd.

This time the bailiff stepped to the front of the courthouse and yelled, "Order in the court. Order in the court," as the judge pounded his gavel.

When things finally quieted down, Judge Murphy spoke first to Grasso. "I warn you," he said. "One more comment like that and you will not only be barred from this court. I will throw you in jail and take away your attorney's license. Do I make myself clear, Mr Grasso?"

"Yes, your honor," he said.

Then the judge looked out at the crowd and said, "As for the rest of you. It is a privilege for you to be able to sit here in court and observe the practice of justice in our city. But if there are any more such outbursts, I will clear the courtroom, and we will continue with only the witnesses and jury present. This is my courtroom, and I intend to keep it orderly." Looking back at Grasso, he said, "You may continue your cross examination of the witness."

"No further questions," he said.

The next witness was Lieutenant Grady, who testified about the interrogation of the suspect at the police station. He also testified that the murder weapon was determined to have been "police positive." He said that meant it was a

32-30 style weapon used only by policemen and some security personnel. Asked how it could have come into the possession of the defendant, he said that several years ago a patrolman named John Wren had been slain in the same neighborhood. Wren's revolver was missing and had never been found. The police had compared the identification of the weapon used by Mr. Russo to that of the missing revolver, and found that it was a match. It was thought that Mr. Russo may have been involved in that shooting as well."

"Objection," called the defense lawyer. "You don't know any of that stuff. You're just spinning tales. The defendant didn't even live here then."

"Objection sustained," said the judge. "The jury will disregard those speculations."

Next, Patrolmen O'Connell and Hanrahan, along with Flynn, the drug store owner, testified that Russo was indeed the man that had been taken into custody the day of the murder. Five local residents also testified that they had witnessed the event, described what they had seen from different points of view, and identified the defendant as the man who had done it. Surprisingly, the defendant's attorney, Nicolo Grasso, did little or nothing to challenge any of the prosecution witnesses. He continued to lean back in his chair and twirl the toothpick in his mouth. Father Luigi found himself wondering what kind of trick he might have in store that allowed him to be so smug in the face of what seemed to be overwhelming evidence. And he wondered if it could have anything to do with the two jurors who continued to make eye contact with the man across the room.

The final witness for the prosecution was Mrs. Lucia Ciccia, the widow of the slain man. Father Luigi stood and stepped into the aisle to allow her to approach the bench. Before standing, she reached into her purse and took out a man's fedora hat. Holding her cross in one hand and the hat in the other, she walked thru the swinging gate that separated the spectators from the trial participants, and strode to the witness box with a determined look on her face. When asked to swear on the Bible her oath to tell the truth, she placed her left hand -- still holding the man's hat -- on the Bible, and raised her right hand -- lifting the cross high.

Prosecutor Gorski elicited the basics from her: she and Frank had known each other in Sicily before coming to America fifteen years ago, but had waited to get married until Frank was able to support a family; they had four children, ages 3 to 10; Frank was a wonderful husband and father; he worked hard at various jobs until he was able to start his own candy business; they weren't rich, but always had food on the table; he was an usher at St. Philip Church and active in the Knights of Columbus; and a kind, gentle man who would never hurt a flea. Then Gorski leaned in and asked very quietly, "And how are you getting along now, Mrs. Ciccia?"

At this question, the widow seemed to shrink in the witness chair, which already looked several sizes too large for her tiny frame, but now almost seemed to swallow her whole.

"Only by the grace of God," she sobbed, "and the help of Father Luigi and the good sisters. I don't know how we can do it. What will we do?" she asked, and looked imploringly at the prosecutor.

Then suddenly she shifted her gaze to the defendant, and her expression turned to one of violent anger. She stood to face him and raised her left hand, thrusting the fedora hat into the air. The hat had a ragged hole in its side, covered with dried blood.

"Look what you did to my Frank," she cried. "Look what you did!" Then she held the large cross next to it shouting, "I pray that God strikes you down for what you have done!"

At this the room erupted in sound. Niccolo Grasso almost swallowed his toothpick as he leapt to his feet to shout, "Objection! Objection!" But his shouts were drowned by the din in the room, which included the sound of the judge pounding his gavel and the bailiff calling, "Order in the court! Order in the court!" Some members of the jury sat open mouthed at this display, some turned away from the sight, and two put their heads into their hands either to cry or to pray.

When order was finally restored, an angry judge said, "The motion of the defense is sustained." Then he turned to the widow and said, "I sympathize for your loss, Mrs. Ciccia, but such demonstrations cannot be tolerated in a court of law. Mr. Gorski, please control your witness."

"Yes, your honor," he replied. "I have no further questions.

When Grasso declined to question the witness, she was dismissed, still clutching the hat and the cross in her hands, to return to her seat between the priest and the two cousins.

At this point the judge called a recess for lunch. The jury was dismissed from the room first. Before leaving the room himself, the judge told the spectators that they were free to go also, but that no seats could be reserved. If they left and returned later, they would simply have to wait in line to get in. This evoked a series of groans from the crowd, but the judge did not bother to gavel them down. He simply stood and exited by the same door that he had entered, as the bailiff stepped forward to announce, "The 21st Circuit Court of the State of Illinois is now in recess, to return at 1:30 pm sharp." The teams for the prosecution and defense went out, but none of the spectators left the room.

After what seemed to be an interminably long wait for those who were stuck in the uncomfortable benches, the trial finally resumed in the early afternoon. The teams for the prosecutor and defense returned. Then the bailiff and judge reentered at precisely 1:30 pm, along with the jury. When all had assembled the bailiff called the court in session, and the judge informed the defense that they were free to call their witnesses.

Nicolo Grasso called only three witnesses to the stand. The first, a Mr. Vito Marino, testified that the murderer was a much shorter, stouter man than the defendant. The second, Luca Privitera, testified that he had seen the defendant in the parade downtown during the time of the murder. The third, Uberto Gurrieri, said that he was Joseph Russo's supervisor on the railroad, that he was a good and dependable worker, and that he would never do such a thing. Father Luigi noted that none of the three looked directly into the eyes of the prosecuting attorney, and seemed to be reciting lines that they had memorized for the occasion. No matter what questions they were asked, they simply repeated what they had said previously. He also noted that the defendant simply looked forward with a vacant expression on his face, and that the two jurors whom he had noted previously continued to steal periodic glances at the same spectator in the rear. After the last of the three witnesses, Grasso said simply, "Your honor, the defense rests."

Following summary statements from the two attorneys, the judge instructed the jury that they were to rule on the charge of first degree murder, a crime punishable by hanging, and they were dismissed to render a verdict. Once again the judge and bailiff left the room, but the others stayed in their places. Two hours later the bailiff and judge reentered the room and the jury was brought back to their places. The judge asked if they had reached a verdict on the charge of murder in the first degree. The foreman, a bank teller named Michael Milligan, said they were unable to reach a unanimous verdict. They were deadlocked, with 10 voting guilty, 2 voting not guilty. This news caused another stir in the crowd, requiring some time to quiet down.

Judge Murphy gave the jury a long, hard look. Father Luigi tried to comfort Mrs. Ciccia, who was bent over and sobbing uncontrolledly. He noted that the two jurors who had been glancing at a man in the back of the room seemed to be inordinately interested either in a spot on the ceiling across the room or their own fingernails. After the jury was dismissed to return to their deliberations, the judge spoke privately to the bailiff and left the room. The bailiff then gathered the prosecutor and defender to accompany him to the judge's chamber. They returned after about 30 minutes, Grasso trying to suppress a smirk from his face, Gorski looking like he was ready to punch someone. An hour later, the judge reentered the courtroom and the jury was returned to their places.

"Have you reached a verdict?" the judge asked.

The foreman answered, "We have your honor." The defendant was asked to rise, and he stood along with his attorney.

"And what is your verdict?" asked the judge.

"On the charge of murder in the second degree, we find the defendant guilty as charged, your honor," said the foreman.

This announcement elicited many surprised looks and murmurs from the crowd.

Judge Murphy then turned to the defendant and said, "Mr. Joseph Russo, this court declares you guilty of murder in the second degree. I therefore remand you into custody, to serve a sentence of fourteen years in the state penitentiary. Officers, you may remove the prisoner. Members of the jury, I thank you for your service. I hereby declare this session of the 21st District Court to be closed."

Shock and confusion filled the room at this pronouncement. How could it only be 14 years? Why second degree? He deserves to be hanged. How could anyone say he was not guilty?

Handcuffs were put on the prisoner as his attorney whispered something in his ear. He was given only a moment to get a hug from his brother and sister, then led out of the courtroom with two officers clearing the way in front of him, one leading him by the elbow, and another following behind. The judge and court reporter left from the room behind the bench, followed by the members of the jury, who were escorted by the bailiff, as the remaining officers began herding the spectators from the room.

Mrs. Ciccia cried on Fa. Luigi's shoulder for some time, as the crowd slowly and noisily disbursed from the courtroom. He saw no need to hurry her along, since he could tell that it would be some time before she would be able to walk from the courthouse without jostling thru crowds of people. In addition, he didn't think that she would be anxious to deal with all of the reporters who would be pressing her with questions.

But suddenly she pushed herself back from the priest and, still sobbing, cried out, "Get me out of here. I can't breathe in here. Where is the justice? Get me out of this horrible place. Get me out of here."

She stood, the priest rising with her. He took her arm and led her into the aisle towards the rear doors. The two nephews went around them to take the lead, clearing a few people who were blocking the way down the aisle.

They walked down the hallway, down the stairs, and out the main entrance doors, passing people who turned to look at the aggrieved widow. Some turned angrily when the nephews pushed past them, but quickly made room when they saw that it was the widow who wanted to get thru.

On the steps in front of the courthouse, Nicolo Grasso was enjoying the spotlight, as he answered questions from a group of about 20 reporters and half that many photographers. Another slightly smaller group had cornered Prosecutor Gorski further down the steps. When some from both groups noticed that the widow was leaving the building, they broke off and hurried to her instead.

The questions and camera flashes came fast and furious. "What do you think of the verdict, Mrs. Ciccia?" "Did he get what he deserved?" "How are your children handling this?" "What will you do now?" "Was this a Black Hand murder?" "Was this a fair trial?"

She paid no attention to the questions, but noticing the defense attorney, headed towards him with a determined look. Father Luigi felt her strength suddenly returning as she pushed thru the reporters in the direction of the attorney for the defense. She got an angry look on her face and lifted up the cross and hat that she had displayed on the witness stand.

"You evil man," she said, holding the hat and cross in front of him. "May God strike you dead, along with that killer. You are just as bad as him, maybe worse. How can you speak up for a man like that? Have you no feelings?

What are we to do now? How can I care for his children? They no longer have a father."

Grasso at first attempted to answer her accusations, saying that he was sorry for her loss, but that his client was not guilty. But he quickly saw that the widow was not about to engage in a discussion, and reluctantly ceded his spot, walking thru the reporters and down the steps. The widow continued after him.

Father Luigi, who was no longer needed to support the widow, nevertheless stayed at her side. Scanning the large crowd on the steps and the sidewalk in front of the building, he noticed the man from the rear of the courtroom now standing on the street corner, leaning into a lamppost. Around the corner of the building came the two jurors who had regularly glanced at this man during the trial. When the mystery man caught their eye, he turned and crossed the street, heading east away from the courthouse on the other side. The two jurors looked around to see if anyone was watching them as they followed him across the street, maintaining a discreet distance. All three disappeared from view around the next corner.

Chapter 8

The Law Tries Again

"So a couple of people on the jury held out, and they had to settle for a second degree murder charge," said Marco. "But he still was given fourteen years. What happened?

"Another long story," said John. "In the meantime, I've got to make a quick stop in the little boys' room. You sure you're up for more of this tonight?"

"You bet, Uncle John," he answered. "I find this most en-lightening. While you're about your business, I'll get us each another cold one."

He walked to the front of the house and out the front door, stood on the front stoop and did a variety of stretches as he looked up and down the street. A young man hurried out of a house to the east, jumped into a car parked at the curb, and drove off down the street at a quicker pace than was wise for this narrow side street. Other than that, the street was very quiet. After a few more stretches, he went back inside, pulled a couple of Buds out of the refrigerator, and returned to the back porch.

Uncle John was already waiting back in his usual spot. "Ahhh," he said. "The pause that refreshes. Send me over one of those Buds." After Marco slid one across the table, both men took a good swig. Then John took a cigar out of his breast pocket and went thru his usual lighting ritual.

"So Marco," he said, "have you seen that old friend of yours since you're home? Danny, I think his name was. Always liked him."

"Yeah," he answered. As a matter of fact I'll see him this week. His brother's getting married on Saturday and I'm invited. They want me to go to his bachelor party on Friday night too."

"That sounds like fun," said John. "You bringing a young lady with you to the wedding?"

"No. I never had a girl waiting when I was off in the service, and I haven't been home long enough to meet anybody."

"Maybe you'll find a good one at this college you're going to."

"Could be, but don't hold your breath, Uncle John. They're all quite a bit younger, and this school tends to attract the very religious types, if you know what I mean."

"Since when do you have a problem with that? Your father went to mass two, three times a week. I know you weren't raised Catholic, but you did the Sunday School route and all that, and you're going to a religious school aren't you?" asked John.

"No problem at all," said Marco. "It's just a matter of degree, that's all. Anyway Danny wants to fix me up with a cousin of his from Texas."

"From Texas? John asked. "Whee haw! I hear those Southern belles are really something. Sounds promising."

"Maybe," answered Marco. "But I'm afraid that anybody that Danny and his brother would recommend is someone who would be way too wild for my taste."

"Sounds to me like you're being awfully picky. You know what I think? I think that one of these days you're going to run into somebody who'll knock you off your feet, and then it won't matter one bit whether she's a gangster's moll or a woman who lives for church suppers. You'll be a goner. Mark my words."

He reached into his pants pocket for his wallet, opened it up, pulled out a bill and put it on the table. "There," he said. "Twenty dollars says that's what's going to happen."

Marco laughed and said, "You're probably right, Uncle John, but put your money away. You're just trying to divert me from the information I'm looking for. How did my great uncle get out of prison?"

"Okay, okay," he said. "Get ready for an even longer story this time. And it's a doozy . . ."

114

Chicago, May, 1920
Second Trial; A Busy Weekend;
St. Louis Beckons

"Jesus, Mary & Joseph," said Sgt. Byrne. "You can't be serious. How the hell could that bastard be gettin' a new trial? He should have been hung after the first one. It was a bloody shame that he got off as light as he did after killing that poor man in cold blood like he did."

Byrne was sitting across from Lieut. Grady's desk in Grady's office. Asst. States Attorney Martin Gorski sat next to him.

"Bloody shame is right," said Gorski, as Byrne stood up and began pacing around the small office. "We had him dead to rights. No way he should have got off as light as he did, and now we've got to do the whole damn thing all over again."

"What's the basis of giving him a new trial?" asked Grady.

"They claimed the widow prejudiced the jury by carrying Ciccia's bloody hat and a crucifix into the witness box and waving it at them like she did. Hell, I thought it was the best part of the whole damn trial," said Gorski.

"You and me both, Marty," answered Grady. "You and me both. That jury needed to be reminded of what they were dealing with. I thought you did a great job with that trial."

115

"What I want to know," asked Byrne, continuing his pacing even though he could only get in four steps in each direction in the tiny office. "What I want to know is how anybody in the appeals court would even give the time of day to that sleeze-bag lawyer, Grasso. Makes my skin crawl, just thinking about him."

"Oh, we're way past him," said Gorski. "Guess who's representing him now? The Honorable Charles N. Goodnow, former state court judge." Gorski made a point of overemphasizing the word "honorable."

"You gotta be kidding me," said Byrne. "How'd he get a heavy hitter like that?"

"You tell me," said Gorski.

"Word on the street is that D'Andrea has suddenly taken an interest in supporting this young man, who has been treated so unfairly by the courts," said Grady.

"Saints preserve us," said Byrne.

"Who's D'Andrea?" asked Gorski.

"The former ward committeeman," answered Grady. "He no longer has the official office, but there's no doubt about who still runs the show. He says, 'jump,' and the alderman and anybody else connected with the organization asks, 'how high?'"

"You talking about the Republican Party organization or the Black Hand?" asked Gorski.

"Hmmf," said Byrne. "One and the same thing, Martin. One and the same thing."

"Well," said Grady. "I guess we've got to do the whole thing over again."

"Yeah," said Gorski, "and we almost didn't even get that much. My boss had decided to *nolle prosse* the case, and just let him go. We had a big fight over it and I almost quit."

"Not prosecute? Has the man gone daft?" asked Byrne, finally sitting back down, as if in shock.

"He doesn't think we'll be able to get as many witnesses this time around, besides which the opposition has had a lot of time to intimidate anybody who would be gutsy enough to come forward," said Gorski. "Luckily the Tribune and a couple of other papers got wind of the story. After they started reporting on it, he figured he'd better retry the case after all."

"Well," said Grady, "I guess you've got your work cut out for you."

"Huh," replied Gorski. "Don't I wish. This time around he's bringing in Tom Reilly as prosecutor. Bob Rollo from my office will assist him. Crowe told me I'm too emotionally involved in the case."

"It's about high time somebody got emotional about it," said Byrne. "Jesus, Mary and Joseph."

"Who's Tom Reilly?" asked Grady.

"Reilly & Cashen," answered Gorski. "Got offices in the Cunard Building. Not a bad guy, but he doesn't have all that much criminal experience. Plus, he's not going to be making near the money on this case as he does when he's working for all of his Gold Coast clients. I don't think he'll put in anyway near the effort that'll be required to get the job done."

"So what's in it for the States Attorney?" wondered Grady.

"He's up for reelection this year," answered Gorski.

Byrne stood up and banged his fist on the wall as he stormed out of the office.

*   *   *

James Martin stepped up onto the Western Avenue bus, paid his fare, and like the good citizen he was, moved to a seat towards the rear. He was a short man of medium build, with light brown hair whose every strand was kept in place with hair gel. He wore an inexpensive but very neat brown suit, starched white shirt, and wide green tie. A

118

brown derby hat with a black hat band sat lightly on his head. He was in a group of several people who got on at the same time, but he didn't pay much attention to the others. His mind was on the events of his day. As the bus pulled away from the curb and headed north, he turned his face towards the window, but didn't really notice anything outside either.

Early that morning he had left his north side home and taken this same bus route south to Grand Ave, where he transferred to a bus going east. He got off at Racine St., walked a block south to Hubbard, and turned west to his destination -- the Cook County Criminal Court Building. He had received a summons to appear for jury duty, and he always believed in doing his civic duty. It took all morning for the jury to be selected, most of which he spent sitting quietly in a room full of a wide assortment of people sitting on uncomfortable benches. He had never served on a jury, and hated taking off from his job as a bookkeeper at Marshall Field's Department Store, but he knew how important it was that every citizen be judged by a jury of his peers.

They were called six at a time to follow an official from the waiting room into the courtroom. There they were questioned by attorneys for the prosecution and the defense, in front of the judge, the Hon. John J. Sullivan. Martin was surprised to find himself selected for the jury. He had mixed feelings about it. He hated the probability of missing more days of work. Company policy allowed for it, but his wife would not be happy about the loss of wages, and his supervisor would overload him with work when he returned, in order to make him pay. On the other hand, he was intrigued at the possibility of observing a murder trial and even participating in rendering a judgment. The case had been written about in several newspapers, and his friends and neighbors would all be pumping him for information. It would make him a minor local celebrity for a time.

It was past noon when the last juror was seated. Then those selected were taken into the jury room and brought sandwiches and root beer for lunch. In the afternoon, the jury was seated again and the trial began with taking evidence. It seemed to Martin that the case was pretty clear cut. Sergeant Byrne's testimony had been quite compelling, and could be enough on its own to convict the killer. Other witnesses confirmed his account. Martin knew that the first trial had ended with a guilty verdict on a charge of second degree murder, and that ten of the jurors had actually voted in favor of hanging the man for murder in the first degree. From what he had heard so far, he could understand why.

Thru it all, the accused man, Russo, had mostly sat staring at the wall, showing no emotion. On one side sat his lawyer, who apparently was a former judge. He wore an expensive looking dark blue suit, looked very distinguished, and spoke in very refined English. Martin wondered how an immigrant could obtain such legal help. He knew that he certainly would not have been able to afford it. On the other side of Russo was a man who looked familiar, but Martin couldn't quite place him. He thought he had seen his picture in the papers somewhere, but couldn't quite remember why or when.

After Judge Sullivan recessed the trial until the following week, Martin was glad to head home. He snapped his attention from the trial back to his surroundings. The bus had come as far north as Belmont Street, and he eagerly looked out the window to see the entrance of Riverview Gardens Amusement Park. He was looking forward to spending some time there on Saturday with his wife, Emily, and their two boys. James Jr. was eleven years old; Edward was nine. Just a boy at heart, their father enjoyed riding the roller coasters and eating cotton candy at least as much as his sons did. Emily loved going to Riverview as well, mostly because she loved her husband and her boys, and nothing brought her more joy than seeing them all together and happy. Passing by the amusement park in the bus, Martin craned his neck to see the roller coaster tracks rising high above street level, with cars full of riders who screamed as they rode past. Two years ago Riverview had built The Whip, which was supposedly the highest and fastest roller coaster in the world. It sure gave him a thrill, and his oldest boy was tall enough to be allowed to ride with him this year. He got excited just thinking about it, and was glad that he had found a house for his family just a few blocks away, so that they could easily walk there as often as possible.

He stood up in his seat and pulled on a black cord above the window. The cord rang a bell in front of the bus, to let the driver know that someone wanted to exit at the next stop. Then he apologized as he climbed over the man who sat next to him in the seat, stepped into the center aisle, and made his way to the rear exit. Several others got up to leave the bus as well. He stepped out onto Western Ave. and turned the corner to walk east on School Street. His house was just a block east and several houses north on Oakley Ave.

As he came to the alley between Western and Oakley, he was surprised when two large, burly men came suddenly across the street and stood in his path. He was alarmed, and turned around, thinking to hurry back to Western Ave., where there would be more people to witness what was happening. But when he turned, he found himself confronted by a tall man in a shiny blue suit with wide pin stripes, and wearing a black fedora hat.

"Don't be in such a hurry, Mr. Martin," he said. "Or can I just call you James? Or how about Jimmy? I like that better. Let's be friends, Jimmy."

"I don't know you," said Martin. "Who are you?" he asked, as the two burly men came in close behind him.

"You can just call me Mr. Nice Guy. How about that? Cause I'm a-gonna be a real nice guy to you, Jimmy. I've got some nice pictures to show you, right here. You're gonna like 'em a whole lot. I know you will."

The man reached in his pocket and took out some photos, showing the top one to Martin. "Look at this fine looking boy," he said. "This must be James Jr. That's right, isn't it, Jimmy? Looks a lot like his father, doesn't he?"

The man showed the picture to the other two men. "Look at that," he said. "Jimmy Jr. looks a lot like his dad, don't he? Don't you think so?"

"Sure does," they answered.

"Here," said the man, handing him the photo. Martin looked stunned as he took the photo and looked at it. "That's it, you take it. I know that boy means a lot to you, Jimmy, doesn't he?"

Martin stood looking shocked and frightened and said nothing. But the man was insistent. "He means a lot you, doesn't he," the man asked, and poked Martin in the chest.

"Yes, yes he does," said Martin.

"You're very proud of him, aren't you?" asked the man.

"Yes," said Martin.

"Yes, what?" asked the man.

"Yes, I'm very proud of him," he answered.

"There, that wasn't so hard, was it?" asked the man. "Now here's another one," he said, placing another in his hand. "Nice picture, don't you think? Who's this?" he asked.

Martin looked at the picture, but said nothing.

"I asked you politely now, didn't I?" the man asked. "Now I'll ask you again," he said, poking Martin again in the chest. "Who's this?"

"Edward," said Martin.

"Edward," said the man. "The youngest son. The smallest. The weakest. I'll bet you have to keep a close eye on that one, don't you?" he asked.

"Yes," said Martin, barely able to speak.

"What's that?" asked the man. "Can't hear you. Speak up," he said, poking him again.

"Yes," said Martin, a bit louder.

"Yes, what?" asked the man.

"Yes, we keep a close eye on him," answered Martin, fighting back tears.

"Good thing you do," said the man. "Never know what kind of trouble kids can get into these days, do you? You keep that picture too, Jimmy. Now I've got another one to show you. Who's that fine looking woman, Jimmy? That couldn't possibly be your wife, could it? Look at this woman, boys," he said, showing the picture to the other men, who made appreciative noises. "How in the world did a puny guy like you ever end up with a woman like that? Umm, umm. A man could sure have a good time with a woman like that, couldn't he boys?" They grunted in response. "Sure would be a shame if something happened to that woman, wouldn't it Jimmy?" he asked. "I said, wouldn't it, Jimmy?"

Martin was no longer able to hold back his tears, as he replied, "Yes. Yes, it would."

"Well," said the man, "this is your lucky day, because we don't want anything to happen to them either, do we boys?" he asked.

"Naw," they replied. "Not us."

"No, we would hate to see something bad happen to that fine family of yours, so we came here today to do you a big favor. We're going to tell you one simple little thing you have to do to make sure that your family is safe and then you got nothing to worry about. You want to know what that one little thing is, Jimmy?" he asked.

"Yes," sobbed Martin.

"Well, you may have heard something about this trial going on right now. There's this good man named Joseph Russo who is on trial for murder, but he's being framed. He's an innocent man. And you wouldn't want to see an innocent man go to jail, or even worse, get hanged for something he didn't do, now would you Jimmy boy?" asked the man.

"No," sobbed Martin.

"No, I'm very sure you wouldn't want to see that happen. So if anybody ever asked you whether you thought he had done it, what would you say, Jimmy?"

"Not guilty," said Martin softly.

"What's that? Speak up, I can't hear you," said the man.

"Not guilty," he said, a little louder.

"Can you hear him, boys?" asked the man.

"No. Can't hear. Too soft," they answered.

"You need to speak up, Jimmy," said the man. "The judge and the jury need to hear you loud and clear."

"Not guilty," said Jimmy.

"That's a little better," said the man. "But still not good enough. The people sitting out there in the courtroom need to hear it too, just so there's no confusion, you understand? Let's try again."

"Not guilty," said Martin, forcing the words out.
"That's better," said the man. "Now you take all these photos with you. They're our special gift to you. They can help remind you of what a special family you have, and how a man has to do whatever he can to take care of his family, to make sure they don't get hurt. Isn't that right, Jimmy? I said, isn't that right, Jimmy."

"That's right," he answered.

"You bet that's right. Well, we've done our good deed for the day, boys. Helped keep a family from getting hurt for no reason at all except being stupid. And you're not stupid, are you, Jimmy?" he asked.

"No," said Jimmy.

"Good," he said. "Let's get going, men. Bye, Jimmy. Bye for now, but we'll be seeing you around. And that's a promise. You can count on us. He can count on us, can't he boys?"

"You bet," they said.

After the men left, Martin began walking slowly towards his home. His heart was beating very fast. He was breathing very quickly as well, almost hyperventilating, and trying to think of a way that he could slip into the house without his

127

family seeing how distressed he was, or noticing the wet trail flowing down the leg of his pants.

*   *   *

Father Bastioni walked south down Cambridge Street, headed towards house number 842. The Lombardi family had invited him to a celebration for their youngest child, Angelina, whom he had baptized at St. Philip just that morning. He always enjoyed these gatherings when he could find the time to attend. Especially he wanted to come today. He wanted to hear what people were saying about the trial.

He slowed down as he passed number 870, where the Cuccia family lived. While there were many people walking briskly on both sides of the street, and children running and playing, there was no sign of life at this house. The priest suspected that the family was at home, just not wanting to be seen. Sadness and gloom seemed to seep out from around the curtains and thru the windows.

Fa. Luigi was especially concerned for Catherine, the fourteen year old daughter. At the beginning of the trial for her father's killer, the girl had waved a revolver in the corridor of the Criminal Court Building, right outside the courtroom, where she announced that she would have her revenge if the court failed. Fortunately he had been there, and had stepped between the girl and a police officer, who had drawn his gun to shoot. The priest had restrained Catherine with the help of another officer. After the revolver was confiscated, Bastioni had convinced the police to let her go home in the care of an uncle, one of the Conzello brothers who were always lurking around the widow and her family. The officers were sympathetic to the girl's situation, and were not anxious to add to her troubles. But tomorrow the trial would resume, and he was worried that the girl might want to sneak in another weapon, and might actually try to use it.

The priest stopped in front of the house for a moment, placed his hand on the front door, and said a brief prayer for the grieving family. Then he returned to his walk down the street. He was still several houses away when he saw that Lucille Lombardo and her cousin Sophia were standing on the sidewalk in front of their house. When they saw him coming, they jumped up and down excitedly, and then started running towards him down the sidewalk.

"Father, father," said Lucille. "We were watching for you. Everyone is so excited." She clapped her hands and kept jumping as the three of them walked towards her house, unable to contain her enthusiasm. "We're all in the back," she said. "There's lots of food, and music, and all my cousins are there, and isn't Angelina the prettiest little girl you've ever seen? Didn't she look wonderful in her white baptismal gown? Mama tells me that I wore the same one in mine. My grandmother made it back in Sicily. You remember my cousin, Sophia, don't you, father? She still hasn't been baptized. In Sicily they lived too far away from the church. You could baptize her too, couldn't you, father? She's not a baby anymore. Do you have to be a baby to be baptized? Would she have to have a white gown? The one Angelina and I wore would never fit her."

Father Luigi laughed, and tried to respond to her questions whenever he could get a word in edgewise, and was glad when they arrived at their destination.

As Lucille led him down the gangway, he could hear music and singing coming from the courtyard behind the house. He recognized the song as *"Abballati, Abballati,"* a song usually sung at weddings, but enjoyed whenever people were gathered for a good time.

> *Dance, dance, single and married men,*
> *And if you do not dance well,*
> *I will not sing or play.*

And dancing they were. The yard was full of people, and most of them were dancing, filling up whatever space was available. In order to enter the courtyard, he had to stay close to the fence that separated them from the adjoining yard. A group of people in that yard were also dancing along.

Lucille called out loudly above the din, "Mama, Mama, Father is here. Father is here!"

Mrs. Lombardo, a plump, round-faced woman with a pleasant face adorned by a huge smile, worked her way towards him and opened her arms wide to give him a big hug. "Father Bastioni," she said, "we are so glad that you could come to our humble home on such a blessed day. Come, come. You must have something to eat."

She led him to a makeshift table made of an old door laid across four stools, one at each corner. The table was covered with food dishes, most probably brought by friends and neighbors. Mrs. Lombardo handed him a plate and pointed out the variety of options. "You must have my eggplant, father," she said. "Everyone says it is the best."

Fa. Luigi thanked her and followed her advise, as she went off to greet others. In truth, he did not consider himself the partying kind, but he loved to watch his people enjoying themselves, and his parishioners always seemed to appreciate his taking the time to come. He was never sure exactly why. Most felt awkward trying to carry on a normal conversation with a priest. So he was usually content to eat the delicious food as he stood where he could observe and listen to conversations. But today he had an added incentive.

He noted that against the fence across from where he had entered were the musicians. Along with a guitarist, a man played the *ciaramedda*, an Italian version of a bagpipe. Another played an *organetto*, a folk accordion. Two teenagers played energetically on jaw harps. And a couple of young girls bobbed around as they beat a rhythm on tambourines.

There were a few chairs against the back of the house across from where he stood. Grandparents and other elders had been given the honors, and younger people periodically brought them food and drinks. Fa. Luigi worked his way thru the dancers to stand by the elders. Not surprisingly, they were talking about the trial. It seemed to be the only topic of conversation these days in the various Italian neighborhoods on the north, west, and south sides of the city. "Did you go to the first trial?" "Do you know anyone who was there?" "Will Joseph Russo get what he deserves and be hanged?" they wondered. The unanimous opinion was that something worse than hanging would be appropriate for the cold blooded killer. "Will someone take up the vendetta and take revenge if he isn't?" "If he's convicted, what effect will that have on the Black Hand?" The priest made a mental note to get to the trial early the next morning. If local gossip was any indication, the crowds would be at least as large this time around.

The tempo and mood of the music changed, as the band began to play *"Sicilia Bedda."* At once the dancing stopped, and it seemed that the whole crowd turned towards the musicians and began to sing along in Italian.

Beautiful Sicily, I can never forget you.
So great is this love, as great as the sea.
I remember my first love, the land that gave me life,
my youth, my mother, and all my friends.

Fa. Luigi joined in the singing, and was surprised at the wave of emotion that came over him. He didn't often think of his homeland. He was too busy with his life in the new world, and the struggles of his people to survive and thrive here. But now he remembered his childhood in Bargecchia, Italy. Pictures of his father, Casimiro, and especially his mother, Luigia, passed before his eyes. He thought of the growing certainty of his calling to the priesthood, his vows to the Order of the Servants of Mary, the ocean journey to the new world, his years of teaching philosophy in Wisconsin and in British Columbia, and finally his appointment here at St. Philip. A feeling of deep love and compassion filled him as he looked out at these people. He knew their struggles and their courage. He knew their goodness and their weakness. He felt their disappointment and their enduring hope. And suddenly he knew that this place and these people were now his true home and calling, and where his ministry would remain and find fulfillment. The possibilities were great in this new land, but so were the difficulties. They could build something here so much better for them than the old country. But life was so much harder for them here than he imagined it would be. And a few of them had brought with them some of the worst of the land they had left behind. His heart ached for them all.

His reveries were rudely interrupted as Lucille Lombardo and her cousin pushed thru the dancers to get to the priest, dragging a man and woman behind her. Judging from their clothing and their humble demeanor, Bastioni could tell that they were recent immigrants.

"Father," she said, "here are Sophia's parents, Mr. & Mrs. LaGattuta. She's my aunt, my father's sister. They want to talk with you about getting Sophia baptized."   Lucille was bouncing up and down as she spoke, and Sophia's eyes were big and wide with hope.

After making arrangements to visit with the couple to make plans for the baptism, Bastioni paid his respects to the seated elders and his Lombardi hosts, and worked his way thru the crowd to the gangway that led back out to Cambridge Street. As he was leaving, the band was playing *"Addio, Lugano Bella,"*

> *Farewell, beautiful Lugano, O sweet, pious land.*
> *Expelled without guilt, the workers go away*
> *And leave singing, with hope in their hearts.*

*   *   *

134

On Monday morning the Ciccia family walked up the stairs of the courthouse and opened the double glass doors leading to the great hallway. Fa. Luigi led Mrs. Ciccia by the arm, as the Conzello brothers held the doors open. Catherine, the fourteen year old daughter, followed close behind them. They were anxious to begin this second day of the trial, hoping that this time there would be a guilty verdict on the charge of first degree murder. Two officers opened a path for them thru the crowd of those waiting for a chance to be allowed into the courtroom. When they came to the courtroom door, a sergeant came forward to stop them.

"I'm sorry, Mrs. Ciccia," he said, "but I'm afraid that your daughter will not be allowed in the courtroom."

The widow became distressed, not understanding what the policeman was saying, and wondering why they were being kept out. She looked up pleadingly to the priest, while Catherine shouted, "No! No! He killed my father. I've got to get in there."

Nick Conzello restrained the girl and whispered something in her ear, while Bastioni explained things to Mrs. Cuccia. She insisted that her daughter had been deprived of a father, and was certainly old enough to see that justice was done.

The sergeant remained adamant, saying that the judge insisted on it, since Catherine had threatened everyone with a firearm last week. Fa. Luigi asked if he could make an appeal to the judge, and that he would vouch for the good behavior of the girl. When the family continued to insist, the sergeant agreed to carry their concerns to the judge. He went thru the courtroom door and was gone for several minutes, during which the priest tried to impress upon the girl that she would have to control her emotions if she expected to be allowed into the trial.

When the sergeant returned, he told them that the judge would allow Catherine into the courtroom, but first she would have to submit herself to a search in his office in order to assure him that she was not carrying a weapon. The sergeant took the girl with him, and the others were ushered to their spot in the first row, behind the desk of the prosecuting attorney.

Once again, the priest sat at the aisle next to Mrs. Cuccia. On her other side was an empty chair for Catherine. The Conzello brothers occupied the next two. Attorneys Thomas Reilly and Robert Crowe turned and greeted the widow, her nephews and the priest. Then they returned to the notes on their table, occasionally conferring with one another.

A man and two women made their way down the aisle to sit in the first row on the defendant's side of the room. Fa. Luigi noted that the man bore a resemblance to the defendant. At the last trial he had learned that it was Joseph

Russo's brother, Pietro, his sister, Lucia, and Pietro's wife, Rose. Their names and appearance indicated that they were also Italian immigrants, but he had not seen them at St. Philip's. Pietro looked a bit shorter than his brother, and his face was not as long and narrow, but the resemblance was plain to see.

As they came to their seats, the two men at the defendant's table turned to greet them. One the priest recognized as Anthony D'Andrea, the former ward committeeman. Word on the street was that he was deeply involved with the Black Hand, and continued to run the political machine from behind the scenes. Why was he here? Bastioni did not like the look of it. The priest had heard that the other man was the attorney for the defense, who was a former judge. How could this railroad worker from out of town obtain such a high-powered defense team? The priest's heart sank, and he began to believe the rumors about the whole trial being a sham.

After the judge entered and the jury was seated, Mrs. Ciccia reached inside her coat and took out the bloody hat and the crucifix, holding one tightly in each hand. Fa. Luigi gave a deep sigh. He had strongly advised her not to bring them again, since they were the cause given for a new trial. However, it began to look like there would have been some other excuse given for a retrial in any case.

The officers at the door began allowing others to enter the room, and it did not take long to fill it. As the others came in, the sergeant brought Catherine out from the door behind the bailiff's table, and brought her to sit beside her mother. "The judge has allowed her to stay," he said. "But he made it plain that she is not to make a sound or do anything else to disrupt the court. If she says or does anything the judge doesn't like, she will not only be removed from the courtroom. She will be sent to juvenile detention. Is that clear, ma'am?"

After some discussion with Fa. Luigi, she said that she understood, and began to speak softly with Catherine, who sat with a sour, angry look on her face.

The priest felt that the beginning of the trial the previous week had been pretty similar to the first one. Lots of pretty conclusive evidence, it seemed to him, although there were a couple of fewer witnesses, which was no surprise.

But as he looked at the jury now, he was puzzled. Something was different, although he wasn't immediately sure what it was. Gradually it became clear to him that it was their demeanor. Last week they had all seemed very attentive, very engaged. They looked liked a group of citizens who were pleased to do their civic duty, and were honored to participate in a trial that had gained such notoriety. Some sat up on the edge of their chairs, not wanting to miss anything. Over the weekend something had changed. Today some of them still showed the same attentiveness, but several were noticeably different. They looked distracted. Like they would rather be anyplace else than in that courtroom. Their gaze wavered about the room, as if their minds were far away.

One man kept squirming in his chair, and looked as if he wanted to get up and walk out of the room. Then the man did something that made the situation dishearteningly clear to Fa. Luigi. He cast a furtive glance to the back of the courtroom. The priest paused for a moment, took a deep breath, and tried to nonchalantly turn and glance around the room. Just as he feared, he saw seated in the rear a very large man wearing a shiny blue suit with wide pin stripes. Sadly, he already knew how this trial would end.

*   *   *

Pietro Russo drove his black Ford Model T down the alley behind the courthouse. His wife, Rose, and his sister, Lucia, sat in the back seat. He saw a police officer standing at a rear door, and drove up to it. The officer looked both ways down the alley, and seeing no one else there, he opened the door. Another officer led Joseph Russo out the door and hurried him over to the passenger seat of the Model T. The car drove to the end of the alley, where Pietro took a hurried look in both directions, then quickly turned west, away from the crowds angrily shouting at the main entrance. Joseph put an arm up on the window, obscuring his view from anyone on the street who might look in their direction. After they had travelled several blocks without incident, the four passengers finally began to breathe more easily and calm their rapidly beating hearts.

"*Grazie, fratello*," said Joseph. "*Grazie.*"

"You're my brother," Pietro answered.

They rode in silence thru busy city streets for a while. Pietro turned south on Western Ave. and took it down to Ogden Ave, heading southwest. They soon came to a highway sign that said "Illinois Rt. 4."

"I'm not familiar with this road," said Joseph. "Where are we headed?"

"St. Louis," answered Pietro.

"St. Louis?" asked Joseph. "Why in the hell would we want to go to St. Louis?"

"Because I just bought some property down there for Rose and me," he answered. "It's out on the edge of town. There's a lot of land. Two big houses, each with four bed-rooms. I figure we can raise vegetables there, make some extra money when I retire from the railroad. Got myself transferred down that way. The boss wasn't too happy about it, but tough. It'll be best for our family."

"You gotta to be kidding me," said Joseph. "St. Louis. You know all my contacts are in Chicago and Grand Haven."

"That's right," he answered. "And so are your enemies."

"Whadda you talk about?" asked Joseph. "I ain't afraid of nobody. What enemies?"

"Joseph," said Pietro. "We're Sicilians. What do we Sicilians do when somebody kills somebody in our family?"

"We bump off the son-of-a-bitch," he answered.

"That's right. And as far as the Ciccia family is concerned, **you're** the son-of-a-bitch. You were busy looking at the ceiling during the whole trial, so I doubt you saw the two big, mean looking guys sitting next to the widow. They never took their eyes off you the whole time, and it didn't look like they were ready to give you a big kiss."

"Hell, I don't care about them," he said.

"No?" said Pietro. "Well, just about everybody in Little Sicily knows that after you shot Ciccia, the two of them went and clipped their fingers in his blood right there on the sidewalk."

"You mean they've got a vendetta on me?" Joseph asked.

"What does that sound like to you?" asked Pietro.

"Hell, I've got friends a whole lot scarier than those two bozos," he answered.

"Yeah," said Pietro, "but while you were changing clothes back there in the courthouse, we were out in front and walking to get the car. And what we saw out there was several hundred Italians screaming for your blood. The cops had to muscle them to force them out of the building. They were ready to go back there and rip you apart, piece by piece. You need to get out of town, Joe. They're not going to let this go. And you're my brother. I want you to live. Rose and I are about to start a family. Who else can I get to be their godfather?"

"St. Louis." said Joseph. "St. Louis. You gotta be joking me."

"It's not so bad down there, believe me," said Pietro. "There's a big area they call The Hill that's a lot like Little Sicily. The Irish even call it Dago Hill. And it's a good place to raise a family."

"I appreciate what you're doing, little brother, but I don't think I can do it. You don't know what I'd be leaving behind. I got connections here. Did you see how they took care of me? Got me that big time lawyer. And that D'Andrea guy, he's a big time pol around here. They told me they'd take care of me, and they did. They did."

142

Pietro sighed. "Look, just go along for a little while, okay? Just until the heat dies down. There's murders up here all the time, and after awhile most of the people will have other things to think about. There won't be so many people looking around for you, so they can rat you out. Give it a little time. Can you do that much?"

Joseph was silent for awhile, then he said, "Okay. Okay, little brother. I'll do it for you, cause it'll make you feel better."

*   *   *

Lieutenant Grady sat at his desk with his head in his hands, as Sergeant Byrnes stormed about the room, banging walls and filing cabinets. Grady didn't make any attempt to calm him down. He felt like doing the same thing himself.

"Why bother to pretend that we're about the law and order business?" Byrnes asked. "I should have just shot the bastard on the spot. I could have claimed he was about to shoot me and I had no choice. The son of a bitch. Not guilty. NOT GUILTY! Seven to five not guilty. They call that justice? Those Italians are good people there, but along comes somebody like that Russo and no wonder they all get called *dagos* and worse. No wonder they have a hard time getting jobs and finding a place to live. And our HON-OR-A-BLE courts and judges — Jesus, Mary and Joseph. Why do we bother, Edward? Why do we bother?"

Grady was silent for a few moments as Byrnes stormed about. Then he lifted his head out of his hands and said, "Let's go get drunk."

*   *   *

Father Luigi sat at the desk in his office, reviewing the financial report from the parish treasurer. His people were very generous in their offerings to the church. Unfortunately, very few were people of means. Their new building was wonderful. It added so much to the worship life of the congregation, had already become the center and anchor of Little Sicily, and really helped to convey their feeling of permanence and security, that they had truly found a new home here in this country. But it would take many years to pay for it, and the upkeep was also substantial. The Servants of Mary, the Servite Order of which he was a member, continued to give substantial support, but the local congregation was expected to assume a growing share of expenses each year.

He always smiled when he thought of the school that was even now under construction across the street, almost finished. One of his favorite activities was recruiting families by giving tours of the grounds where he painted word pictures to describe in glowing terms where the various rooms would be and what would happen there. Soon the Dominican Sisters would be arriving to take charge and get the school up and running by this fall. How wonderful that would be! But it had to be paid for.

He racked his brains trying to think of fund raising ideas. Should they have a parish festival of some kind? St. Bernadette's had one each year that brought crowds from all over and seemed to raise a lot of money. He made a note to contact Fa. Conway about it, to see how they had gotten it started. Church life in this country was very different than back home in Italy. Parishes had a lot more freedom to do things on their own, but along with that came a lot more stress from having to pay for everything. Especially in a parish of poor immigrants.

He gave a great sigh. "Ah, Luigi," he thought. "You knew it wouldn't be easy. That's why you came here. Because the people here need the hope of the gospel and the ministry of the church. And when people questioned you, and asked you how you could possibly accomplish the things that were needed, what did you answer, Luigi? You always said the same thing. You said, 'God will provide.' And he will, Luigi. He will."

A knock at the office door roused him from his musings. "Come in," he said.

Sister Maria Josephina stepped into the room. She was one of the Italian nuns who had come to run the church's kindergarten and nursery, and to assist with running the parish. In truth, the priest didn't know how he could possibly get along without them. He had said more than once that it was really the sisters who ran the church. The nun wore the traditional habit of her order, a flowing black robe with a large, black hood accented by a white cowl.

"I'm sorry to disturb you, Father, but someone has asked to speak with you. Two men, actually, but one seems to do all the talking. Is this a convenient time, or should I make an appointment?"

"This would be fine. You can just send them here. And thank you, sister."

The priest stood and came out from behind his desk when two men entered the office. One was of medium height and build, and wore an expensive looking dark suit, white shirt, and dark blue tie. His black hair was slicked back and looked lately groomed. The other man was slightly shorter, but looked muscular even underneath his brown suit. He wore a white shirt with a green tie that was somewhat casually knotted. Both were carrying fedora hats in their hands. He didn't recognize them as being mass attenders, but they may have been. The numbers of worshippers had increased to the point that he could not get to know everyone, much to his disappointment.

As Fa. Luigi shook their hands, they introduced themselves as Claudio Vicari and Vince Nicolosi. He invited them to sit on two chairs there in front of the desk.

"Thank you for taking the time to see us, Father," said Vicari. "We feel a part of your parish, even though you may not remember seeing us at Sunday mass. We have been here for baptisms, weddings, funerals. We have family members who have benefitted very much from your church. You have become very important to our Italian community."

"Thank you," said the priest. "The church is here to serve all of God's people."

"Anyway, Father," continued Vicari, "even though we are not the regular Sunday morning kind of Catholics, we want to do something special to show our appreciation for your good work here. Since it is a rather large contribution, I wanted to present it to you personally."

He handed across the desk a large, thick envelope. "This is our contribution, Father. You may use it in any way you see fit. I'm sure that this fine building must have cost you a pretty penny. And I know that you are building a school across the street. That will be a fine thing for our community, Father. I will probably send my own children to attend."

"Oh," said the priest, not yet picking up the envelope. "You have children?"

"Yes," he answered. "A boy who is eight and a girl, six. My son, Vito, goes to public school now, but he doesn't like it much and isn't doing as well as I'd like. I think some good, strict nuns are just the thing he needs."

"I see," said Father Luigi. "You may just be right about that. How about you, Mr. Nicolosi? Do you have any children?"

"Naw, not me," he answered. "Least not that I know of," he snickered. Nicolosi glared at him, and he stifled his smile.

"So, father," said Vicari, "I would appreciate it if you would open the envelope and count the donation, please, so's we can be sure of the amount."

"Oh," the priest said. "Would you like a receipt?"

"No," he answered. "That won't be necessary."

Father Luigi opened the envelope and took out two large stacks of bills. On top were five hundreds, which he very seldom saw, certainly not in the collection baskets. The rest were twenties and tens, coming to a total of $2,000.
The priest felt both excited and uneasy at the same time as he straightened the two piles on his desk. "This is very generous, gentlemen," he said. "Very generous, indeed. You must be a very prosperous man, Mr. Vicari."

"Yes, I am," he answered. "This country offers many opportunities for people who are willing to work hard for a living."

"It certainly does," said Fa. Luigi. "What exactly is your occupation, may I ask?"

"I am a business man," he answered.

"Oh," said the priest. "I haven't seen your name on any of the stores around here."

"No, Father," he said. "I guess you'd say I'm more on the wholesale end of things."

"Really? What goods do you deal in?"

"No one special thing," answered Vicari. "I just look for whatever good opportunities come my way, and I make the most of them. A little of this, a little of that. Know what I mean?"

"No," answered the priest. "I'm not sure that I do."

"Well, as I said, Father, you may use this however you see fit," said Vicari as the two men rose from their chairs.

"Are you sure you don't want a receipt?" asked the priest, rising with them.

"No, thank you. That won't be necessary," he said. "We won't take up any more of your time. I'm sure you must be a busy man."

"Thank you for coming," said the priest, "and on behalf of the children of this parish, I thank you for your donation. Let me walk you to the door."

The men walked down a short corridor, past the church office, to a large double door that led to the street. After shaking hands again at the door, the two men left. Fa. Luigi held the door open and watched them as they walked towards a black sedan parked at the curb. Standing on the sidewalk next to the car was a tall man wearing a dark blue suit with wide pin stripes. The man had been looking back and forth down the street as the others left the church building. Now he turned towards them, then opened the rear door for Vicari to get in. Nicolosi walked around to the other side and got in as well. Then the tall man glanced briefly towards the priest, walked around to the driver's side door, got in, and drove off.

Father Luigi stood in the door for some time, looking out at the street. His heart was beating faster than his physical exertions would have required. Finally he closed the door and walked to the church office, stuck his head in the door, and called out, "Sister Maria, I'm going next door for lunch."

The nun peeked out from the storage closet, holding two reams of copy paper in her hands, and replied, "Go right ahead, father. I'll take care of things here."

The priest left the building and walked next door to the church rectory. He sighed as he took off his black suit jacket and hung it on the coat rack in the entryway. A woman's voice came from the rear of the house. "Is that you, father?"

"Yes, Mrs. Svenson. It's me," he answered.

"Tilda, father. Please call me Tilda. I've got your pasta all ready. Come out and get it before it gets cold," she called.

"Yes, I'm coming," he said.

He walked slowly back to the kitchen, where his sixty something cook and housekeeper was walking across the kitchen floor carrying a tray of food. "No, not here, father," she said. Please go to the dining room. It's so much nicer there, and I've already got your place set for you."

The priest sighed again as he followed her obediently thru the door into the dining room. He would have much preferred to eat in the more homey setting of the kitchen, but he was too tired to argue. He knew she meant well.
"I keep trying to learn how you Italians like your pasta, father," she said, as she set a plate of spaghetti on the table. The silverware, napkin, a glass of red wine, and a glass of

water were already there. "You work so hard, and I want it to be just right for you. My neighbor, Mrs. Grasso, is trying to teach me, but she tells me I have a lot to learn."

"Your cooking is just fine," said the priest as he sat at the head of the table. It was a table for six, but he sat there alone. The diocese kept talking about the need for more priests, what with the rapidly growing Italian population in the community, but they never seemed to arrive.

As Tilda returned to the kitchen, and the sound of dishes began, he took a small sip of wine and pecked for a moment at his food. Then he sat back in his chair and sighed yet again. He pushed back his chair, got up, and walked into the parlor, where he picked up a missal from a table next to the comfortable chair where he liked to do his reading. He brought it back to his place at the table, sat down, and opened it to the scripture lessons for the coming Sunday. Holding the book in his left hand, he tried to eat with his right hand at the same time. As a younger man, he had always envisioned that he would be a great preacher, inspiring his congregation to deep faith and powerful deeds of love and service. But usually it was difficult to find anything worth saying at all. Responding to the daily struggles of his people consumed almost all of the time and energy he had to give.

The priest was about half way thru with his meal when Tilda Svenson reentered the dining room. She noted how little food had been eaten and the open book in the priest's hand, and she seemed to be torn between returning to the kitchen or remaining there. Finally she said, "Father, may I speak with you for a moment?"

Bastioni turned towards her, surprised. He closed the book, set down his fork, and said, "Of course, Mrs. Svenson."

She nervously pulled out a chair and sat down, then looked at the priest as she said, "It may not be my place to say so, father, but I have been worried about you lately. You used to be so light hearted. You came in singing a hymn, or even something from Italian opera. Now it seems that you are just worn down by cares. Is there something I can do to help?"

He paused for moment, taken totally by surprise by her remark. "Is it so obvious?" he asked.

"Yes, father," she said. "Others have noticed as well, I'm sure. We all know what a caring man you are, and how much your people depend on you, so it hurts us all to see you so sad. How can I help?"

He looked up at the chandelier on the ceiling before answering. He should just tell her that he was fine, and to stop worrying. But it bothered him that his weariness was so obvious. Maybe he should confide in his bishop, but he had never been that comfortable with the man. Would it be absurd to unburden himself with his Swedish housekeeper? At least she was not a member of his parish. And she seemed to be a very sensible, caring woman. He decided, probably because he did not have the energy to resist, to actually share some of his burden with her.

"You are right, Mrs. Svenson. Tilda," he said. "I have been letting my people's cares weigh me down. It's just that they have so many struggles. I came here because there was nothing for these people back in Sicily. They come here with such high hopes. And I had such high hopes for them."

"Don't you have hopes for them anymore, father?" she asked.

He sighed. "Oh, yes. Yes, I guess I still do. But life here is so much harder than I thought it would be. Jobs are difficult, dangerous, and hard to get. Then just when someone thinks they are getting somewhere, they lose their job, and cannot support their family. Or they are injured, or even die in some kind of accident and their family has no way to survive. There are schools here, but the children, especially the boys, don't want to go. They would rather be doing something to make a little money, and many of the families need them to go out and get a job so they can put food on their table. And worst of all, some of our people have turned to lives of crime. They remember how things were in the old country, when a few cruel and powerful men controlled everything, and they dream of becoming such men themselves. I am sorry to go on this way. I know that there are many good people here, and that many of our people are doing well."

"You know, father," said Tilda, "my people have been here a little longer. It was that way for them in the beginning as well. But it gets better. My husband, Karl-Erik, took a long time to find his place when he first came to America. He spent years moving around the country. Mostly he worked on farms. He had aunts and uncles and cousins who had farms here. In Iowa. In Nebraska. In Texas even. They all welcomed him and offered him work, but he was not cut out to be a farmer. He came back to Chicago and worked at the Stockyards for awhile. Like you say, it was hard work. It didn't pay much. And lots of people got hurt there. Every day when he was gone at work, I prayed and I prayed that he would come home safe. So many of our neighbors had gotten hurt there. But then somebody told him that McCormick Harvesting Machines was hiring people. He went there and got a job running a big machine. Now the company's even bigger, and it's called International Harvester. It's a union job too, so the pay is pretty good. Good enough so that we could finally get married. So you see, father, your people will find a way too. I know they will. They just need you to keep believing in them."

Father Bastioni was smiling at her. He had never heard her say more than a few words before.

Tilda suddenly became very self-conscious. She looked away, stood up, and pushed her chair back under the table. "Oh, listen to me, going on and on like that. I'm sorry, father. I don't know what got into me."

"No," said the priest. "Thank you for sharing, Tilda. I never knew so much of your story before. It's exactly what I needed to hear. But I think I'm finished eating now. You may clear the place if you wish."

He stood up, taking the missal with him, and went to his reading chair in the parlor, keeping his place as he walked. Once again he looked at the text which he planned to preach on the coming Sunday. The words seemed to haunt him. They seemed to speak to him with a special power.

"He looked forward to the city that has foundations, whose architect and builder is God."

The priest read the haunting words once again, and as he looked up towards the ceiling, his thoughts returned to the day in 1908 when he was ordained a priest in the Order of the Servants of Mary. He could clearly picture the cathedral there in Orvieto, Italy. He remembered the pride on the face of his mother that day, and the sadness his father tried to hide, not just over the fact that his son and namesake would soon be leaving for America and would give them no grandchildren, but also that the son's surname had been changed from Gemigani to Bastioni.

Father Luigi gave a deep sigh, and returned his attention to the text in front of him. "Ah," he thought wistfully, "it had all seemed so clear and so noble then." He went on further in the text.

"If they had been thinking of the land they left behind, they would have had the opportunity to return. But as it is, they desire a better country, that is, a heavenly one."

Would his people have been able to return, he wondered? Would they have wanted to? Certainly not these Sicilians. What did they have to go back to? But why did so many insist on bringing the worst of the old country with them to the new one?

"He looked forward to the city that has foundations, whose architect and builder is God."

The priest stared at the passage for a moment, then put it down into his lap. Abraham was looking for a city whose builder and maker is God, he thought. What would that look like? A city of justice and peace. A city where we treat our neighbors with love and respect. A city where there is enough for everyone. A city where the children are joyful and thriving. A city where immigrants and poor people are treated with dignity and respect. A city where people can live in safety. A city where working people can earn a living wage.

Could Chicago become such a city? Could St. Phillip be such a community? What would it take? There was so much opportunity here, so much possibility. But also so much suffering and cruelty. So much inequality and injustice.

Suddenly he realized that he could not keep the money the men had given him. It could be put to good use in building the school, of course. But he felt that somehow that money would tarnish and cheapen the very purpose and value of the school. It must be a school built on love, not murder. Perhaps he should burn it. Or tell the police about the two men who brought it. But what good would that do? He really had nothing but suspicions to share. The money should really go to the Ciccia family. But they would never accept it if they had any idea where it came from. He decided that he would tell the police about the two men. It might help them in their dealings with the Black Hand to know who was behind some of the murders. And he would give the money to the men in the church's St. Vincent De-Paul Society. They could give the Ciccia family a regular amount every week as a gift from the parish community.

He sighed and sat back in his chair, closed his eyes and tilted his head back. Then he took some deep breaths, put his head in his hands, and wept.

Chapter 9
Life, Love Go On
St. Louis, 1976

Marco came up to a gate that led into a large, rectangular courtyard at the side of St. Stanislaus Church. A tall, black, wrought-iron fence surrounded the area on two sides. The other two sides abutted the church building. Just inside the fence, tall bushes gave the space a modicum of privacy and the hint of a natural setting, hiding the brick buildings and grim city streets in the neighborhood where the church was located. He entered along with a stream of people who had just left the wedding ceremony in the church sanctuary. Marco had sat alone near the rear of the church, on the groom's side. While he knew Danny's family members, they had either been in the wedding party or sitting in the first few pews in front.

Inside the courtyard there were some long tables set in a line parallel with the church wall. Several warming trays were there, and servers were going back and forth thru a door to the building as they filled the trays. At the end of the line of tables was a bar from which people had started getting drinks. The other church wall came out at a right angle. In front of that wall was what looked like a typical wedding band: keyboard, bass, drums, guitar, and a female vocalist. The rest of the courtyard was mostly grass, with lots of tables and chairs spread around, and an open space in front of the band for dancing. Colored, inflated balloons were flying from the bushes.

The band was playing a song that sounded very familiar to Marco, but he couldn't quite figure out what it was. A few middle-aged couples were dancing to it energetically. Finally it came to him. The song was "Just Because." Marco knew it as an Elvis Presley rock song, but this band made it sound like "The Beer Barrel Polka," and that's the kind of dance that was being done. Marco laughed to himself as he thought, "I guess Danny knew what he was talking about when he suggested I might be afraid to dance a polka."

"Hey, Marco," someone said. He turned and saw two other friends, Richie and David, both of whom had dates. They introduced them as Janice and Pat. The men went to get drinks while the women looked for a spot at one of the tables. The men all got beers and picked up chardonnay for the women. All of them wanted to hear about Marco's time in the military.

"Not much to tell, really," he said. Most of it was being stuck out in this remote area of Wyoming, where there was not much to do unless you liked hunting for whitetail deer."

"Wyoming?" asked David. "Come on, air force guy. I always pictured you over in Nam, spraying napalm on the V.C."

"Hardly," grunted Marco. "And it's glad I am. I would have had a hard time with those orders. My job was safe and pretty boring."

"Safe and boring?" asked Richie. "Weren't you guarding nuclear missiles or something? That sounds pretty exciting." That comment got everybody's attention, and they all looked at Marco expectantly.

"Pretty exciting for the first hundred hours or so," he answered. "Then it just becomes drudgery. You just sit there for hours at a time staring at screens and instruments, and hoping that nothing ever happens. And it doesn't. At least it hasn't yet, thank God."

"Wow," said David. "I didn't realize that's what you were doing, man. You mean, if there was a nuclear war, you'd of been the guy pressing the button?"

"Me or one of the others there," he answered. "Actually there is this whole protocol you have to go thru, and it would end up with three guys coming to an agreement, and they would all have to enter their codes at the same time. And before that the order would have to come from the president, and it would have to be verified that's where the order came from. It's pretty complicated, but even so, it could all happen in just a couple of minutes. And I'm very happy to say I never actually had to do it, because if I had, none of us would probably have been here today."

"Oh, but man," said Richie, "what a sense of power! And responsibility!"

"That's the whole problem," said Marco. "You sit there hour after hour, day after day, with nothing ever happening. But you have to keep ultra alert and ready the whole time, because if something ever **does** happen, the future of the whole world might depend on what you do or don't do in that one split second. Lots of guys can't take the pressure. Probably two-thirds of the people there are in therapy after the first couple of weeks. Some people can't handle it at all. They start to go bonkers and have to be removed."

"How long did you have to stay there?" asked Pat.

"Two years," he answered.

"Wow," she said. "I could never have done it."

"Just be glad you didn't have to," he answered.

Marco was glad that the band gave a signal to get everyone's attention. They all turned towards the gate, where the wedding party was entering. The little flower girl came in first, to the usual "Oohs and aahs," followed by six pairs of groomsmen and bridesmaids. Then everyone stood to applaud for the bride and groom. As Marco stood, out of the corner of his eye he was distracted by a glimpse of someone at a nearby table. As he clapped, he looked over in her direction. She looked to be about his age, a little bit shorter than him, a nice figure, dark brown hair, wearing a light green summery dress. Did he know her from some-where? He didn't think so, but there was something about her.

Later, after the toasting, and after everyone had received their food, Danny came over to greet his friends. Then he took Marco aside. "Say man," he said. "You've got to meet our cousin Melissa. She really is something." He took Marco by the arm and started moving him thru the crowd towards the dance floor. In the middle of the area where several couples were dancing to "The Pennsylvania Polka," there was a young woman in a very short, tight fit-ting, red dress. Her hair was almost the same color, and though she did not appear to have a partner, she was demonstrating some very provocative moves to what ap-peared to be a very different kind of dance than a polka.

After Danny gave a whistle and called her name to get her attention, she danced her way over to them. "Come on, Danny," she said. "Let's dance."

"You bet," he answered. "But this is the guy I've been telling you about. My best friend, Marco. I wanted you to meet him."

Marco thought of shaking her hand, but her hands and her body had continued moving the whole time, so he just said, "Happy to meet you, Melissa."

"Well, howdy," she said.

Somehow when she said the word, "Howdy," the look in her eye, the expression on her face, and the movements of her body made it sound like an invitation into her boudoir. "I hear you're a football player and you used to be a soldier boy like Danny," she said. "I hope you like to dance more than my cousin does, because I'm ready for a good time. Do you know how to do 'The Hustle?' I've been trying to get this band to play something besides a polka."

"No," said Marco. "I'm afraid I don't. Where I was stationed out in Wyoming, there was only one place to hear music anywhere near us, and all they had was a country band."

"Well I **love** country," she said. "Can you do the Texas two-step?"

"I'm afraid not," he answered.

"How about YMCA?" she asked. "You know that one? Everybody knows that one."

"No, sorry." Marco turned to Danny for help, but his friend had disappeared into the crowd.

"Well you just stay right here," she said. "I'll get them to play something real fun, and I'll teach you to do it."

164

Marco looked around again for Danny as she went up to the band, but still didn't see where he had gone. After Melissa came back, she took his arm and dragged him into the dance area. "They're going to play 'YMCA'," she said. "All you have to do is put up your arms like this to make a Y, then like this for an M, then a C and an A like this. The rest is free style. It's a lot of fun. You'll see."

Marco never felt very comfortable with anything but a slow dance. Still, he did his best, and by the end of the song thought he was doing a pretty acceptable YMCA. He couldn't come close to the moves Melissa was putting on, however. After the song ended, she gave him a big smile, put her hands on her hips, and said, "Now wasn't that fun? I knew you could do it. Listen, I'm going to the ladies room, but I'll be back right quick. You stay right here now."

Marco finally saw Danny talking a few tables away, and he headed right over to him. Danny said, "Say, Marco, how about that Melissa? She's really something, isn't she?"

"That she is, Danny," he answered. "But what is she, about fifteen years old?"

"Sixteen," he answered. "But she's real mature for her age. They grow up fast down there in Texas. Go ahead, have some fun."

"I'm not sure that's such a good idea," said Marco. "But who's that woman there?" he asked, pointing to the woman he had noticed earlier.

"Oh," said Danny. "That's my cousin Marsha. I always think of her as somebody older, but actually she's about our age. I guess just a whole lot more mature. You want to meet her?"

"Uhm," said Marco. "I think I would."

They walked over to the nearby table, where Danny introduced him to his cousin, Marsha Carpentier, along with her parents and younger brother. "Say folks, I want you all to meet my best friend since way back in sixth grade, Marco Russo. He's the guy I always talk about. We enlisted the same day, but he went air force and I went army."

They all engaged in small talk for a few moments until Danny excused himself, saying that he had to get back to his duties in the wedding party. Marco started to leave as well, but Marsha said, "Why don't you sit down and join us for awhile. It must be awkward to come to a wedding where everybody else is family and you don't know anybody."

"Oh, no," said Marco. "I've known Danny and his brother so long that I've gotten to know all their other friends and a lot of the family as well. They're all pretty easy to get along with. But I'd be happy to sit with you for awhile," he said, while pulling out a chair next to Marsha.

The conversation from that point was mostly Gerald Carpentier, Marsha's father, quizzing Marco about his education, his military experience, his religion, and his job prospects. Marco got the impression that Marsha's father didn't particularly like any of his answers. Marsha seemed embarrassed by this, and asked her father to leave him alone.

Finally Marco noticed that the band had started to play a slow song, "Deep Purple," and took the opportunity to ask Marsha to dance. She seemed relieved and accepted with a smile. As they got up and headed towards the dance area, Marco was surprised to notice that her father had followed right behind them. He tried to ignore the man as he began to dance with Marsha, but Mr. Carpentier followed them out onto the dance area and kept staring at Marco with dark blue eyes that seemed to have almost turned black.

"Don't pay any attention to him," said Marsha. "He's old school Methodist. Doesn't approve of either drinking or dancing."

"He must be having a gay old time here, then," answered Marco. My family never had much problem with either, especially the Italian side, but I have to admit I've never seen so much booze at a church wedding before."

"You've got that right," she agreed. "It's flowing quite freely."

Marco felt very comfortable talking and dancing with this woman, and so he gently pulled her in a little closer, and brought in his right arm a little tighter around her back. She eased right in to the new position, but out of the corner of his eye, Marco noticed her father also moving in closer. He turned towards the man, and saw him staring menacingly at him with those darkened eyes.

Marsha noticed what her father was doing and laughed lightly while she shook her head. "Don't worry about him," she said. "He's very protective, but basically harmless. I've been living on my own for a long time now anyhow."

Marco was not intimidated by evil eyed looks. He had experienced the same treatment many times from his own father and his uncles, so he just gave it right back. Then he turned back to Marsha and said, "I'm heading up to Chicago tomorrow, but I'll be back here in a few days. Maybe we can get together then.'

"I think I'd like that," she said.

Chapter 10
Let's Do What We Can

Marco emerged from the underground subway in Downtown Chicago. Cars, busses and taxicabs whizzed past on State Street, horns beeping, tires squealing. A traffic cop on the corner blew his whistle and stepped out into the street to stop the State Street traffic and get it started on Madison Avenue. The last of the pedestrian traffic hustled along to get across Madison Avenue, as the crowd that had been waiting on the corner quickly started to cross State St. in both directions. It looked to Marco like a wall of people crossing east would crash into the crowd crossing west, but the two groups adroitly wove their way thru each other to the other side. "Downtown St. Louis is nothing like this," he thought.

He worked his way into the crush of people. Remembering Franny's instructions, he walked one block to Dearborn St., then turned north. As he walked down Dearborn Street past tall steel and glass bank buildings, he began to see parts of an open area in the next block. "That must be Daley Plaza," he thought. He crossed the next street and found himself in the plaza. He stopped to look around and orient himself by the description he had been given. On the north end of the plaza was a tall, very modern skyscraper that must be the Civic Center. In spite of the size of the building, the first thing that grabbed his attention was the rusty steel sculpture that stood in front of it.

"Must be the Picasso," he thought. As he walked towards it, he found himself laughing and liking it in spite of himself. Franny had told him that the city had ridiculed it at first, but that over time it had become a beloved symbol. How had that Chicago columnist, Royko, described it? "Its eyes are like the eyes of every slum owner who made a buck off the small and weak. And of every building inspector who took a wad from a slum owner to make it all possible... You'd think he'd been riding the 'L' all his life." How appropriate, Marco thought.

Marco turned to look around the plaza, and saw a large group gathered towards the west, Clark St. side. Most were African-American, and many carried signs saying things like:

"SCHOOLS, NOT TRAILERS",
"OUR KIDS NEED A SCHOOL", or
"SUPPORT OUR KIDS".

He started walking in their direction, and noticed Franny and Richard Parker looking across Clark St. towards a mammoth, brownstone, classically designed building on the other side. He recognized among the crowd several people from the NCO action earlier in the week, and decided to join them.

Soon Parker joined the crowd of sign-carriers, and Franny came over to the NCO group. "Okay, so here's the plan," she said. "They're still waiting for more people. They've got two busloads of school children coming, and a lot of parents along with them. When they get here, we all line up and cross over there on the south end of the plaza. Our group will be towards the rear. The line will wait for a green light to cross, but of course, we won't all make it across before the light changes. We keep going anyway. Parker talked with the cops, and they're going to make sure everybody makes it across okay. The mayor's office is on the fourth floor, and we want to get as many people as possible up there, but we don't know what they'll allow. Parker's folks go up first, because this is their action, their community. We're just here for support. But they're really glad that we came. It shows they have wider support from all around the city. Some of you remember how they supported us in our battle with Comm. Ed. So thanks for coming. That's how people power works."

She noticed something from the corner of her eye, and turned towards City Hall. Two yellow school busses had pulled up in front of the entrance. Richard Parker was jogging thru traffic to cross over to them. Two women got out of the busses and met him on the sidewalk. He looked back across the street and signaled to someone to get the people started crossing the street. People began forming a line four people wide and heading towards the corner crosswalk. At the same time, several adults started bringing children out of the school busses, and lining them up by twos in a long line outside city hall. They ranged in age from roughly seven to twelve, and were surprisingly orderly. They held up signs that read,

"I NEED A SCHOOL."

Marco, Franny and the NCO folks brought up the rear. By the time they got to the corner, the light had changed. Two police officers had stopped the traffic on Clark St. Marco could see that the drivers were not happy for the delay, but were looking at the demonstrators and the signs, trying to figure out what the commotion was all about. A group of adults led the way into City Hall. Then the children were brought in, once again in very orderly lines. The rest of the adults went next, with the NCO crowd bringing up the rear.

They passed thru two sets of glass doors to enter a long, wide hallway with wide, marble stairs on both sides. There was a matching set of stairs on the far side of the building, with another set of doors leading out to LaSalle St. Elevator operators and police officers stood in front of the elevators and at the bottom of each set of stairs. The hard, marble floors and walls made every sound reverberate thru the entire space. The children seemed awed to be in this space. Some kept looking around and saying, "Wow!"

Richard Parker was in conversation with a policeman who was obviously an officer. After a time, the officer entered the elevator and the doors closed. Marco noticed that there was a dial with an arrow that resembled the big hand of a clock above each elevator door. It followed the progress of the elevator the officer had entered up to the fourth floor, the highest floor, where it stopped. It stayed there for what seemed an eternity where the children were concerned. When they began to fidget, the adults allowed them to sit down.

Finally the arrow began to move down again, and the same officer came out, along with a young man in a suit and tie, who looked to be in his late twenties, and a woman in a business suit who might have been in her forties. The three went to speak with Parker and two of the others in his group. They returned to the elevator. Parker and the two people with him joined them in the elevator, after he had motioned for Franny and two other adults to join them as well. Then the elevator returned to the fourth floor.

Another twenty minutes went by, as the crowd in the hall-way grew more and more restless. The whole time a steady stream of citizens who were not part of the demon-stration kept entering and leaving the building, going up and down the stairs and the elevators, and entering and leaving the various offices, winding their way thru the demonstrators. While a few of them seemed to wonder what was going on, and even stopped to ask, most just seemed to consider this another day in city hall, looking straight ahead, their minds on their own business.

When the elevator eventually returned, the group who had gone up exited with smiles on their faces, some of them pumping their hands in the air. The group who had been waiting crowded around Richard Parker to hear what he had to say. He spoke in a loud, booming voice, turning his head from side to side so that all could hear him.

"We met with Mayor Daley, his chief of staff, and his secretary. The mayor listened to our complaints, and said that the education of our children is one of the most important things that his city does. Note that he referred to Chicago as **his** city."

This drew a big laugh from the crowd.

"But he said that he shared our concerns, and that he would make them a priority. He instructed his chief of staff to work with me to schedule a meeting with the Superintendent of Schools, the Department of Buildings, and the Zoning Commission within the next two weeks, after which he wanted a full report of where things stood. He promised that no city agency would drag its feet in dealing with this issue. This is just what we hoped for!"

The crowd cheered loudly.

"But we're far from done yet," Parker continued. "We have to keep at it until our new school is a reality, because it is amazing how quickly things can come to a halt if the people don't keep the pressure on. Will you stay with me?" he asked. "Will you help me convince the mayor that we are serious, and that we are not going away until we've got our school?"

"We want a school. We want a school," the people chanted.

After the police officer came up to Parker and whispered in his ear, he quieted the crowd and announced, "Thank you all for coming today. We've made a big step towards getting our new school. But now we have to leave so that we don't continue to block the hallway. Let's send the children out first, please."

Marco had been separated from Franny in the crowd. Now he worked his way towards her. She was engaging the MCO people in helping to direct the children out the Clark Street door to their waiting buses. He had to lean over to speak into her ear. "Listen, Franny," he said. "I've got to get going. Heading back home for the weekend to pick up some stuff I'll need when classes start. Want to talk some more to Uncle John too.   But thanks for contributing so much to my education. Let's get together when I come back to town."

"Hey, anytime, Marco. The more bodies the merrier when you're calling on Hizzoner. I'd love to hear more about your time with Uncle Sam too, and where you're headed now."

Marco gave her a hug and made a quick exit on the LaSalle Street side.

*   *   *

Back in St. Louis, as Marco walked down the street towards his uncle's house, he kept thinking about all that had happened up in Chicago. Still digesting it all, he tripped on an uneven spot on the sidewalk and almost fell. "Okay, Mr. Athlete, get with it," he said to himself.

He was greeted with the usual warm welcome by his Aunt Lucia in the front room. She was full of questions about Chicago, college, and Franny. Marco answered them all, but without going into a lot of detail, until after a bit she said, "Oh, listen to me taking up all your time. You're here to talk to your Uncle John, not me. Go on now, he's back there in his usual spot. He's been waiting for you."

She stepped aside and waved him past, but when he came into the dining room, standing there blocking his way thru was his Aunt Virginia, and she was a different matter all together. She stood with her arms folded defiantly in front of her ample bosom, wearing a dark scowl on her face, and blocking his way thru towards the back porch.

"Whatta you tryin' to do, Marco?" she asked. "I heard about you digging around in old dirt from the way back times. Whatta you wanna do that for? Leave it alone, Marco. This is a respectable family, and we had to work hard to get that way. Whatta you tryin' to do? "

Now she unfolded her arms and waved an index finger at his face. "You've had a pretty damn good life, you know that? You ever have to worry where your next meal was coming from? Huh? Did you?"

"No Aunt Virginia. I didn't," he answered.

"You bet your booty you didn't. You've had a great family, people who watched out for you, took care of you, made sure you had everything you need. And now, what, you're trying to drag us all thru the mud? Is that how you repay all of us?"

"That's not what I'm trying to do," he replied, shaking his head.

"Then what? Whatta you tryin' to do? Tell me."

"I just want to know the truth, what really happened," he answered.

"What truth?" she said, waving a finger at him again. "Here's the truth. You're a damn lucky boy to have been raised the way you were, and you ought to be grateful every single day for what you've had. So stop trying to make us look like scum, because we ain't. If you're ashamed of this family, you're welcome to leave it anytime you want."

The distraught woman looked ready to continue until she had backed Marco out of the house, but Lucia stepped in to defend him. "That's enough," she said. "I won't have this kind of talk in my house."

A male voice called out from the back porch, "Leave Marco alone, Virginia. He came to see me, and he's always welcome in my house. Come on back here, Marco, and bring a couple of cold ones with you."

His aunt frowned and squinted her eyes, but stopped talking and moved aside to let him pass. Marco went around her into the kitchen, where he opened the refrigerator, took out two Buds and took them onto the back porch. Once more he was struck by the fact that his uncle was again sitting in the exact same spot. He had a fleeting thought that this was his uncle's permanent location, and arguably the most consistent and dependable fact of his life.

After going over the highlights of his Chicago visit, as he had done with Aunt Lucia, Marco got down to the question that had been burning in his mind all along. "Uncle John," he asked, "what really happened to my grandfather?"

Right on cue the man pulled out a cigar from a pack sitting on the table, tapped it down three times, bit off the end and spit it into an ashtray, put the stogie into his mouth, struck up a match, lit up slowly and carefully, took a drag, blew the smoke over his shoulder out the window screen, and contemplated the cigar he held between his thumb and two fingers as he began to speak.

"It happened back in 1925," he said. "I don't remember anything about it, of course, because I was just 3 years old at the time. But I sure saw the results. Changed everything in our family. There were eight of us kids, and our father was supporting everybody with his job for the railroad. He was on the road a lot, so our mother was the main parent by far, and let me tell you, she was a force to be reckoned with. Actually they had eleven kids, but the first one died right after birth. The two born just before me died also. So there were eight left. I was the youngest boy. Pauline was after me. She was not quite two when it happened.

179

"So anyway, right away the three oldest boys had to leave school and work. That was Charles, Joseph, and Vincenzo -- Charlie, Joe, and Vince. Charlie was sixteen, Joe was fourteen, Vince was only eleven."

"Vince had to quit school when he was eleven?" asked Marco incredulously.

"Yeah, 'fraid, so," he answered. "See, it's a funny thing. Us younger kids had a bad habit. We liked to eat. Plus, there was still a mortgage on the house. So anyway, they went out on the street and hustled whatever work they could get. That was when Grandma Rose really got to work on growing vegetables on that property there on Manchester Road where your mom still lives. Buying that place turned out to be one of the smartest things gramps ever did. The boys helped with it too. So did I when I got old enough. They scraped up enough to buy a beat down old truck and started selling produce all around the area. The truck kept breaking down, which actually turned out to be a good thing, because Charlie learned how to be a mechanic out of necessity. That led later on to us opening a used car lot there on the property. So we got by.

"And every once in a while our Uncle Joe would send us something. Not much, but it helped out a little bit. Our mom took the money, but she always looked mad about it.

She held it out from her body like it was dirty or smelly or something. If we didn't need it so bad, she would have thrown it back in his face or burned it in the fireplace. She was not exactly fond of Uncle Joe."

"Even though she named my father after him?" asked Marco.

"She always blamed Uncle Joe for your father's death." John puffed on his cigar.

"I thought my father died in a train accident," said Marco.

"Well," answered John, "there might have been a lot more to it than that. . ."

Chapter 11

Some Answers at a Funeral

St. Louis, 1925

Rose Russo was washing dishes in the kitchen when she heard the doorbell ring. "Mary," she called out. "Answer the door." Then she remembered that her daughter, her eldest child, had gotten married just a week ago. How she missed that girl already. The three oldest boys were never at home, always running around the neighborhood somewhere. Truth be told, they were not much help around the house anyway. Her next oldest girl, Virginia, was nine. She was capable enough, but was probably upstairs in the bedroom lost in a book. It would take half a dozen calls just to get her attention. Then it would be another several minutes before she would finally make it downstairs. Rose might as well answer it herself. She dried her hands on her apron, pushed the hair back from her face, and went to open the door.

Two men she didn't know were standing there on the front porch. They wore dark woolen overcoats and each held a derby hat in his hand. She could see that under their coats they wore suits and ties. "Can I help you?" she asked, wondering who in the world they might be.

182

They introduced themselves as James Moore and Mason Rutledge from the railroad office, and asked if they could please come in. They had some news about her husband, Pietro.

Rose's back immediately stiffened up, and she took in a deep breath. She hesitated a moment before she silently stepped back, holding the door open for them to enter into the small vestibule. A feeling of foreboding kept her from extending her usually warm welcome to anyone who came to their door.

"I'm afraid we have some bad news for you, Mrs. Russo," said Moore. "Your husband, Pietro, has been in an accident."

"What do you mean, an accident?" she asked. "Is he alright?"

"Well, ma'am," he said, "I'm afraid he got caught between two freight cars when he was switching them off."

She cut in, saying, "Switching them off? He hasn't done that kind of work for years. He's been a supervisor for six years now. If he still had to do that kind of dangerous work, he would have quit a long time ago."

183

"You're right, ma'am," he answered. "We don't know why he was doing it. The company is investigating the whole event to find out exactly what happened. We're going to get to the bottom of it."

"Well, why don't you just ask him, then? I'm sure he'll be able to explain the whole thing. My husband is such a hard-working, conscientious man. He always wants things to be done just right. He probably stepped in because the other men weren't doing it right. I told him and told him . . ." She paused because she noticed that the two men were looking at each other with expressions on their faces that let her know things might be even worse than she had been imagining. "He's alright, isn't he?" she asked. "How bad is it?"

Moore looked sadly at her and said, "I'm afraid that the two cars came together with a tremendous amount of force, ma'am. They crushed him pretty bad. Then it took some time to get the cars separated again so they could help him. The men tried their best, ma'am, and they called for an ambulance right away, but I'm afraid that nothing could be done. Your husband died, ma'am."

"Oh, no!" said Rose, holding her hands up to her face. "No! No!" she screamed, and began stomping around the room, holding her head between her hands. Then she asked, "Where did this happen?"

"In the train yard in Effingham, ma'am," said Moore.

"It all happened very fast," said Rutledge. "He didn't suffer for long."

"He didn't suffer long," she said. "He didn't suffer long. He didn't suffer long. That's fine. But what about us? What about his eight remaining children? How much will they have to suffer? How **long** will they have to suffer? Oh, my God! His youngest is two years old. You railroad people, all you think about is getting your precious freight and your rich passengers going on time. You don't care one bit for your workers. I kept telling him that. I kept telling him that. Where is he? Where is he?"

"He's at a funeral home there in Effingham, Mrs. Russo. They will transport him here as soon as you let us know where you would like him to be," said Moore.

"Fazio's, I guess," she said. "Fazio's. What am I doing sending my husband to Fazio's?" she cried. "He's too young for this. I'm too young for this. What will we do?"

"You'll be hearing from Mr. Thomas from the business office soon, Mrs. Russo," said Moore. "He will help you with financial arrangements. The railroad will pay for funeral expenses, of course. And there will be a pension payment as well. It's the least we can do."

"The least you can do," she said. "The least you can do. Oh, God, what am I going to do? Answer me that question, please. What am I going to do?"

"Sorry for your loss, ma'am," said Rutledge, as the two men quickly left the house.

*   *   *

Rose sat on the sofa in her living room next to Pietro's sister, Lucia. Rose's sister, Mary Campisi, sat on a lounge chair. All three were looking at another chair, which was empty. Rose's eldest child, Mary, named after her aunt, stood in the center of the room and spoke earnestly to her mother.

"I'm almost sixteen, ma," she said. "I don't need school anymore. I can start doing laundry for people. My friend Nelly does that, and she made ten dollars last week! My friend Betsy even got a job at the bookbindery over there

186

on Chicago Avenue by the river. Guess how much she makes? Over twenty dollars a week! Twenty dollars, mom!"

Rose gave a deep sigh, and held up her hand for her daughter to stop. "Please, Mary," she said. "Not now. Not now. Have some respect. I appreciate that you want to help out. You're the oldest child, and you feel responsible. That's a good thing, Mary. But your father is not even in the ground yet. That's all I can deal with right now. You know that your father would be heartbroken to hear that his oldest daughter, who he loved so much, would have to quit school because he was not here to support us any more. You know that, don't you, Mary?"

Mary hung her head, and sobbed softly as she said, "Yes, momma, I know. That's why I want to help so much. I miss him so, and I want to help."

"Come here, child," said Rose, and held out her arms.

Mary came to her and leaned over to return her mother's hug, then cried softly onto her mother's shoulder.

"There will be time later to speak of these things," said Rose. "For now, we'll just remember what a fine man your

father was, and how much he loved you and all of his children. He was especially proud of you, Mary. You were his
first child, and he always thought you were the prettiest
and smartest girl there ever was. He thought you could
even be a doctor or a lawyer someday. He often told me
how glad he was that we had come to this country, because even though he had to work so hard, he knew that
his children could become whatever they wanted here, if
they worked hard enough for it. So let's not talk about you
leaving school, Mary. Not now. Let's just show our respects for your father for now. We'll figure the rest of it out
later."

"Okay, momma," said Mary, and kissed her mother on the
cheek before leaving the room.

Meanwhile Mary Campisi had heard a sound from the
street, and looked out the window. "A car just pulled up in
front," she said. "Somebody's getting out and walking this
way. I think it's Pietro's brother."

Lucia said, "I'll get the door," and went to open it.

She invited Joseph Russo into the house, giving him a hug
at the door. Joseph walked into the living room, looking
very distraught. "I came as soon as I could," he said to
Rose. "I can't believe my little brother is dead, my brother

Pietro. You know, I used to call him 'Little Pea' when he was a kid. I guess I still thought of him as my little brother, even though he ended up being my boss at the railroad."

He went over to Rose, but when she did not stand to greet him, he took her hand and brought it to his lips. Then he went to sit in the empty chair, but Rose immediately said, "No, Joseph. Not that chair. That was my Pietro's chair." Then she sobbed as she repeated, "My Pietro's chair."

Joseph stopped and turned to take the chair that his sister had been sitting in. Lucia returned to the living room and sat next to Mary Campisi on the couch.

"You know I'll do anything I can to help out," said Joseph. "You need any money? You need me to go get you anything? Need Lucia and me to go shopping? I'm still in shock. My little brother, Pietro," he sobbed. "I was always afraid that railroad would get him someday. I always told him to be careful. Be careful, Pietro, I told him. So do you need help with arrangements? Is there anything I can do to help?"

"No thank you," said Rose. "Everything has been taken care of. Father Falzone will say the funeral mass at St. Anthony's on Friday. The burial will be at Sts. Peter & Paul

Cemetery. Then we'll come back here for a meal. Every-thing has been taken care of."

"That's good, Rose," said Joseph. "That's good. You were always real good about organizing stuff. But there **is** one thing I wanted to talk with you about, Rose. One thing I'd like to do."

Rose's back stiffened as she answered, "And what is that?"

"I want to put an obituary in the paper. The Post here in St. Louis and the Tribune up in Chicago. You know, I think it's only right that it should be in both places, you know?" he said.

Rose paused a moment, and then said, "That should be fine. But I would like you to show me what you have writ-ten before you submit it. Will you do that?"

"Sure, sure, Rose," he answered. "Whatever you want. Whatever you want. But there is one thing that is very im-portant to me that I want it to say. I want it to say that the deceased was Joseph Russo instead of Pietro."

Rose jumped to her feet as both Mary and Lucia looked at Joseph incredulously. "What did you say?" exclaimed Rose. "How could you even **think** of such a thing?" she asked. "I knew there would be something. Get out of my house! Get out of here right now!"

"Now hold on, just a minute," said Joseph, holding up his hands in defense. "Just hold on a minute. You don't really care what's in the newspapers, do you? You weren't even planning to put anything in there, were you? None of our friends and relatives pay attention to what's in there. They find out at church, and thru their friends and family. Hell, most of 'em don't read English anyway. So it won't make a difference. But it could really help me out. I could really use your help here, Rose."

"I knew it," said Rose. "I knew it would be something outrageous. You're really something, do you know that, Joseph Russo? You're quite a work of art, you are. Now get out of my house!"

"Now just hold on a minute," he said. "Hear me out. There are some really bad people out to get me. They're after me all the time. That's why I have to keep moving all the time. No matter where I go, they're trying to track me down. They're out to get me. I don't know why. But

191

they're real bad people, Rose, you got to believe me. So I've been thinking, if they think I'm dead they might finally let it go. I might finally have some peace and be able to settle down someplace. And what would it matter to Pietro? It wouldn't hurt him none. He's already up in heaven." He crossed himself as he said, "My brother, what a saint he was. And he would be willing to do this for me. You know he would, don't you, Rose?"

"Your brother was a fool to do all the things he did for you," she answered. "He had to cover for you all the time. Always getting you out of trouble. Always making alibis for you and the sorry excuse for a human being that you are."

"Now wait just a minute, Rose. We were brothers and we loved each other. Who got him his job with the railroad when he came over here from the old country? Who did that, Rose? He ended up doing better there than I did, got promoted ahead of me, when I'm the one who got him the job in the first place. But was I mad about that? No way. I was happy for him, 'cause he's family. We're family, Rose, and we help each other. Family always comes first. My brother Pietro would always do whatever he could to help our family, and he would want this done for me. You know that, don't you Rose?"

"Here's what I know," answered Rose. "My husband died because of **you**," she said as she pointed her finger at him. "That was no accident that happened in that railroad yard. You know that as well as I do. Somebody killed my Pietro because **you** killed that Ciccia man, that poor man who never did nothing to hurt anybody, that poor man who had a wife and children to support. **You** killed that man, and you should have been hanged for it. **You** should have paid for it, not my Pietro, not me, not our children. And now you want to take away from him even the dignity of his own funeral! You call that family? I call it despicable. I call it beneath contempt. Get out of my house, Joseph Russo. Get out right now! I never want to see your sorry face again, do you hear me?"

As she spoke, Rose began backing Joseph towards the door. Lucia and Mary moved in to both support her and restrain her as she continued to push Joseph towards the door. He held up both hands to indicate that he was leaving, and backed towards the door. As he opened it and began his exit, he turned back and said, "Family, Rose. Family."

*   *   *

Father Falzone stood at the head of the casket, wearing a black cassock with a black stole over his shoulders. In one hand he sprinkled earth over the casket that had been lowered into the grave, while with the other he held his missal, from which he read in Italian the words of committal:

> Into your hands, Father of mercies,
> we commend our brother Pietro,
> earth to earth, ashes to ashes, dust to dust,
> in the sure and certain hope that,
> together with all who have died in Christ,
> he will rise with him on the last day.

Then he extended his hand in blessing over the grave and looked with compassion on the family members gathered around the gravesite, especially the children, as he raised his hand in blessing.

> Eternal rest grant unto him, O Lord,
> And let perpetual light shine upon him.
> May he rest in peace. Amen.
> May his soul and the souls of all the faithful
> departed, through the mercy of God, rest in
> peace. Amen.
>
> May the peace of God, which is beyond all
> understanding, keep your hearts and minds in
> the knowledge and love of God and of his Son,
> our Lord Jesus Christ. Amen.

The people joined him in making the sign of the cross as he gave the final benediction.

> May almighty God bless you,

the Father, and the Son, + and the Holy Spirit. Amen.

He let the people know that the services for Pietro Russo were concluded, and that the family thanked them for coming, and invited all to join them at the family home for refreshment. Then he stepped around the grave to give his condolences to the family members standing closest by, and stepped off to the side to allow others to comfort them. As he stood watching, he pondered the unusual circumstances of this funeral.

The priest had noticed an undercurrent of tension throughout the entire funeral, both at St. Anthony's and here at the cemetery. He had at first assumed it was because of the unhappy circumstances of the man's death. It is always difficult to deal with such an unexpected and tragic blow, especially to a family with eight children. His heart went out to them.

The Russo family had been active in the parish ever since they moved from Chicago six years previously. He had baptized their youngest three children: Anthony, John, and Pauline. Two others had died at birth. The older five all attended the parish school, or had done so before going to high school. Rose regularly brought them all to mass, with the oldest, Mary, helping to corral the younger ones. The oldest boys, Charles and Joseph, were a real handful, and Father Falzone worried about how they would do without their father to keep them in line. Pietro had obviously commanded their respect, and he too had attended mass regularly, though he was often out of town with the railroad or working on a Sunday. To add to all their sadness, the oldest children would probably have to quit school and go to work to support the family. What choice do they have?

So the family had plenty of reason for sadness. But it had become clear that there was even more to it than that. The widow seemed to be unhappy that her brother-in-law, Joseph, was there, and she had not allowed him to sit in the same pew at St. Anthony's during the funeral service. The widow seemed to be close to Pietro's sister, Lucia, however, who sat next to her here as she had at the church. So Joseph had sat behind them at church, and here at the graveside he stood at the rear of the crowd of some thirty or so people that had come here in the funeral procession. "Why is she so angry with him?" the priest wondered. "Could she be holding the brother responsible somehow for the accident?" Nerves are often frayed in such a situation, but this seemed excessive.

Fa. Falzone had also noted unusual, furtive behavior on the part of the brother. Both in church and out here, he frequently turned and looked about, as though he was expecting someone. Or was he afraid that someone was looking for him?

A short, heavyset, balding man in a black suit came to him from off to the side. Antonio Costa was the director of the funeral home most often used by area Italians. The man usually did a good job, and considered his work as almost a religious calling, but Falzone was sometimes irked that Tony seemed to think that his ministrations were more important than the prayers of the funeral service. Costa stood by the priest and looked out at the crowd as he spoke from the side of his mouth.

"Anytime you're ready, Padre," he said. "You can ride back with me."

"Let's wait for a while, Tony," he answered. "Some of the people may want to talk a bit. I don't want to hurry them."

"I hear you. This is a tough one, for sure. Uhm, uhm. Lots of bad feelings there, on top of everything else."

"Oh?" asked the priest.

"Oh, yeah," Tony answered. "Word on the street is that the widow don't believe the accident was an accident at all.

Thinks that somebody was out to get the brother but got the wrong Russo by mistake."

"Oh, really?" said the priest.

"Yep. And that's not the half of it. A director I know up in Chicago tells me that the brother, that Joseph Russo, did a Black Hand hit on a guy up there about five, six years ago. Went on trial for it twice, but got off both times. It's a big story in Little Sicily up there. Anyway, supposedly a couple of the guy's nephews dipped their blood in the dead guy's, and they've been after Joseph ever since."

The priest just shook his head sadly. Just then a middle-aged couple walked up to him. The woman, a member of the parish whose name he couldn't quite recall, reached out and took his hand in hers. "It was a lovely mass, Father," she said. "Thank you. Thank you. Such a comfort for that poor family."

The man spoke next. "I've been talking to the St. Vincent de Paul guys, Father, and we're going to make sure that the family gets the help they need."

"Thank you," said the priest. "The family needs to know that we care about one another, especially at a time like this."

After they had returned to the rest of the crowd, Costa said, "Anyway, there's even more to it than that, Father. I've been working with the family for all the other arrangements -- the cemetery plot, the gravestone, you know. So here's the real kicker, Padre. You just had a funeral for Pietro Russo, but the cemetery's records and the name on the gravestone are gonna say something different. They're going to say 'JOSEPH Russo.'"

Chapter 12

War and Aftermath

"Well, that clears up one big mystery for me," said Marco. "Maybe more than one, now that I think about it. I always wondered why nobody in our family seemed to ever want to talk about my great-uncle Joe. And whatever they did say was never exactly flattering. So did the trick work for him? Did he manage to break off the vendetta?"

"Well, maybe for a little while," answered John. "But I sincerely doubt that one hit was the only thing Uncle Joe ever did that was less than legal. But he managed to evade the law and all the other people after him until 1933. Somebody caught up with him outside of Cincinnati, and put a few slugs into him. Wasn't the cops though. Probably wasn't the Ciccia boys either. Rumor has it that it was a hit put out by the Nicolosi family."

"The Nicolosi family?" asked Marco. "Nicolosi, like the family that has several car dealerships all over town? Nicolosi Pontiac. Nicolosi Cadillac. Nicolosi Chevrolet."

"The very same," answered John. "Turned out to be a good way for them to launder their ill-gotten gains. Now they're pillars of the community. Big charity givers. Send all their kids to exclusive Catholic high schools, then on to Wash. U. or the Jesuits at St. Louis U. Even got a couple into Ivy League schools.

"Say, Marco," he went on. "I happen to have a couple of tickets to the Cardinals game tomorrow. Our dear friends, the Cubs, are in town. My wife usually goes with me, but really, she could care less about sports. How'd you like to go with me instead?"

"Sounds great, Uncle John, if you're sure Aunt Lucia won't mind."

"Nah," he answered, waving his cigar hand in the air. "She'll be relieved that she can stay home and talk to her girlfriends on the phone."

*   *   *

"Why are people standing and cheering for Rick Monday?" asked Marco. He and his Uncle John were seated in the second balcony, first base side of Busch Stadium. It was a long way up, but afforded a good view of the entire field. Not that they could see much at the moment. Many of the people around them had stood up to cheer, and blocked their view of the field.

"Because he's the guy that stopped those two protestors from burning a flag out in left field at Dodger Stadium at a game back in April, " he answered. "Didn't you hear about that?"

"Oh yeah. I remember hearing something about it now. And I suppose, with this being the Bicentennial year and everything, people are especially patriotic these days. Even so, it seems weird to have Cardinals fans cheering for a Cub player. Especially here at Busch Stadium, and in a year where they're beating us in the standings."

"I know what you mean, Marco," said John. "Notice that I did not join them. Not that I'm unpatriotic, mind you, but it would take more than that to make me cheer for one of the Cubs. But you're a military man. You might have a different point of view."

"To tell you the truth, Uncle John," said Marco, "the biggest problem I would have with somebody burning the flag is that the war's over now. Been over for a year. By the end of the war, I was very much against it too."

The crowd yelled and stood up, as Monday hit a high fly ball, deep into right center field. The Cards' right fielder, Willie Crawford hustled back and camped under it, hauling it in just in front of the warning track. The crowd cheered and sat back down.

"You surprise me, Marco," said John. "You seemed really glad to enlist, so I always figured you supported the war."

"I did at first," he answered. "But I saw a lot of body bags coming home, and several of my high school friends never made it back. I think I would have felt differently if I thought it was accomplishing anything worthwhile, but I just didn't see it. My friend Danny was over there, and he's hinted that there was a lot of bad shit going on there, but he doesn't want to talk about it. Says I'm better off not knowing, and I was lucky to be stationed here, stateside."

The crowd cheered again, as Bob Forsch struck out Jose Cardinal to end the top of the first inning. "That Forsch can sure pitch," said Marco.

"Well, maybe." answered John. "Maybe. After he won 15 games last year, I thought he'd really take off this year. But so far he's been pretty mediocre. Everybody thought he was going to be the ace of this team, but now I'm not so sure. And it looks like it will be a struggle for us to be even a five hundred team this year. You know the worst part about it?"

"No. What's the worst part?"

"Being behind the Cubbies in the standings," said John.

"I hear that," laughed Marco.

"Strike three!" yelled the home plate umpire.

People all around them booed. "You need glasses!" they shouted. "If Forsch threw it, it would be a ball." "Get yourself a seeing eye dog!"

"That Ray Burris is a pretty tough pitcher," said John. "He got a gift on that call for sure, but he's been pitching tough."

"Yeah," said Marco. "He's **their** ace all right. I think you're right. The Cards don't really have one this year. You can't call Forsch an ace. At least not yet, I'm afraid."

"Hmph," said John. "No hitting either. I can't believe they traded to get Kessinger at short. He's a decent fielder, but he couldn't hit his way out of a paper bag."

"Yeah, I think we must be coming to the end of the Schoendienst era," said Marco. "Time to rebuild."

"Hate to say it," said John, "but I think you're right. By the way, Marco. I wanted to tell you that I've enjoyed talking to you about all this old family history shit. I'm honored that I'm the guy you decided to talk to about it, and I hope that I've helped clear up some things for you."

"Yes, you have," he answered, "and I really appreciate it. I figured you'd be the guy who would give me the straight dope. But I have to tell you, I've still got a lot on my mind."

"You do? What do you mean?"

"Well, first of all, could we talk some about my father? That's something else I never got a satisfactory answer to. I know he was hurt during the war and everything, and that's why he was on disability, but he would never talk about it. Wouldn't let my mother talk about it either, or he'd get real mad. And I know it affected him a lot, because sometimes he would just fly off the handle. He'd lose his temper for no apparent reason. And my mother was just always real protective about him. 'He's your father,' she'd say. 'Just be patient with him. He loves you very much, you know.' And I get that, I really do. But I know there's more to the story than that. And even when he died, nobody really explained to me what was going on."

"Okay. Let's talk about your father. But not here. Why don't we leave and head to that bar on South Broadway. We're down 4 to 1 here, and it ain't going to get any better anyway . . ."

*　　*　　*

Belgium, December 17, 1944

Sergeant Joseph Russo of the 285th Field Artillery was busy getting the privates who worked under him in the mess tent to get a move on, cleaning up after breakfast. They were more likely to throw wet dishtowels at each other than use them to wipe clean the folding tables or actually wash the dishes. Now that the allies seemed to be steadily pushing the Krauts back towards Germany, he had allowed the young men, most of whom were still in their late teens, to lighten up a bit, but they could easily get out of hand. And after all, they were still at war.

"Hey, Benson," he called out. "Where do you think you are? At a Sunday School picnic? Get a move on. We've got to clean up here and get out to the guns."

"All right, Sarge. Hold your horses. I've just got one more thing to do here," said Pvt. Benson, as he jumped over a chair, knocking it down as he went, and chased Pvt. Curtis between the tables, trying to snap him with the wet towel.

Russo just shook his head and wondered how he ended up baby sitting on the front lines of the war. But as usual, the thought made him smile. He had asked for it, after all. He had a fairly cushy job stateside, running a mess hall at Fort Campbell, Missouri, not very far from home. He could easily make it home on a weekend pass. Might have made it thru the whole war that way. But no, not him.

He could still picture that asshole of a Lieutenant. One of those little guys who liked to throw his weight around. Thought he was hot stuff just because he came out of college and got commissioned as a Second Looie. The mess was Russo's to run, but Lieut. Masters was always ordering his men around, sometimes even giving them orders that were the exact opposite of what Russo had told them to do.

One day it was just too much. Masters was chewing out one of his men over nothing, threatening to cancel his upcoming leave, calling him names, ordering him to do 100 push ups. Russo had gone over and stood between the two men. He looked at Masters and said, "I've told you many times, Lieutenant. If you have a problem, go thru me."

"Out of my way, sergeant," he said, and tried to step around him. Russo sidestepped to block his way.

"I'm ordering you, sergeant," said Masters. "Get out of my way!"

The whole mess full of men was now looking their way, wondering what would happen next. It was the best entertainment they had had in weeks.

After that, things had happened very quickly. Russo had a vague recollection of the whole mess standing up cheering, as he grabbed the lieutenant's shirt at the neck with his right hand and the man's belt buckle with his left, picked him up, hauled him out the back of the tent, and with strength he didn't even realize he had, threw him into a dumpster. It was perhaps the proudest moment of his life, and made him a hero to all the other men.

Of course, it had also meant facing a court marshal. Lieut. Masters had brought charges, and stood before the colonel looking very smug, expecting Russo to get at least jail time, if not drawn and quartered. Russo could tell, however, that the colonel had a hard time to keep from laughing over the story of what he had done. He began to hope for the best.

What he heard was this: "Sergeant, if you want to fight, we need you over in Germany. Pack up your gear. You leave tonight to be transferred to the 285th in Belgium."

Russo thought to himself that if given another chance, he'd do the same thing again. But back to the present, he thought. "All right, girls," he said. "That's enough. Time to . . ."

That's when they heard the sound of incoming shells.

The privates threw down their dishrags and went running towards their duty assignments. Russo ran out of the mess tent and headed straight towards the artillery. He hadn't heard their own guns answer the enemy's yet, and he hurried to help. Outside the tent, the camp area was filled with men running in all directions. Some were headed towards tents to get their gear, some to other tents to run communications or to get orders from officers. Most headed towards the gun emplacements.

Russo was moving quickly across the center of the camp when a large shell hit. Along with men all around him, he flew into the air and when he landed, his head hit a boulder. He lifted his head and saw bodies strewn all around him. It looked like he was the only man in his outfit left alive. Then he passed out.

*　　*　　*

Six months later he woke up in an army hospital outside of London. It was a surreal experience. He didn't know where he was or why he was there. He didn't feel a lot of pain beyond a steady headache, but he was restrained so that his movements were severely limited. His neck was also held in place, so that his only head movement was to open and close his mouth or move his eyes. It took him over an hour to remember that he had been in Belgium, and that his company had come under attack.

The nurses were very nice and attentive, but they couldn't really tell him much of anything, except that he had to keep as still as possible, and that he was on a strict regimen of medications. He was in a ward with about a dozen other men who were in various states of recovery from a variety of injuries. None of them were from his platoon.

When word got out that he had regained consciousness, a team of three doctors came to examine him. They were thrilled that he had revived, but warned him that he still had a long way to go, and he needed to keep as immobile as possible because he was recovering from a very serious head wound. When he asked for more information, they told him that his skull had been badly fractured, and they had replaced some skull fragments with a metal plate.

They were still not sure how much brain damage he might have suffered, and in any case, he had to allow the plate to settle completely. Any movements could cause more damage. They would be watching him closely in the days ahead, and would gradually increase his mobility when it was safe to do so.

It was a shock, to say the least. But he was alive. None of the doctors could tell him anything about his unit either. Finally a chaplain came by. After they prayed together, the chaplain promised to find out what happened to the 285th. The next day the man returned with some news. His unit had been one of the first attacked in what was now being called the Battle of the Bulge. The Germans had mounted a huge attack to try to turn around the momentum of the war. The allied forces had withstood massive attacks, and had managed to hold their ground, but there were very huge casualties suffered by both sides.

The chaplain had one humorous story to report. It seems that the 101st Airborne was surrounded and pinned down by vastly superior forces, but they dug in and refused to be driven out. Under a flag of truce, the Nazis demanded that they surrender. The Germans were totally confused by the reply sent by the commanding officer of the 101st, however. His reply was, "Nuts." None of them could figure out what that strange message meant, but it became clear that the Yanks were not about to surrender. And they didn't. They managed to hold on for many days, until the Germans finally backed out at the end of January.

News of his own company was not so good, however. Just as he had feared, he was the only one who had survived. After waiting for this information to sink in, the chaplain assured Russo that his family had been notified of his situation. Due to the wartime situation, they were unable to visit him in England, but were anxious to welcome him home. Now that he was conscious again, he would soon be able to make the journey.

*　　*　　*

St. Louis, 1976

"He had a metal plate in his head?" asked Marco. "I had no idea."

"None of us knew about it either," answered his Uncle John. "Nobody in the family knew until about two weeks before he died. When he was in the hospital -- get this -- this doctor comes in and says he'd like to run an experiment on your dad's brain. Then he says, 'You know, he has a metal plate in his head from the war.' Get that. All those years, and nobody knew."

"Nobody knew he had a metal plate in his head?" asked Marco.

"Nobody knew," he said. "Not your mom, nobody. I'm not even totally sure your dad knew it."

"What did he say about it?" asked Marco.

"He said, 'The next person who works on my brain will be the mortician.' He wasn't about to let anybody mess around with him anymore."

"I never had a clue," said Marco. "You would never know he had a problem except when he got off his meds. At least that's what my mom said was the problem. When he got off his meds was when he could get mean, lose his temper for no reason at all. Then you knew it was time to get out of his way. It was like he was a different person all of a sudden."

"Yeah," said John. "That's why they gave him 100% disability. Gave him a bronze star, a purple heart, a national defense medal -- and 100% disability. He was more emotionally disabled than physically. His nerves were shot. And it's no wonder. Went thru all that. I heard later that when he was first in recovery they had to keep him on a suicide watch."

"Oh, man," said Marco. "I had no idea. I wish I had known this stuff sooner. I might have understood him better. Listen, I've got to get going. Got a date tonight."

"A date?" asked his uncle. "Who's the courageous woman who's brave enough to be seen in your company? Anybody I know?"

"Afraid not," he answered. "Met her at Danny's brother's wedding last week."

"Uh oh," said John. "Don't you know it's dangerous to go out with a woman you meet at a wedding? The setting seems to put ideas in a woman's head. What's her name, and by the way, is she Italian?"

"No she's not," said Marco. "Name's Marsha. Marsha Carpentier."

"Carpentier," John mused. "Carpentier. Don't think I've ever known anybody with that name. What kind of name is that? I guess your ma poisoned you against finding a good Italian girl."

"She's an American, Uncle John. You ought to know by now that I don't like to judge people by their ethnic background. We haven't talked much about that kind of thing so far, but actually, her people came here from the Alsace-Lorraine region in Europe."

"I think I heard something about that area during the big war, but I don't remember much about it. Wasn't there a lot of fighting there? Her last name sounds French," he said.

"Yeah, it's right on the border between France and Germany, and it's been kicked back and forth lots of times.

And you're right. Her people were basically French. But like I said, she's an American girl, just like I'm an American guy. It's very early in our relationship, and maybe nothing will come out of it. So don't go talking to people about it, okay?" he asked.

"Who me?" asked John, in mocked astonishment.

Marco laughed and said, "But I'm not finished with you yet. We still haven't gotten to what are probably the most important questions that I have."

"And what might those be?" asked John.

"Those might have to do with what is still going on with some of our family members today," answered Marco.

Chapter 13

What about now?

"So how was your hot date?" asked Uncle John.

"Hot is not the word that I would use," answered Marco. They were back in their familiar spots on the back porch, each sipping a beer. It was a typically very hot, very humid night in late June St. Louis. Fortunately a bit of a breeze came thru the screened windows of the back porch, making things a bit more bearable. Marco had thoughts of suggesting they go inside to the air conditioning, but decided that the comfortable and confidential relationship they had developed on the back porch made it worth putting up with the heat and humidity.

"So what did you do?" asked John.

"We ate out. Went to a movie," he answered. "Pretty standard stuff."

"So where'd you eat? What movie? *Mamma mia*, You've got all these questions for me, want all these details about stuff that happened God knows when, but when I ask you about something that happened last week you answer me like a fourteen year old. Ate out. Went to a movie. What kind of an answer is that?" asked John.

"I'm sorry, Uncle John," answered Marco. "I guess I'm a little nervous about it because I think I really like this girl, but I still hardly know her."

"Okay," he said. "Let's just start with some basic stuff. Like, she's French . . ."

"Ethnic background," interrupted Marco. "Ethnic background. Like I said, she's an American girl. Don't think she has any family connections back in Europe, at least there's no indication of that. No mention of speaking French, nothing like that. She grew up an ordinary American kid, just like me."

"So her background is French. Does that mean she's catholic?" He asked. "I hope."

"No, Uncle John. Turns out she was raised Methodist, like me. But that's not a big issue for either of us."

"That's what I was afraid of," said John. "Another heathen heretic. Figures."

Marco laughed. "As if that meant anything to you. Aunt Lucia can't even get you to mass on Christmas and Easter."

"Just kidding, Marco," he said. "You know I never was part of the religious fanatic side of the family. Always stuck up for your father and mother not raising you Catholic. But what else? Does she work? Go to school? Shoot craps for a living? Model for nudie magazines?"

"She's office manager for a small distribution company. Keeps the books, does the payroll, that kind of stuff."

"So how soon do I get to meet this little lady?" he asked.

"Whoa! Way too soon for that, Uncle John," said Marco. Besides, I'm not ready to scare her off yet. But you're distracting me from what I really want to talk about tonight."

"Oh, really?" he answered. "And what, pray tell, might that be?"

"What's really been bothering me is wondering if the family underworld history is all really in the past."

John paused, took a drag of his cigar, and turned to blow the smoke out the porch screen. "Why would you be wondering about that? You heard what your Aunt Virginia said last time you were here. This is a respectable family now. You were given a good, honest upbringing, with lots to feel good about and nothing to be ashamed of."

"I know all that, Uncle John. I feel grateful for having great parents who gave me a good upbringing. And I have a lot of respect for you and for most of family. But over the years there have just been lots of things that didn't quite add up. It helped that you explained the stuff about my great uncle Joe. But there are more recent things too."

"Like what?" John asked.

"Well, first of all I remember things from when I was a kid growing up over there on Manchester. Of course it was just our families in those two houses by the truck farm, with the factory across the road. But just up the hill was that neighborhood with all the houses, Dogtown. How did it ever get that name, anyhow?"

"I have no idea," answered John.

"Anyway, that was my neighborhood growing up, and you'd think I'd have made a lot of friends up there. There were lots of kids my age. But from a very early age, I had the feeling that the other families were afraid of us. Some of them even hated us. They tried to hide it, but you could just feel it. I think some of the parents told their kids not to have anything to do with me. So I think that's one of the reasons I like my friend, Danny, so much. Way back in fourth grade he was about the only kid who would be friends with me.

"So that's one thing. Then one time I was with Uncle Charlie and we stopped to visit a friend of his. Guy named Tony G, who ran a little furniture store. So we just went in and shot the bull with him for awhile, until a customer came in. They spoke Italian, so I didn't get much of the conversation. After we left, Charlie told me the guy was rumored to be big in the local mob. He said he didn't believe it, because Tony G was too dumb, and the mob wouldn't want him. But later I found out the G stood for Gardano, and lots of people think he really is big in the mob. And here's the thing, Uncle John. The way he talked about it gave me the definite impression that Uncle Charlie knew who the real power people in the mob were, and he knew how they operated, and he knew what they were up to.

"Then there was the time that Danny and I went together to enlist. Part of the process was that we had to go downtown to the Comptroller's Office. So we go in the office, and there's a long counter there, with one guy standing there, looking through a big book or ledger or something. Behind him are several other desks with people working. The biggest desk was back under the windows on the far side of the office. There was a sign on that one that said, "Paul Berra, City Treasurer." So anyway, we're standing there for quite awhile and nobody's paying any attention to us, not even the guy who's standing right there in front of us. So if you know my friend Danny, he doesn't tolerate that kind of nonsense for long, and he's a big guy, about 6'3", 240 pounds. So he starts making these obnoxious comments, like 'Marco, you were right. These invisibility cloaks really work. We're standing right here, and nobody can see us,' stuff like that. So finally the guy at the counter looks up from his book, gives us this phony smile, more like a smirk, and says, 'How can I help you?'

"So we told him why we were there, and he asked our names. So we told him our names, and apparently the treasurer guy, Paul Berra, must have heard our names. Because when he heard **my** name, Russo, his head snapped up. It happened so quick that I noticed and looked his way. And I swear to God, Uncle John, that man looked scared. He looked scared. And right away he called the counter guy back to his desk and whispered some stuff in his ear. And while he was talking, the guy looked up at me standing by the counter, and he got this really serious look on his face. Then he came back to us.

"After that we were treated like rock stars or something. He couldn't do enough for us. For awhile I thought he was going to offer to shine my shoes or something. Later I mentioned something about it to Uncle Charlie, and he said, 'Paul Berra. Paul Berra. I used to change that kid's diapers.'"

219

"So that's another one. And then I don't think I told you what happened the morning after you and I talked the first time. The next morning there was a lot of noise outside the house. There was a big white panel truck parked out there and a couple of cop cars. And Charlie's kids were there talking to the cops. So I went down to find out what was going on. It turns out that the truck was full of stolen liquor from California. Supposedly the cousins just found it sitting there in the morning, so they called the police. And the cops were trying to get them for possession of stolen goods, even though they were the ones who called it in. Anyway the FBI even showed up, and it all finally got straightened out. But you know, Uncle John, I keep thinking there is a reason somebody thought that our lot would be a good place to drop off stolen goods. And there was a reason that the cops were so quick to suspect my cousins for being involved. And I also think that the auto parts business they run is really a chop shop.

"So I'd hate to see my mother lose her house because our family property is being used for illegal activities. And, bottom line, I don't think that all of the mob activity connected to our family ended back in the 20's."

John took a big swig of his Budweiser, tilted his head back, and smacked his lips. "Ah," he said. "Nothing like a cold beer on a hot summer night. Of course, this one ain't so cold anymore. But it still tastes mighty fine." It was quiet for some time.

Finally John said, "Marco, are you familiar with the word '*Campanilismo*'?

"No, Uncle John," he answered. I'm afraid I'm not. As you know, I never learned that much Italian because my mother doesn't speak it."

He nodded and went on, "That's right. Italian. *Campanilismo*. It's a word that means something like what the union people mean when they say 'solidarity.' You know like that union song, 'Solidarity forever, for the union makes us strong.' It means that this world can be tough, and none of us can make it on our own. So we've got to stick together. We've got to take care of one another. So when our people came over to this country, what did we do? We settled in areas where there were other people from back home already living here. And I don't just mean other Italians. I mean other people from Sicily. Other people from *Porjoreali*, that little town where our people came from. Because those people understand you. And I don't just mean you all speak Italian. Those people know how you think, and understand your way of looking at the world, and why you do things the way you do. And even if you don't agree with those people about a lot of things, even if you'd never invite them over for Sunday dinner, even if you don't even like them very much -- they are still your people. And when you need help, those are the people you can count on to help you. And when **they** need help, **you** are one of the people **they** are going to count on.

"*Campanilismo*. It's a good word, don't you think, Marco?"

"Yeah," answered Marco. "I think I hear what you're saying, but . . ."

"And even more important than that," John went on, "even deeper than that, is *familia. Familia.* Family. Other people, other relationships, other things come and go, Marco. Nowadays you can't even count on a marriage to last. But family. Family is what we will always need to count on. You don't have to agree with the things your cousins do, Marco. You don't have to do the things they do. You don't have to be buddies with them. You're not like them. You have lived a better life than they have, and you have a brighter future ahead of you. Your father always shielded you from some things. But they are still family. Don't forget that, Marco. And if you ever find yourself in trouble some day -- and I hope it never will be so -- but if you ever find yourself in trouble some day, those cousins of yours will be the first ones to come and help you out.

"I have always thought there was something special about you, Marco. I have always been proud to be your uncle. And I look forward to seeing what you do with yourself now that your tour with Uncle Sam is over. I want you to go your own way, and be your own man. Just don't forget about family. We need each other, Marco."

They sat and drank quietly, and Marco suddenly realized that it had gotten very dark as they were talking. He looked across at his uncle, who was now mostly just a dark outline on the unlighted porch. Finally he spoke.

"You know I love you, Uncle John. The reason you're the one I come to talk to is that I feel like you've always been straight with me. And I understand what you're saying. I do. I know that in the old country, family was the only thing you could count on. I know that when our people were new immigrants, those connections were all they had. I know that, and I appreciate that. And I also know how important family is. I'm very grateful for the parents I've had, and for lots of relatives who have always been very good to me and supported me.

"But the reason our people came here from Sicily — the reason anybody comes here from another country — is that they want something better. They don't want to live in a place where you can work long, hard hours to make some kind of a life for yourself and your family, only to have somebody else take it away, either because they control the courts and the police, or because they can hire thugs with guns. They want something better. They want a chance to make something of themselves. They want to live in a place where there's justice and freedom.

"That's one of the things I learned from my father. He would never talk about the battles and the destruction in the war. But he did tell me that in the army he worked with all kinds of people: black and white; Italians and Swedes; hill billies and city slickers; you name it. And they were all religions: Catholics and Presbyterians; Jews and Baptists; Buddhists and atheists. And he told me that there's good and bad in all of them, but that most of them just want a fair shake, and to be treated with a little respect.

"And then there was the way my father ran his little deli and grocery store. I don't think he ever turned anyone away who was short on money, or who needed something to eat. He extended credit to his customers all the time. I remember one particular family that had ten kids. They owed my father a lot of money, but he never denied them anything they needed, even though it was pretty clear, even to me as a kid, that these people would never be able to pay him back. I asked him one time why he did it, and he said, 'That man's children have got to eat, and it's the right thing to do to help them out.' A generation or so later, that family is doing very well. Some of them even got rich. And there wasn't a week that went by that I didn't hear my father say something like, 'Thank God for what we have.'

"And that's what I think too, Uncle John. We've still got a lot of problems in this country, but at least here we can try to make things a little better. But we're not going to help by being junior mafioso, or small time hoods."

Marco stopped speaking and looked down at the floor, suddenly embarrassed that he had spoken up so forcefully, and surprised at himself for expressing these strong feelings he was not even aware that he had.

His uncle chuckled and said, "Marco, Marco. So you want to change the world, do you? Well, I wish you luck with that. But I guess that is what youth is for." Then he raised his glass to give his nephew a salute. "I commend you for your idealism," he said, "but don't count your family out. You might find out that there's more support for you there than you realize."

Marco looked down at his beer, then gave a big sigh and continued.

"All of that's true, Uncle John, but I just don't get it.   How can people in the same family, the same community, turn out so differently? My grandfather and my great uncle. My father and my Uncle Charlie. They had the same background. Same family. Same conditions. But their values and way of living were so different. It always seemed so plain to me that we all need to work together to make this world a better place, but I'm not sure that kind of thought has ever crossed their minds. How can we be so alike and still seem to live in a different universe?"

John took the time for two draws on his cigar before answering. Then he said, "I heard this Indian story one time — I guess I should say Native American or something — that said inside each one of us are two wolves, a good one and an evil one. And they are always at war with each other."

Marco thought about that for a moment. Then he looked at his uncle and asked, "Which one of them wins?"

John took a big swig of beer, smacked his lips, and said, "The one you feed."

They sat and drank quietly, and Marco suddenly realized that it had gotten very dark as they were talking. But it was a peaceful dark. A comfortable dark. It felt as if a heavy weight had been lifted from his shoulders. Marco took a deep breath and realized how much he loved his Uncle John.

Finally Marco said, "Well, tomorrow it's back to Chicago. Football

225

practice begins right after the 4th. I think I'm going with Franny down to the big 4th of July celebration in downtown Chicago. It's supposed to be a really big thing there. They have it down at the lakefront in Grant Park. Starts off with what they call 'Taste of Chicago,' with over a hundred food booths from all these great restaurants. Then the symphony gives a concert in the band shell there, and they finish off with fireworks. A lot of is probably similar to what we do in St. Louis, but of course in Chicago every-thing is four times as big. And this year is the Bicentennial, so they're really going overboard on everything. You doing anything special, Uncle John?"

"Nah," he answered. "I can usually see a lot of the fireworks from right here on my back porch. Lucia will probably want to watch some of it on tv. Maybe at midnight we'll go out on the front porch and bang some pots and pans. That'll be enough for me."

Marco lifted his beer can and started to take a drink, but was suddenly interrupted by a fit of laughter that caused him to quickly put down his beer and place a hand over his mouth.

"What's so funny?" asked John.

"I'm sorry, but I just had this image of you and Aunt Lucia stand-ing out on your front porch in your pajamas, banging on pots and pans, and it was just too funny."

John feigned being insulted, but then he began to chuckle and said, "You know, that would be a pretty funny thing to do. I think I'm going to insist on wearing our pajamas this year when we do it. I'll make sure that we're loud enough to wake up that old grouch, Salvatore, who lives across the street.

After some more laughter and a time of peaceful silence, Marco stood to go and said, "Well, thanks so much for your time and your wisdom. It really means a lot to me."

*　　*　　*

Chapter 14
Bicentennial

Marco got off the Lake Street "L" at Wabash and Randolph in downtown Chicago, walked down the stairs to street level, and after getting his bearings, turned east on Randolph towards Michigan Avenue. He found himself already in a crowd of people. Apparently the prediction of record crowds was coming true. He let the crowd carry him along, although the movement was very slow. Approaching Michigan Ave., he saw the reason why. A second stream of people was coming up a stairway emerging from below the street level, creating a logjam where the two streams of pedestrians came together. When he finally got as far as the stairway, he saw that it was the terminus of the Illinois Central Railroad. People were coming from all directions to celebrate the bicentennial. Fortunately the crowd was able to keep moving across Michigan Avenue into Grant Park, because the Chicago Police were holding up auto traffic in both directions, and were urging people to cross even against a traffic light that had turned red. So they surged across the street, went over a bridge that crossed railroad tracks below, came into the park, and turned south to their right.

Marco was glad that he was not one of those who hated crowds. Some people he knew went into panic mode in a crowd like this -- although he had to admit that he had never been in a crowd quite like this one. But he actually found the experience of rolling along in a human tidal wave to be pretty thrilling. One thing gave him pause, however. He was supposed to meet Franny somewhere down here. When she had suggested it in their phone call, it had seemed pretty simple and straightforward. Little did he know. He began to look for signs of her in the crowd.

They were supposed to meet at the far end of the grassy field that spread out before the band shell. Marco began to doubt their odds of actually finding one another. It did seem that the crowd was headed in the right direction, however, because he caught sight of the top of a band shell when he stood up on his tiptoes to look over the crowd. When they got closer, most of the crowd kept going straight ahead, to where food trucks and port-a-potties lined up on the grass off the right side of the sidewalk they travelled on. A sizable number of the crowd took a path headed off to the left, and Marco decided to turn with them. It seemed to him that would take him in the right direction.

Now headed east, he caught occasional glimpses of Lake Michigan thru the crowd ahead of him. Off to his right, looking thru trees that lined the sidewalk, he saw large, impressive buildings on a peninsula that jutted out into the lake. From pictures he had seen, he thought he could identify them as the planetarium, the aquarium, and the Field Museum of Natural History. He hadn't yet been able to visit any of them, but began to think he should do so as soon as he got the chance. At another intersection, the

229

crowd turned right and headed south again. Now on his left he saw that they had come to a wide highway, with several lanes of traffic headed in both directions parallel to the lake. This must be the famed Lake Shore Drive. On the other side of the drive there were people walking on a path right beside the water. Marco was impressed by his view of Grant Park Harbor and Lake Michigan beyond it. Numerous sailboats filled the harbor, some with white triangular sails unfurled. A few were moving slowly to enter or leave the harbor area. Marco had to apologize for stepping on the heels of a woman in front of him, and decided he needed to watch where he was going.

Coming to another intersection, some people headed right, some kept going straight, and some walked onto the grassy field that indeed seemed to be facing the band shell. Marco headed in that direction and stopped on the grass to look around, but all he saw was the blur of a sea of humanity. He began to resign himself to being down here alone. But not wanting to give up too quickly, he kept looking around in all directions, occasionally being jostled by the passing crowds.

"Marco! Marco! Over here!" someone called. It was a man's voice. He looked in the direction of the call, and saw someone waving a baseball cap at him. He worked his way thru the crowd towards the man, though he didn't know who it could be. Coming closer, he began to recognize him as one of the NCO organizers. What was his name again? Peter something? No, Petro something? He couldn't remember, but the man seemed happy to have seen him, and the feeling was mutual.

"Hi," said the man, and waved him over towards a blanket spread out on the grass. A blond woman sitting on a folding camp chair turned towards him and smiled. There were also what looked like a picnic basket and a couple of brown paper shopping bags sitting on the blanket, along with another folding camp chair. "You may not remember me," the man said. "I'm Petrusiac from NCO. Met you at our staff meeting and at that action to the alderman's office. Come on over. We've been saving a spot for you. This is my wife, Tricia."

They exchanged greetings, and Marco said, "Yeah, I remember you. But I'm glad you said your name for me. I probably would have mangled it otherwise. And I was really glad to hear somebody calling my name. I didn't think I'd ever be able find my cousin in this crowd."

"I hear you," said Petrusiac. "Fran was worried about that too, so she asked me to keep an eye out for you while she went with the rest of the crew to get some beer and food at the food carts over there. They should be back pretty soon. By the way, Marco, I want to introduce you to my wife, Tricia. Tricia, this is Fran's cousin, Marco."

Tricia stuck out her hand and said, "Glad to meet you, Marco. Welcome to Chicago."

"Thanks," he answered. "Happy to meet you too."

Petrusiac sat on the other camp chair and said, "Sorry, we only brought two chairs. But the blanket is all yours. There's some chips and other stuff in the grocery bags. Help yourself."

"Maybe later," said Marco, as he looked around the crowd. "I've been wondering. I assume that Petrusiac is your last name. Does everybody call you that?"

He laughed and replied, "Yeah, pretty much everybody. It's okay by me. My first name is Bob, which never seemed very interesting to me. Not sure exactly when the last name took over. Back in grade school lots of kids called me 'Polack,' which I did not particularly appreciate. I got in way too many fights over that one than I wanted."

"So you're Polish then?" asked Marco.

"Well, the name might be, I'm not really sure. But actually I'm a mixture of Polish, German, Czech, and a little Russian. Real East European mish-mash. You, however, must be as pure Italian as Fran, who is very proud of the fact, by the way."

"Actually my mother's background is German," said Marco. "I've always felt like I was half in, half out of the Italian side of the family."

Just then Franny appeared with three men, all of them holding plates of food and plastic glasses of beer. "Hey Marco," she said. "Glad you found us. You remember Jim, Bill, and Blake?" she asked, nodding in the direction of the three. "Here, can you hold this while I sit down?"

Marco held a couple of plates while the others sat down. Then he joined them on the blanket. Blake remained standing, looking first towards the west at the high rise Chicago skyline, turning around to look at the museums to the south, then the harbor and lake to the east, and Navy Pier and more high rises to the north.

Bill looked up at him and said, "Blake, you look like one of those country yokels who's never been to the big city before. Didn't your mommy and daddy ever bring you down here from Blue Island?"

Blake kept looking around as he answered. "Actually only once or twice. People out in the southwest suburbs avoid coming into the city unless it's absolutely necessary. But this is awesome. Truly awesome."

"Why is that?" asked Jim. "Blue Island is not that far out. And there's so much here to come to. Living in the city is great."

"That's what I keep telling people out there, but they don't want to hear it. I'm doing organizing in Blue Island, but we actually moved further out to Orland Park a few years ago. The Island was getting too urbanized for folks."

"So what's their problem?" asked Bill.

"Well," answered Blake, "when I told my uncle I was com-ing down here he thought I was nuts. 'Nothin' but you-know-whats down there,' he said. Actually, he used the 'n' word."

"So what did you say?" asked Jim.

"I told him I was down here just last week, and that's not true. There's all kinds of people down here. In fact, most-ly white folks. Nothing dangerous about it at all. Do you know what he answered? He said 'Nope. No way. Nothin' but you-know-whos down there. You're taking your life into your own hands going down there.' That was the end of the discussion. It's like talking to a wall."

"My mind's made up. Don't confuse me with the facts," said Bill. "I think I'm glad he's staying out there in the wasteland. We've got enough going on already, without having that kind of attitude to deal with."

Conversation turned to lighter topics as food and drinks were passed around. "You want a hot dog, Marco?" asked Tricia, passing over a plate.

"Uhm," he replied. "I've never been particularly fond of hot dogs."

"Take it, Marco," said Franny. "She's talking about Chicago style hot dogs. It's a whole different thing here than St. Louis or other places." (Franny counted off on her fingers as she described the delights of a Chicago style hot dog.) " All beef, kosher franks; onion; relish; tomato; pickle; spicy mustard; and a few sport peppers to give it some kick. All on a sesame seed bun. Try it. You'll like it."

Marco took the plate, thanked Tricia, and looked it over, as if trying to figure out how to proceed. The others watched, smiling, as he put the plate down and reached with both hands to pick up the hot dog. They laughed at his futile attempt to lift it without letting anything spill out, and then trying to figure out how to get his mouth around it for a bite.

"Just go at it, Marco," laughed Petrusiac. "Whatever falls out you can pick up later."

"Yeah," said Bill. "Jim here finishes up by putting the plate on the table -- or the ground as may be the case --- and lapping it up like a dog."

It was not clear who started it, but soon they were all call-ing out, "Go, Marco, go Marco," as he took copious bites, ignoring the bits of onion and relish that fell onto his plate, and the mustard that stuck to his lips and chin. Then everyone had a good laugh.

"Now you're a real Chicagoan," said Bill.

"So is Marco one of your crew of intrepid organizers?" asked Tricia.

"I think he is now," said Jim. "He's already survived a mid-night staff meeting with Bob Lynn and been with us on a couple of actions. So he's lost his virginity. Might as well make it official."

"No, no way," said Marco, while wiping his chin with a pa-per napkin. "I just wanted to see what Franny has been up to. And I really appreciate you letting me hang around. I feel like I've learned a lot. I've got a lot of respect for what you're doing, but I don't think it's for me."

"Had you ever been involved in politics or activism before?" asked Petrusiac.

"Just once," answered Marco. "I helped out a little when my uncle ran for State Senator in 1970."

"You did?" asked Franny. "I never knew that. I knew that Uncle Charlie had run for some office and lost, but I was

236

still like a freshman or sophomore in high school then and didn't pay much attention. "

"It wasn't that much, actually," said Marco. "Just helped put out some campaign posters."

"What made him run for office?" asked Petrusiac.

"Well," answered Marco, "it was really to get even with a guy who had crossed him. Our family has some property on a major street, and Uncle Charlie used it for business purposes. He had a plumbing supply for awhile, a used car dealership -- small time stuff. But it's really valuable land. There's a big steel factory right across the street, and people have been talking about putting in a strip mall around there for years. So some local politicians wanted to get hold of the property. They rezoned the property on the sly, and one day we get this letter that says there can't be a business there.

"So my uncle knew this state rep named Mazuka, Italian guy. He talked to him about it, and Mazuka said, "Charlie, don't worry about it. I'll take care of it." But it turns out this Mazuka guy probably had his own hand in the cookie jar, and the rezoning went thru anyway. So the family took the city to court. There ended up being a ten year court battle over it. My family fought it all the way to the Missouri Supreme Court. We lost the case, but it got a lot of bad publicity for the city, so they decided to leave the property alone after all.

"Anyway, it really got to my uncle, and he wanted to get even with Mazuka. One day I heard him talking to a friend about it, and he said to him, "They would never have gotten away with that in the 30's.""

"Whoa," said Bill.

Blake got a puzzled look on his face and asked, "What did he mean? What would have been different in the 30's?"

Everyone laughed, and Bill patted Blake on the back.
"They're Italians, Blake," he said. "So I ask you, who were the most famous Italians during the prohibition era?"

Blake got a sheepish look on his face and said simply, "Oh."

"So anyhow," continued Marco, "this Mazuka decided to run for state senator. In the primary he was up against this Irishman named Lawrence Lee. And of course, in that part of town, if you win the primary you win the election. Sometimes the Republicans don't even put up a candidate. But the polls were showing Mazuka in the lead, mostly because he was getting all of the Italian vote. So one day this Lee guy runs into Uncle Charlie and talks him into getting into the race. He offers to pay for his yard signs plus another $3,000 to support his campaign."

At this comment, everybody gave a big whoop and laughed long and hard. All except Blake, who asked, "Why would he do that? Why talk somebody into running against him and even finance his opponent?"

"To split the Italian vote," said Marco patiently.

Blake still looked confused, but Petrusiac went on and said, "That's great, Marco. But you said you got involved in the campaign. What exactly did you do?"

"It wasn't that much, actually. But some of it was pretty exciting . . .

St. Louis, Spring 1970

"I don't get it, Uncle Charlie," said Marco. "Why do I need to stand on the roof of the truck? Not exactly safe, and I'm not sure that it's legal."

"Because we need to get those signs up as high as possible," answered Charles Russo. "Otherwise Mazuka and his cronies just go around and pull them all down. Even the cops do it, cause he's got them in his pocket. The city workers. The phone company. Whoever. So Vince is going to drive, and whenever he pulls up to a lamp post, you climb up there, reach up as high as you can, and use the staple gun to put it in place. Don't worry about using too many staples. Just make sure they're up there good and tight."

"Yeah, but they'll be harder to see and read way up there," said Marco. "Besides, they can still take them down."

"Sure they can still take them down," said Charlie. "But **will** they? If they're in easy reach, all these cronies will just grab them whenever they go by. No big deal. But if they're up high enough it's not so easy. In fact, it's down right inconvenient. I figure most of the time they'll just ignore them. Too much trouble. They can always claim they didn't see it. Catch my drift?"

"I hear you, Uncle. I'll get them up good and high."

Marco climbed into the back of the pickup and tried to make himself as comfortable as possible. His cousin Vince, who had been waiting in the driver's seat, backed up, turned, and headed out of the parking area of the family property onto Manchester Road, where he turned left towards the city. Uncle Charlie got in his car and headed the other direction on Manchester.

Starting in the next block, Vince stopped at every telephone post so that the truck was right up next to the post. Then Marco climbed up on top of the roof, so he could get the poster up as high as possible. At the first stop, Marco reached as high as he possibly could with the campaign poster. He even stood on his tiptoes and leaned over the side of the truck in order to get full extension. With his left hand he held the poster in place, while with his right he tried to shoot in the staples. What he quickly discovered was that it was difficult to shoot the staple into the post at the proper angle when he was so far extended. So he gave a big push upward with his body and a hard push inward with his right hand, and nearly fell off of the truck.

"What the hell you doing up there?" yelled Vince. "That too tough a job for you, little Marco? We've got about a thousand of these to get out tonight, you know."

"Hold your horses," he answered. "Not as easy as it looks, but I think I'm getting the hang of it." Marco tried again, this time not trying to extend himself so far, and the poster went in more easily. He slid down off the roof into the bed of the truck, tapped on top of the cab, and said, "Got it, let's go."

Marco barked, "'Bout time'," and pulled away from the curb. They had placed roughly thirty of the posters when a truck passed by slowly on the other side of the street. The lettering on the side of the truck identified it as "City of St. Louis. Forestry Division." After traveling about a block past them, the truck made a sudden u-turn and headed in their direction.

Marco banged on the back of the cab and yelled out, "Vince, I think that city truck is after us."

Vince checked his mirrors. Apparently agreeing with Marco, he sped up and made a quick left turn onto the next side street, throwing Marco hard into the side of the truck bed. "Hey! You trying to kill me?" he yelled.

The city truck followed them around the turn, now obviously in pursuit. After a few blocks, Vince made another hard left turn. Fortunately Marco was better prepared this time, but it still jarred. After a third hard left, the pickup came back to Manchester. This time Vince made a right turn and sped down the road headed back the way they had come. The city truck continued to follow them. Two blocks down they passed Charlie's car going in the other direction. There was another man in the car with him. Apparently noticing that the city truck was following Vince and Marco, Charlie also made a u-turn and followed after the city truck. Vince made straight for the family property, turned into the lot, and pulled into a small, dead end alley that ran between the two houses on the property. He came to a stop where the alley ended at a low brick wall. The city vehicle stopped right behind them. Right behind them came Charlie's car, which trapped the city truck in between them.

Marco watched from the truck bed as Vince got out of the cab, Charlie and his passenger got out of the car, and two of Vince's brothers appeared holding the tools they had been using in the auto shop. The four of them surrounded the cab of the city truck, whose occupants looked absolutely terrified.

"What you doing, following them?" asked Charlie. "You're trespassing. You ain't allowed on this property."

The driver screwed up his courage and said, "We just wanted to let them know that it's against the law to put up political posters on telephone poles."

Charlie glared at them silently for a long moment, as his sons struck the palms of their bare hands with their tools, and then he said, "Okay. So you told them. Now I'm going to back my car out of your way, and when I do, I expect you to get the hell off of my property, and don't ever come back. Is that clear?"

The driver nodded. "I asked you a question," said Charlie. "Is that clear?"

"Yes, sir," the driver answered.

Charlie got back in his car and pulled it out of the way. The city driver backed carefully out and drove slowly out of the lot. Charlie walked over to the pickup and said, "Well, I guess you might as well knock it off for tonight. You can get back on it tomorrow." Then he got back in his car and drove off with his passenger. Marco never found out who the man was.

Chicago Bicentennial, 1976

"Great story, Marco," said Petrusiac. "Really terrific."

"But did it work?" asked Jim. "Did Mazuko lose?"

"You bet," answered Marco. "Get this. The final vote count was:

Lee:	13,000
Mazuka:	12,500
Russo:	980

So the handful of Italian votes my uncle took away from Mazuka let Lee win the primary and go on to the state senate. After the election, my uncle went looking for Mazuko. He found him at O'Shea's, this bar where he usually hung out. Mazuko was sitting at the bar, in tears. So he sat down next to him and said, 'You rat. I got even. Don't ever double cross me again. A few decades back it would have been a lot more severe.'"

Bill and Jim clapped and whooped. Blake looked like he was still trying to put it all together.

Franny said, "I never heard any of this stuff. Didn't know what I was missing. So Marco, did that experience give you a taste for politics?"

"A little bit," he answered. "It was kind of fun and exciting, even if hanging around with those particular cousins always makes me nervous. So I guess, yes, every once in a while I have thoughts of it, but right now I'm just focused on football and finishing my degree."

"Well let me know if you ever get serious about it," she said. "I think you might be a natural. But anyway, I heard a couple of you wondering why we came down here so early, when the program doesn't start for hours yet. Well, one of the reasons is that, as you can see, if we came much later we'd never have found a spot to lay a blanket down here. Another reason is that we've got time to talk. Get to know each other better and what makes us tick. Petrusiac, I've never told you this directly, but I have a lot of respect for you and the way you go about your business. And you've been at it a lot longer than the rest of us. So if you're willing, I'd like to hear a little of what got you into organizing, and how you've stuck with it for so long."

"Uhm," he said, and looked at his wife, "sure. Why not? Some of it is just to feel like I'm part of what's going on in the world, not just a spectator. Like every time I come down to this park, it reminds me of when I was down here during the '68 Democratic Convention."

"Whoa, that explains a lot," joked Bill. "You got your head beat in by the cops. Never been the same."

After everybody laughed, including Petrusiac, he said, "Actually I missed that part. I came down in the late afternoon. There was a huge crowd here. People were gathered in clumps all around the park. They tended to congregate in groups. There was an SDS crowd, a SNCC group, CORE, SCLC, even the Catholic Workers. The Yippies were probably the biggest group, and Jerry Rubin has gotten pretty well known, but to call them an organization would be hardly accurate.

"So I was glad I had come, but later in the day, when it got dark, the mood became much more dark and ominous. There was this tension in the air, and people were getting angrier all the time. People started doing stuff like shooting off firecrackers. It sounded like gunfire. There were several bonfires started, and groups congregated around them, chanting slogans that got angrier and angrier, waving flags.

"So I walked to the east side of the park, and there was a long line of police there in riot gear, wearing these light blue helmets and holding billy clubs. Some of them were hitting their clubs into their hands, like they were warming up for what happened later. Just couldn't wait to use them. But most of all, they looked like an army that was getting ready to charge.

"So anyway, it became more and more clear to me that both sides were just aching for a confrontation. It was only a matter of time before it all blew up. I wasn't at all sure that was a good idea, but in any case, I didn't think that I needed to be there. So I went home and ended up watching it all on tv."

"Wow," said Jim. "What do you think now? Was it a good idea?"

"It got us Richard Nixon as president," he answered. "What do you think?" That thought quieted the group for awhile.

"But that experience convinced me that efforts to change things need to be carefully organized, with clear objectives and appropriate tactics. Just blowing everything up is very juvenile, and never a good idea."

"But you were already involved in organizing before then," said Fran. What got you started?"

"That's another long story," answered Petrusiac. "I was a college student working a summer job with 7-Up when Martin Luther King came to Chicago in 1966. But before I talk anymore, I'm getting pretty hungry again. Who wants to go for some pizza and beer?"

That suggestion drew a unanimous and positive response from the group. Marco volunteered to go. "I need to move around and stretch a little anyway," he said. "Who likes thin crust?"

Loud groans immediately erupted from the group, along with various dismissive hand gestures and comments such as "Oh, no!", "You've got to be kidding me," and the like.

Fran laughed thru it all, and finally said, "You've got to understand. Marco is from St. Louis. Marco, once you get used to Chicago pizza, you'll understand why people here don't think the stuff we get back home should even be dignified by the name 'pizza.' Chicago deep dish is the only real thing. And I have to agree. After getting used to Chicago style pizza, I can hardly eat the stuff we get back home."

"You bet," said Bill. "Here in Chicago, we're gifted. You know those cities where it's hard to find good pizza? Here, it's hard to find bad pizza. We don't eat our pizza in floppy triangles on street corners. We don't eat it like barbarians, folding it in half. Chicago pizza won't ruin your necktie from grease sloshing off the top of your pizza slice."

"Oh, really?" said Jim. "Since when do you ever wear a necktie? I've never seen you in anything but old faded jeans and a tee shirt."

"Ah, you know what I mean," Bill answered.

Drake asked, "Are there really pizza trucks out here? I didn't see any."

"I guess you didn't." said Jim. "You were too busy gawking at the skyscrapers across Michigan Ave. A few times I thought we'd lose you."

"I think I saw an Uno's truck and an Eduardo's," said Fran. "Anybody got a preference?"

"Yeah," said Petrusiac. "Whichever one has the shortest line. Let's split up. Three of us get pizzas and three get beers. Tricia can hold down the fort."

The lines were long, but eventually they all made it back to the blanket with arms full of provisions. Beers and pizza boxes were passed around, and everybody dug in. After awhile, Bill asked, "So Petrusiac, you started to tell us what got you into organizing."

"Yeah," he answered. "As I was saying . . ."

Tricia interrupted and said, "Hold on now. Finish your slice of pizza first. You'll be spitting it out over everybody." She turned to Bill and said, "I hope you realize what you've done. Once he gets started on this topic, you may not be able to get him to shut up."

"We've still got plenty of time before the concert starts," he answered.

Petrusiac swallowed his last bite of pizza, washed it down with a few swigs of beer, and started in. "As I was saying, before I was so rudely interrupted," he said, looking at Tricia with a mock-angry expression, "MLK came here to Chicago in 1966. I had always admired him, but pretty much thought of him as somebody who was dealing with

those issues, down in **those** states that had segregation. Didn't think it had that much to do with us northerners. But then he and his organization, SCLC, came up here. They were invited by a coalition of several local civil rights groups to address the issue of residential segregation. Because even though we didn't have segregation laws on the books, it was still true that black folks could only buy homes in certain parts of the city. *Defacto* segregation is what they called it. And all you have to do is look at a map of the city to see where people live, and you realize that it's true. It's really obvious, but I had never thought about it before. That's just the way things were.

"Anyway, they started to have marches in some all white neighborhoods of the city, saying that black folks should be able to move wherever they were able to buy a house, not just in certain neighborhoods. And that made a lot of sense to me. I agreed with it, I supported it, but it still seemed to me to be **their** issue, not mine. Not ours. Know what I mean? And I looked at King as a great spokesman for **those** people.

"But then one weekend I drove down to Miami University, Miami of Ohio that is, to see Tricia. She was a student there. So when I was driving back, I was listening to the radio and there was this news report that while the marchers were going peacefully thru a neighborhood on the southwest side, there was this huge angry crowd that came out against them. Then somebody threw a brick that hit Dr. King in the head. The report said that he went down onto one knee, and he was protected by people around him. Then he got up and continued on the march, and it seemed initially that he would be okay.

"So when I heard this, it did something to me. It really upset me that there could be so much evil hatred in this city that I love. I had always thought of Chicago as a place where all different kinds of people from all over the world live together in peace. Sure we tend to live in our own ethnic neighborhoods. That's one of the great things about the city. Everybody knows where the Greek neighborhoods are, and the Italian neighborhoods, and the German neighborhoods, and the Mexican neighborhoods. And so maybe you say, 'Tonight let's go to Greek town.' So you go down to south Halsted Street, and there's four or five Greek restaurants there, and they're all terrific, and you pick one to go to. Then you have your *saganaki*, and your *taramasalada,* your *moussaka* or your *pasticcio*; you wash it down with *Roditis*, and have some *baklava* for dessert. And you feel like you've just taken a quick vacation to Athens."

"I don't know what any of those things are," said Drake, to snickers and shaking heads by the others.

"Stick with me, buddy," said Petrusiac, patting him on the back. "Anyway, of course we were always teasing people from the other ethnic groups. Like, say Drake, do you know why they don't have ice cubes in Poland any more?"

"Really?" he answered. "Why not?"

"Because the old lady who had the recipe died." Groans ensued all around.

"So we had all these ways of needling one another," he went on, "but everybody knew not to take it seriously. But this reaction to Dr. King and the march was something else. It was mean and nasty, and totally unacceptable. So I decided that I couldn't just stay on the sidelines anymore. I had to be out there to support the marchers.

"So I found out where the marchers gathered, and the next weekend I joined them. I drove to this big Missionary Baptist Church -- I think the building had originally been Catholic -- around 47th and Indiana -- and truthfully I was a little nervous about it. The neighborhood looked pretty rough. But I saw some people going in, and I found a parking spot, so I pulled into the spot. . . .

Chapter 15

Inspiration: South Chicago, 1966

Petrusiac got out of his car and looked around. He had parked next to a vacant lot, kiddie-corner from Mt. Carmel Missionary Baptist Church, a very large, brown brick building, with a large, arch-shaped stained glass window rising high over the huge double doors leading into the church. The window depicted Jesus looking down from a hilltop, with his hands held out before him in mercy, and beams of light shining out from around his head.

Turning his gaze to the neighborhood around him, Petrusiac noticed that there were a few other vacant lots around. Most of the buildings were two story brick homes, probably dating back to the early 1920's. A few were boarded up. Many looked to be in immaculate condition, obviously well cared for. Some appeared to have been altered into two-flats.

As he walked across the street, others came from different directions, all converging at the front doors. Shortly before they arrived, a large African-American man wearing a dark brown suit opened a door and motioned people in. "Some seating still available in the balcony," he said.

As Petrusiac neared the church, he could hear singing coming out the windows, and now out of the open door as well. The song was unfamiliar to him, but sounded like it might have been a spiritual. "Keep your hands on the plow," the people were singing. "Hold on. Hold on." Someone was singing verses that he couldn't yet make out. Then the large crowd responded with the chorus. He followed others up several stairs to a gathering area outside the main sanctuary. Then they were directed up stairs on either side.

Coming out thru another doorway, he found himself on the top of the balcony, which was almost full to the back. He worked his way thru several people to an open chair near the center of the balcony, and remained standing so that he could see clearly. He looked down and across several rows of chairs permanently bolted to the floor, all of which were occupied. Some people were seated. Others were standing and singing emotionally. The balcony continued around both sides of the sanctuary below, and it was full all the way around.

Beyond the railing that protected the front of the balcony, he saw that the sanctuary below was also completely full. Beyond the crowd was a dais, a raised area with several benches and chairs, all occupied by people he assumed were part of the program. Behind them was a large white altar, surmounted by a huge crucifix. On either side were paintings of Biblical scenes. One was of St. Peter holding a set of keys. The other was Mary, the mother of Jesus, kneeling before an angel.

A tall, light skinned man climbed several stairs to the raised pulpit and looked out at the crowd. As he did so, the song came to a climactic ending, everyone singing loudly, "Hold on! Hold On!" and clapping until they were calmed down and invited to be seated. Then he said, "Hold on, brothers and sisters. That's what we've got to do. Hold on. And today we're doing more than just holding on. Today we're moving on out!"

After allowing an enthusiastic response to those words, he continued. "Now brothers and sisters, I want to introduce the Rev. James Bevel, of the SCLC staff. As you may know, Brother Bevel has been working with a renters' strike in New York City, but we asked him to come here and help us out for awhile. I know you're going to love his message. So let's give it up for Brother Bevel!"

He walked down the steps and leaned over to give a hug to a medium height, medium skinned man, who then proceeded to the pulpit to loud cheers and clapping. Petrusiac was surprised to see that he wore a *yarmulke* on his head. "Is he a Jew?" he wondered.

Bevel apparently knew that the *yarmulke* often drew questions from people, so after bringing greetings from brothers and sisters in the struggle in NYC, he explained that he wore a *yarmulke* to show solidarity with the Jewish people. "We're all in this together," he said, drawing another long round of applause. He went on to prepare the crowd for what they were about to face out in the streets. He explained the concept of non-violent resistance, and then led them in a response.

"When they scream hatred at you, what do you give back?" he asked.

"LOVE!" they cried.

"When they spit in your face, what do you give back?"

"LOVE!" they cried.

"When they throw rocks and bottles at you, what do you throw back?"

"LOVE!" they cried.

"When they call you a dirty, low-down nigger, what do you call back?"

"LOVE!" they cried.

"When a police officer grabs your arm, throws you on the ground, and drags you off to the paddy wagon, what do give back?"

"LOVE!" they cried.

"That's what the Bible tells us," he said, "and that's what we're going to do. Pay back evil with a blessing. What are we going to do?

"Pay back evil with a blessing!" they answered.

As the people cheered and Bevel walked down from the pulpit, a young African-American man with a guitar stepped forward and began to sing and play, "We shall not, we shall not be moved." The crowd joined in enthusiastically.

Petrusiac stood to sing and clap with the others, but mostly he was looking out with wonder on the crowd that packed the church. He saw several groups of nuns in their religious habits; at least twenty men wearing *yarmulkes*; catholic priests and protestant ministers wearing clerical collars; men and women of all ages, even some with young children; some men with the new hair style called the "Afro," others wearing African styled hats, and women in flowing African styled dresses. He had never seen anything like it, and he was amazed. By the end of the song, he found himself singing and clapping along, and realized that he was very glad to be there.

The man who appeared to be the MC climbed into the pulpit again. Petrusiac looked hopefully across the stage, thinking it might be time for Martin Luther King to appear. He was certainly ready to hear the great man in person. But this time the introduction was for the Rev. Jessie Jackson. Petrusiac was only vaguely conscious of having heard the name before, but most of the crowd was very familiar with the name, rising to clap and cheer loudly.

Rev. Jackson, a tall, strong looking man with a powerful presence about him, looked around as though he was taking charge of each section of the church and each person in it. He took some time to let the cheers quiet down a bit before beginning to speak. It seemed like everyone there was on the edge of their seats, waiting to hear what he would say.

Petrusiac had never experienced anything like it. He had been totally struck and mesmerized by the preaching (and no doubt about it, the man had delivered a sermon) of James Bevel. The kind of preaching he was used to had been calm and theological. It had encouraged faith in God and faithful living, focusing mostly on family life and helping your neighbor in individual ways or by contributing to a good cause. Bevel's had been powerful and engaging. His words had gone thru the crowd like volts of electricity, turning that diverse group of people into a mighty army, ready to rise up as one to go out and change the world.

Petrusiac was amazed to find that the response to Jesse Jackson was even more powerful. In fact, he had the distinct impression that there was a rivalry going on between Jackson and Bevel over who could get the crowd more hyped up. Jackson spoke of the reason and necessity for the march. He used colorful examples to show that segregation was not just in the south, but just as real in the northern cities of the nation, even if more subtle. He told them that even though they were not among the wealthy and powerful of this world, they were precious in God's sight, and that together they could make things change. Then he really got people going when in a response that most of the people there already knew:

"I am!" he shouted. "**I am!**" they answered.

"Somebody!" he shouted.

"**Somebody!**" they answered.

"I am!"   **"I am!"**

"Somebody!"   **"Somebody!"**

He repeated until everyone was standing and shouting, and he continued as he stepped down from the pulpit, and as the guitarist came forward to start everyone singing.

> "Oh, freedom. Oh, freedom.
> Oh, freedom over me.
> And before I'd be a slave,
> I'll be buried in my grave,
> And go home to my Lord and be free."

The verses continued:
> "No more Jim Crowe . . .
> "No segregation . . .

Petrusiac was surprised to find himself singing, moving and clapping loudly with everyone else. They had been going on for an hour and a half by now, and Dr. King had not come yet. He began to wonder if he really would be there after all. But now he didn't know if it mattered. The crowd was fired up and ready. He thought he had just come to learn and observe, but now he found himself ready to go out with them and change the world. The people were ready to go.

But then suddenly, even though the room was already filled with sound and energy, the volume became even greater. It swelled so much that he felt totally engulfed by it. At first he wondered why everyone got even louder, and stopped singing to cheer and clap ever more wildly. Many were jumping up and down with unrestrained exuberance.

He looked more closely and saw what it was. Dr. King had come. He entered the sanctuary thru a door to the right of the altar. Then he made his way across towards the pulpit, but had to move slowly because each of the many people on the dais wanted to touch him in some way: shake his hand, pat him on the back, give him a hug, whatever they could. It was as if they hoped to take into themselves some of his strength, some of his power, some of his charisma. He acknowledged a few of them briefly, but continued to move slowly onward, looking as though he carried the weight of millions on his back, which perhaps he did.

Finally in the pulpit, King had to wait for some time before things had quieted to the point where he could be heard. He looked out at the people and began very slowly, thanking them for being there, and for their many prayers since he had been hit by a brick the previous week. He assured them that he was fine.

"It would take a lot more than a few bricks to stop us," he said. "Down in Alabama, they sicked their dogs on us, and that didn't stop us." The crowd erupted. "They beat us with their bully clubs, and that didn't stop us. They ran us down with their horses and whipped us with their crops, and that didn't stop us. They knocked us down with their water cannons, and that didn't stop us. They kicked us, and stomped on us, and dragged us into their paddy wagons, and that didn't stop us. They locked us up in their filthy jails, and that didn't stop us. They dragged us before their hateful, racist judges, and that didn't stop us. So no, no, no, brothers and sisters, a few bricks are not going to stop us. Until the rights of the black man are recognized to be just as sacred as the rights of the white man, we are going to keep on keeping on. I'm gonna keep on a walkin', keep on a talkin', marching on to freedom land."

Now the crowd really went wild, and Petrusiac found himself caught up in their exuberance. King continued for another forty-five minutes, and he found every moment to be thrilling. It was not just King's powerful words. There was a presence about the man that Petrusiac could not define except perhaps by an old word he had never heard outside of church: holy. There was something holy, something very sacred about hearing the words of this man, in this place, among these people, and for this cause that made him feel almost as though he had been transported into another time and another place. He felt like he was seeing a vision of what could be, what the world could be like, what the world **should** be like. And he was surprised by the wave of emotion that swept over him. He felt himself on the verge of tears, which embarrassed him. But he looked around and realized that no one was looking at him. They were all mesmerized by the preacher, and by the power of the moment.

Finally King returned to the purpose of their being there today, and the march that was ahead of them. He reminded them they would face great anger and terrible hatred, but they must not give in to these destructive feelings themselves. He told them that they were not doing this to defeat their opponents, but to love them. They were doing this to set their opponents free, for the chains of racism bind the white man as well as the black man. No matter what was said or done to them, there was to be no retaliation. Nothing must make them become the very thing that they hated. They were to return evil only with love. Then he spoke words that came to Petrusiac as a revelation, and stuck in his mind.

"Darkness cannot drive out darkness: only light can do that," said King. "Hate cannot drive out hate: only love can do that. The beauty of nonviolence is that in its own way and in its own time it seeks to break the chain reaction of evil. And so our goal is never to defeat our enemy, but always to gain his love and trust."

Petrusiac continued to think on those words as King completed his message, finally concluding by leading them into "We Shall Overcome," as he and the others on the dais began a procession out of the church building. "We shall overcome," the people sang. "We shall live in peace. We'll walk hand in hand. Black and white together -- NOW." Then came a verse that seemed especially to speak to him. "We are not afraid -- TODAY." He had thought to just be an observer, but now he knew that he would be going with these people on the march. He didn't know exactly where they were going, or how they were getting there, but somehow it didn't seem to matter. He just went with the flow of the crowd, as finally the people in the balcony were the last ones to be ushered out of the church.

In front of the church there was a row of yellow school busses. The remaining people were ushered into them. As soon as a bus was filled up, it drove off. Only the last of the balcony people remained, so a lot of busses must have already left. Petrusiac ended up towards the rear of a bus, seated next to an elderly African-American man who wore a brown suit, white shirt, and green tie. He held a black fedora hat in his hand. Petrusiac felt under-dressed.

The bus headed west on 47th Street to the Dan Ryan Expressway and entered on the southbound ramp. "Do you know where we're going to march?" Petrusiac asked the man sharing his seat.

"No, I don't rightly know," the man answered.

A woman seated in front of them turned around and said, "We're going right back to Marquette Park. Same place he got hit by the brick. Straight into the lion's mouth," she said, laughing.

The woman seated next to her also laughed and said, "Are you sure? I thought we was headed straight into the fiery furnace." They all had a good laugh at that, which Petrusiac thought was probably at least partially to hide their very realistic apprehension.

The bus exited the Dan Ryan at 63rd Street and headed west. They passed an elevated train station that was identified as the Englewood Station. Petrusiac was not familiar with this part of town, but recognized the name as the end of the line for one of the city's rapid transit lines. There was a fairly new shopping center there, but as they headed west along 63rd Street, there was a slow but steady deterioration of the condition of the property. 63rd was clearly a commercial street, with lots of small storefronts, many of which were empty and boarded up.

At Western Ave., the street was blocked by police cars. Busses were turning left onto Western. As they made the turn, he looked down 63rd and saw that the street was crowded with people. Marchers were in the street, and there appeared to be many people all around watching them and making a lot of noise. It all went by very quickly as the bus continued to 64th Street and turned west. About mid block they stopped in front of a vacant lot and were ushered out of the bus. There were marshals guiding them, and police officers wearing riot helmets and carrying bully clubs stood around looking for any signs of trouble. They were guided across the vacant lot and the alley behind it, then into a gangway that ran between two buildings.

As Petrusiac emerged from the gangway onto 63rd Street, he was approached by a thin, elderly woman wearing a babushka. She looked like somebody's grandmother. But as she came up towards him, he saw that her wrinkled face was knotted up in a sneer. It could well have been the most hateful look he had ever seen. He thought that she was about to say something to him, but instead she just came close and spit on him. Then she turned and walked the other way. He was stunned, but he had to keep moving with the group, which was now merging with other marchers who were already walking west down 63rd Street. As he walked, he tried unsuccessfully to wipe spittle from the front of his shirt.

Looking up and around as he joined the flow of marchers, he noticed first that the sidewalks on both sides of the street were lined with crowds of people shouting and jeering at them. Fortunately the noise was so great that he could not hear any of the things that were being said. Next he noted that windows were open in many apartments and offices in the upper stories of the buildings they were passing, which were mostly small shops and local businesses. People were leaning out of the windows to curse and shout at them. Then, to his further surprise and shock, he saw that there were many young men on the rooftops of these buildings, not only yelling, but also throwing stones. He even heard a few firecrackers exploding. The worst thing about the firecrackers was that one's first thought upon hearing them was of gunfire. At various times a group of marchers would flinch from the rocks or the firecrackers, but they kept moving steadily, resolutely forward, and nowhere did anyone turn to respond to the hecklers.

It was only a four block walk from where the march began at Western Avenue until they turned south onto California, but to Petrusiac it seemed like an eternity. He was a man who had always avoided conflict. He considered himself a peacemaker, who always tried to smooth over disagreements. He just wanted people to get along, and didn't see why they couldn't. He was shocked to discover that what he considered to be a very basic right -- that people should be able to buy a house wherever they wanted to and could afford to -- could elicit such a violent response. And it was a revelation to him to find this intense hatred here, in the north, in the city he loved. This idea of non-violent resistance had far deeper implications than he had ever imagined.

California Avenue had some storefronts, but there were mostly apartment buildings. They still faced crowds of hecklers, but not as many. Petrusiac was relieved that he could breathe a bit easier, but he was still anxious to have this come to an end. He had quite enough for one day. He couldn't imagine how African-Americans could face this kind of intense, unwarranted hatred on a regular basis.

They continued on California to Marquette Boulevard, the equivalent of 67th Street, where they came to a large park. A sign on the corner said, "Marquette Park." The police blocked off traffic on the boulevard, so that the marchers could cross and enter a road leading into the park. They followed the winding road past grass and trees, and Petrusiac found himself taking deep breaths, full of relief. He became aware that a tightness in his chest was beginning to let go. He hadn't even been conscious that it was there.

"Thank God," he thought. "We survived."

His sense of relief turned out to be premature. The road came to an end in a parking area outside of tennis courts that were surrounded by high, chain-link fences. There the group came to a halt. Word slowly filtered around that they were to wait there for the busses. Unfortunately, this was not to be a peaceful wait. He felt like they had been cornered here, and that they had been led into a trap. On their right was the high wall of fencing around the tennis courts. To their left, across the parking area, was a grass covered hill. The hill was crowded with over one hundred people who were shouting, heckling, and throwing things at them, just as they had done on 63rd Street. Rather than a place of refuge, this felt more like a cattle pen. He felt like a cow who had been penned here in preparation for slaughter. He hoped the busses would arrive soon.

After a time, a group of young men among the hecklers realized that they had another way to get at the marchers.

They circled around the tennis courts to the other side, where the entrance gates were. From inside the courts they could approach within a few feet of the marchers, shouting their insults from close by, rattling the chain-link fencing, and giving the marchers the clear impression that they were surrounded, with no way out. The handful of police who were present gave all of their attention to the people on the hill, ignoring the young men in the courts.

Where were the busses? The time dragged along, with no let up in the harassment. Petrusiac was astounded by the self-control of the people around him. Not one single person responded to the disgusting insults hurled their way. Not one single person picked up a rock to throw it back at the hecklers.

Petrusiac looked at the young men in the tennis courts. They were calling the marchers savages, apes, gorillas. But he looked at them making their obscene gestures, rattling the fences, and yelling incredibly hateful things, as opposed to his group, staying solid in spite of every provocation thrown at them, and he thought, "My God, who are the savages here? Don't they realize what they look and sound like?" Suddenly his pent up emotion got to him and he approached the fence. He began to mimic the young men in the tennis courts, hoping to make them see what they looked like. Immediately he realized what a mistake that had been. It only encouraged them. They were ecstatic that they had finally gotten a response from one of the marchers, and they doubled their efforts.

Petrusiac turned, walked back to the others in his group, and determined to just ignore the young men. But where were the busses?

Later on he calculated that it had taken just short of an hour for the busses to arrive. It had seemed like an eternity. When his bus finally arrived back at Mt. Carmel Missionary Baptist, Petrusiac felt a great sense of relief. They had made it. For the first time in hours, he could breathe freely. He felt safe. It felt good to be alive. He wondered if this was how soldiers felt after surviving a great battle. And he realized with amazement that he was feeling all of this, this tremendous sense of relief and freedom, because of leaving a lily-white neighborhood and returning to the security of the ghetto.

What was it that Dr. King had said? "Darkness cannot drive out darkness: only light can do that," said King. "Hate cannot drive out hate: only love can do that."

*   *   *

Grant Park, Chicago 1976

"Wow!" said Blake. "You actually heard Dr. King? And you marched with him?"

"Yes, I did," answered Petrusiac. "And it really changed me. I had always admired King, but I looked at it like he was a great spokesperson for 'those people.' But after that experience I realized that no, he was speaking for me too. He was lifting up a vision of the kind of country I want to see us become. He was challenging all of us to live up to our ideals, you know, life, liberty and the pursuit of happiness; all people crated equal. It was like in that meeting I got a vision of what that could really look like. And on that march I got an indication of what it would take and how hard it would be. But I knew that it was worth it. And I knew I had to be part of the effort. That's how I got into organizing."

"But you didn't get into a Civil Rights organization," said Bill. "You got into community organizing. How come?"

"Well, for one thing, most of the work needs to be done in the white neighborhoods. And when people start to work with their neighbors on the issues that really matter to them, they find out that everybody wants the same things, and we're all in it together."

Fran joined in. "Yeah, did you see what happened when we went to Alderman O'Malley's? When we took on the

270

issue of a junkyard on Chicago Avenue, look who came together to work on it. We started out with the Ukranians, because they've been the majority in that neighborhood for years. But we ended up with lots of Italians, Polish, Irish, you name it. Then when some of the new Mexicans started showing up, they were just included like more neighbors helping us fight the junkyard. A few years ago, there would have been block clubs getting together to try to keep Mexicans from coming into our neighborhood. Not many blacks living there yet, but it won't be long. And when they do, our folks have learned that we need everybody working together to get things done, and they'll be included with everybody else."

"Hopefully," said Jim.

"Yes, hopefully," she laughed, and poked him in the ribs.

"So, Marco," asked Tricia, "what are you studying in college?"

"Well," he answered, "Trinity is primarily a teacher's college. I'm hoping to get a teaching position somewhere I can also coach football. That's what I really want to do."

"No kidding?" said Bill. "You mean Fran hasn't convinced you to major in Poly Sci and get into organizing, like she's doing?"

As Marco just looked down and shook his head, Fran said, "I wasn't trying to do that. But you know what?" she asked, looking at Marco, "He would actually be good at it. He knows how to talk to all kinds of people. He's a good listener. And best of all, he really cares."

"Hey," said Tricia. "I think the orchestra's getting ready to play."

Right on cue, the sounds of the 'Stars and Stripes Forever' began to emanate from the large speakers set up on poles all around the grassy area, broadcasting the music from the distant band shell. The group settled themselves on chairs and blankets to listen.

CHAPTER 16

How Quickly Things Can Change

Marco lined up as the right side linebacker. It was third down, and with eight yards to go, they were expecting a pass. As he watched their opponents line up over the center, something caught his attention. The offensive end set up further outside than he had been previously. Marco took note and moved two more steps further out himself. In response, the offensive end also shifted two steps further out. Marco waited until the quarterback called "set," then moved back further inside, drawing a nervous movement from the offensive end.

That was the "tell" he was looking for. He quickly turned and made a hand motion, signaling to the defensive halfback behind him that "they're coming our way". Then he moved up closer to the line of scrimmage, just outside of his own defensive end.

The quarterback barked his signals and the ball was snapped. The quarterback took the ball and immediately made a quick pitch to his speedy left halfback, who was already running towards the sideline. He gathered the ball in stride, expecting to sprint around the left side, with his own left end blocking out the defensive linebacker. But

Marco was already there in the backfield. Even so, the halfback almost got around him. So he dove for the man's legs, stretching out his body full length and grabbing for his ankles. He just caught him, not enough to grab hold of him, but enough to trip him up, so that he fell for a nine yard loss.

The homecoming crowd roared with delight, but Marco's cry was one of pain. His right knee was bent across his left leg at an unnatural angle, and the offensive end was lying on it, pinning him down. The man had turned inside in a futile effort to block Marco out of the play, but he did succeed in knocking him out of the game. And as it turned out, in putting an early end to his football days.

*   *   *

Two days later, Marco was lying in a hospital bed. His right leg was in a hard cast, from his thigh down to his ankle, and held up in the air by a metal chain attached to a post rising from the foot of the bed. He was still in pain, in spite of the meds, and his back ached constantly. His severely limited ability to move or shift positions meant that he was constantly uncomfortable and unable to do anything about it. Angry and miserable, he couldn't remember ever feeling so helpless or frustrated.

Suddenly his mother came into the room, a comforting smile hiding the worry Marco knew she was feeling. "Marco, Marco," she said. "I'm so happy to see you, and so glad that you are okay." Inhibited by the contraption on his leg, she bent over to kiss him on his cheek."

"What do you mean, 'Okay?'" he asked. "My knee will never be the same again. My football days are over, and I don't know what that will mean for my scholarship. I'm really all bummed out, mom." He groaned and tried to shift positions, pushing up on his elbows to relieve pressure on his back for a moment, then slowly settled back in bed. "But thanks for coming, anyway," he added.

"Don't worry about all that right now, Marco," she said. "We'll figure it all out. I'm sure we can work something out with the college. But first, all you have to do is get better."

"Yeah, I know," he said. "But I can't help thinking about it. Thanks for coming, mom. I'm glad you're here. But you really didn't have to come all the way up from St. Louis. Did you take the train?"

"No," she answered, "We drove."

"You drove?" he asked, incredulous. "You've always said you'd never drive in Chicago. Even when somebody else drives, you cover your eyes because the traffic makes you so nervous."

"Oh, I know, I know," she said. "And I still feel that way, believe me. But your lovely friend came with me, thank God, and she graciously agreed to drive when we got near to the city." As she spoke, she turned with a smile to the petite brunette who had entered the room with her.

Marco looked at her incredulously. Had she been there all along? Those pills they were giving him must have been affecting him more than he had realized. "Marsha," he said, and blushed as their eyes met. "How did you . . . ?"

The women looked at each other and laughed. His mother said, "Everybody has been worried about you, you know. As soon as the school called me, I called your cousin Frances, since she could get over here the quickest. She did come to see you didn't she?"

"Yeah," he answered, "right away that night. I wasn't a whole lot of company, I'm afraid. When I wasn't in some sort of medical procedure, I was too hopped up on pain killers to be very conversational."

"That's what she told us," his mother continued. "But she did mention that you had a friend who should be told about

276

it. She thought her name was Marsha, but wasn't sure, and she didn't know a last name anyway. But she suggested I ask your Uncle John, since you've been talking with him a lot lately. Well he didn't know anything either, but he remembered that you met her thru your friend Danny. So I called Danny and found out that Marsha is his cousin. And of course he knew how to contact her. So you see, you've become quite the topic of conversation lately."

Marco just shook his head and looked down as the two women laughed. Then he looked up at Marsha, his eyes shining, fixed on the hair soft around her face, and said, "I'm sorry," even though he realized he was not sorry at all that she was there.

"Don't be silly," she said lightly, not wanting to betray what her eyes saw -- larger-than-life Marco, looking helpless and still in the bed. "I would have come anyway, once I found out about it. But it's a lot more fun to come with somebody else, and I've enjoyed getting to know your mother."

The older woman smiled and agreed. "We did have fun on our drive, and it didn't hurt that we shared some good stories about a certain football player . . . "

"You mean EX – football player," Marco interrupted, stating what his visitors were avoiding. Turning red, he went on, "So you two had fun. Well, I'm glad to know that something humorous has come out of all this."

As Marsha approached to give him a kiss, his cousin Fran poked her head around the curtain and looked in. She said, "Hey there, big guy." She grinned while appraising the young woman standing by him, and said, "Looks like you're doing a little better today. Good to see you, Aunt Molly. And you must be Marsha."

As Marco's mother introduced the two younger women and the three spoke together, a smiling nurse entered and walked around to the far side of the bed, where she checked his IV bag and monitors. She was a tall African-American woman of about the same age as Marsha and Fran. While disconnecting his IV and other devises, she said, "Well, Marco, I knew you would be attracting a crowd of young women back here. You said no, but I knew it would happen. I told you so."

As the women laughed, Marco turned red, looked away, and said, "Cut it out now, guys," he said, feeling uncomfortable with the women's laughter. "You're embarrassing me. Mom, this is Keisha, my favorite nurse. Keisha, this is my mother, Molly, my cousin, Frances, and my friend, Marsha. Actually, all the nurses here are very nice. The doctors and therapists are another matter though."

"Now, now," said Keisha. "You know it's just because they want you to make a full recovery as soon as possible. But that's actually why I'm here. To unplug you, because there will be an orderly here in just a minute, who will be taking you downstairs for some more tests. And I'm afraid only one person will be able to go with you."

The women looked at each other and agreed that Marco's mother should be the one to go with him. "We can just go down to the cafeteria for awhile," said Fran. "I'm starving, and besides, I'd like to get to know Marsha." Looking at Marco she said, "I'll bet we can share a lot of juicy stories about you."

Marco groaned as the women all laughed, and said to the nurse, "Keisha, can you please tell these annoying women that your patient needs some peace and quiet?"

"Oh no," she answered. "You know the doctor wants you to start getting more active and more social. He says you've been feeling sorry for yourself long enough."

When the orderly appeared and wheeled Marco out of the room, Fran and Marsha headed to the cafeteria. Seated at a cramped table in the corner, they sized each other up over sips of coffee. Fran noted Marsha's conservative, below the knee skirt. Her pale green blouse complimented the auburn highlights in her dark hair and eyes. Marsha noticed Fran's creamy skin and her jet black hair falling in waves on a plaid shirt tucked into jeans. Both were comfortable in their impressions of each other and their feelings for the wounded Marco. They shared a concern for him, as he mourned the loss of his beloved football days while recovering from his injury.

"Aunt Molly really appreciated you driving up here with her," Fran offered. "I know she was dying to come, but she gets nervous about driving alone."

"I was glad to do it," Marsha replied softly. "It made things easier for me too. And thank you for making the connection. I know that Marco thinks very highly of you. He's told me a lot about the work you're doing here. He was really impressed, and really respects you for it. And so do I."

"Yeah, Marco and I have always been good buds," said Fran. "We like ribbing each other. We're so different in many ways, but we seem to be on the same wavelength a lot of the time. You know, I would never have brought any of my other myriads of cousins along on an action, but I thought Marco would understand what we're trying to do. And I think he enjoyed it."

"He sure did," said Marsha. "For awhile that was all he could talk about. It's the only thing I've ever seen him get almost as excited about as football."

"You've got to be kidding me," said Fran, "As much as football? No way."

"ALMOST as much, I said. Almost." The two women laughed, but then grew quiet as they remembered that his playing days were over.

"Well, anyway," said Fran. "I'm really glad to finally meet you. Even though Marco is a big, strong guy, he is very tender hearted underneath that tough exterior. So I'm very glad he's found a great girl."

"Thanks, Fran," said Marsha. "I know he's got a good heart. That I do know. But it took me awhile to see it. Did he tell you about how we met?"

"Not much," answered Fran. "Just that it was at Danny's brother's wedding."

"Well, I think he asked Danny to introduce us, then he sat at the same table. People were asking him about his military service, and that was impressive. Then after a while he asked me to dance. But what I really liked was the fact that he stood up to my father right away. My father has scared off a whole lot of men, let me tell you. When he gives you the evil eye, most guys just decide I'm not worth the effort. But Marco just gave it right back. He wasn't intimidated in the least. I liked that."

Fran laughed, and said, "That's Marco all right. I can just see it. But as strong as he is, he's a pushover underneath."

"Yeah, but it took a while to see that," said Marsha. "Have you ever been to one of his football games?"

"No," answered Fran. "I'm not much into football. Marco invited me a few times, but I never went. Now I wish I had."

"Same with me," said Marsha. "He kept asking me to go to one of the Eagles' games, so I finally did. And you wouldn't believe it. He's like a madman out there on the field. I wasn't watching the game really, just Marco. And what I saw kind of frightened me. He's vicious out there. When somebody tried to block him, he just threw him off like a dishrag. When he tackled a running back, it looked like the guy had hit a brick wall. Once I saw him sack a quarterback, and they had to carry the poor guy off on a stretcher. I started to ask myself, 'Who is this guy? What have I got myself into?'"

Now Fran was really laughing. "You're kidding me," she said.

"I am not," said Marsha. "I can see why he got a scholarship to play, but it did make me wonder what he'd do to me if I ever crossed him."

"But he's always very solicitous of women," said Fran. "He's almost chivalrous."

"I know," said Marsha. "But I still wasn't so sure about him till he came to church with us one Sunday."

"Church?" asked Fran. "He went to church with you? This really is serious."

Marsha paused, looked off out the window and said, "It could be. Could be." Looking back at Fran she said, "But here's the thing. The scripture passage that day was that parable where Jesus says that God's going to separate the sheep from the goats. Do you know that one?"

"You mean where people ask, 'When did I see you hungry, or in prison, or naked, or whatever? And he answers,

'Whatever you did for the least of my brothers and sisters, you did to me?' That one?"

"Right, that one," continued Marsha. "Anyway, we've got this new pastor there who's a real social justice guy. My father hates him. Thinks it's too political when he talks about poverty, world hunger, whatever. I think he's great, and most of the people love him, but my father calls the bishop every week to complain. So Pastor Martin was talking about how many people right in our own community don't have enough to eat, and he's giving examples of real families who come to our food pantry every month. Then he starts giving statistics about world hunger, and how many millions that are starving — and the figures are really staggering.

"Anyway, there I was," (here she leaned across closer to Fran) "sitting in between Marco and my father. And on my right, my father is twitching around in his chair like this, and I can just feel him fuming. And I wonder if he's about to pick up a hymnal to throw at the pastor, or just stand up and go storming out of the building, vowing never to return. At the same time, there's Marco sitting on my left, and I can tell he really feels for these people who Pastor Martin is talking about. So much so that I think he might start crying. I think he was trying hard to hold it back."

Fran was enjoying this description so much that she was almost crying with laughter. "That's Marco alright," she said. "I can just see it. That's one of the things I love about him. He really cares about EVERYBODY. Oh, that's beautiful. That's beautiful. So what did you do?"

Marsha paused. Then she said, "I reached out and held Marco's hand. He squeezed real hard." Fran laughed so hard she started crying. Marsha laughed with her.

Marco and his mother were already in the room when they returned. Marco looked back and forth between the two young women. Then he said, "You've been talking about me, haven't you? I'm embarrassed." Then he turned red and looked out the window.

As the women laughed, Fran went up and leaned over to give him a hug. While she did so, she whispered in his ear, "I think she's a keeper."

Chapter 17
A New Path
St. Louis, February 1977

Marco headed towards a cart on the side wall of the room, carrying a large empty pitcher in each hand. He was wearing a white server's uniform, and weaved quickly thru the round tables that filled the banquet hall of the Ramada Inn. They would have to work very quickly and efficiently to serve everyone in the overfilled space on schedule. And along with the quality of the food, the timeliness and efficiency of the service were important to getting good tips as well as repeat business.

As he neared the cart where he would refill his pitchers, he noticed that in between the cart and the door leading to the kitchen, his older brother, Bob, was having a heated conversation with Jack, a sous chef. Jack was holding his chef's hat in his hand, and was gesticulating with it to emphasize whatever point he was making. He was obviously very agitated. Bob was trying to calm him down, not very successfully.

As Marco got closer to the cart, he could hear what Jack was saying.

"Why do you keep that man around?" he asked, waving his hat towards the kitchen. "You know nobody can work with him. Look,

I agreed to help out today as a favor to you, Bob. But I can't do it. I don't need the work so bad I have to put up with his bull crap all day."

Marco listened as he refilled his water pitchers.

"Look," said Bob, holding up both hands as a calming gesture. "I get it, Jack. I hear you. But the man is a great chef. You know that, Jack. Please, please, help me out here. All you have to do is get thru the next hour and a half. That's it. Then I promise, I'll never ask you to work with Clifford again. I promise. Okay? Can you do this, Jack? For me?"

The whole time Bob was talking, Jack was not looking at him, but around and above him, continuing to wave his hat in frustration and shifting his weight from one foot to the other. Finally he said, "I'm sorry, Bob, but I can't do. I'm just not going to put up with his crap any more." Then he took off his white chef's shirt, threw it on the floor next to the wall along with his hat, and stormed out of the room.

Marco put down his pitchers and went to stand next to his brother. "Well, that was interesting. I don't think he likes Clifford," he said.

Bob turned towards him and said, "Looks like I need you in the kitchen again, Marco. You seem to be the only one who can get along with Clifford. How do you do it?"

Marco shrugged and said, "Pretty simple. I listen to him. I pay attention to what he says and do things the way he wants them done. I've actually learned a lot from him."

"Well," said Bob, "I need you to go back in the kitchen and learn some more today."

"Happy to do it," said Marco, but you're already light on servers tonight."

Bob looked out over the crowd, sighed, and said, "I know. How well I know. Guess I'll have to put on an apron and help out myself tonight." Then he turned to Marco and said, "I keep telling you, Marco, I could use your help down here. Let's talk about it later tonight."

Later the two men sat on stools in the Ramada bar. Bob downed a shot of Wild Turkey and started to wash it down with a beer. Marco just nursed a draft beer in a tall, fancy glass.

"So what did you want to talk about?" asked Marco. "You know I come down almost every weekend to help out already."

"Yeah, and I really appreciate it. You've got a way of dealing with people that I don't have, and it can be a big help in this business. I've got regular, steady work for you here anytime you want it. I figure you can't be too serious about whatever you're studying in that college up there, 'cause it's like you can't wait to get back down here every weekend."

"Well, I hate to disappoint you, but it's not your pretty face or magnetic personality that I miss," said Marco.

"Hell, I know that," said Bob. "It's that woman that's got your little heart thumpin'. What's her name again? Martha is it?"

"Marsha," said Marco. "Which you knew very well."

"So anyway, I was thinking you don't need a degree to do the kind of work I do. You're a natural already. I could give you regular, steady work right now. Love to have you. I need a good ramrod. Somebody who can organize the staff, make sure everything is prepared, out of the kitchen, and on time to the tables. I've got the business end down after doing it all these years, and you know how to work with people, motivate them. You'd be great at it. You could move back down here. See Martha or Marsha or whoever every day."

"I don't know, Bob," he answered. "I'll think about it. Now that I know I'll never play football again or be a gym teacher, I've had a hard time keeping up my interest in school. But I do want to get a degree. I figure I could finish it up in a couple of years, maybe less. And it would be a good thing to have. But I'll think about it."

"And here's the thing," said Bob, looking around the room and continuing softly to Marco, "I'm quitting the company and going into business for myself sometime this year. Probably this spring or early summer. Word's not out yet, so keep it under your hat. But I've got a partner, Bill Sykes, who's got lots of contacts around town — politicos, tycoons, you name it. And there's real money in the catering business. Profit margin's almost 50% if you know what you're doing. And I know what I'm doing. This is going to be a real money maker, and you could get in on the ground floor."

"Seems to me there are lots of catering companies already," said Marco, "like the one you work for now."

"You're right, there are," said Bob. "But we're talking about a high end company. The rest are pretty well all basic stuff. You know, mostaccioli, green beans, chicken or beef. We're talking about the high end market. Specialty items. Menus that make people sit up and take notice."

"Clifford," said Marco.

"Clifford," said Bob. "You got it. "I'm telling you, there's a gold mine in that market. And there's a spot for you. I guarantee it."

"I don't know," said Marco. "Sounds tempting. I'll think about it. But I don't think I'm quite ready to give up on college yet."

*　　*　　*

April, 1977

"Oh, Marco, no," said his mother, Molly. "No, you can't quit college now. You're so close. So close. You told me you thought you could even finish up in just one more year. One more year, Marco. I've been so proud of you, the way you've dealt with your injury, and how you haven't let it stop you, even though it ended your plans for being a coach and phys ed teacher. Please believe me, Marco. Just hang in there one more year. You'll never regret it, I promise you."

They were sitting at her kitchen table, mugs of coffee in their hands.

Marco watched the steam coming up from his mug, took a deep breath, and lifted his head to look directly at his mother. "I know you want what's best for me, mom, and I appreciate your concern. But I've made up my mind. I already let the college know I won't be back in the fall."

"This is about Marsha, isn't it?" said his mother, after a pause.

"She' s part of it, yes."

"Did she put you up to this?"

"No, she did not. She told me that she would support whatever I wanted to do. Besides, I thought you liked Marsha."

"I do like Marsha, you know that. I thinks she's a lovely girl, and she's probably a good match for you, Marco. But she'll still be around a year from now. I'm very disappointed that she did not convince you to finish your degree first. Have you talked about getting married?"

"Yes we have. We're thinking about some time in August. Nothing fancy, just something simple."

After another pause, she asked, "And do you really think that working for your brother is a good idea? He's had these big ideas before, you know. So far none of them have worked out. He's doing well with the company he's with right now. It's the most steady work he's ever had. I hate to see him take such a big risk. The food business is very volatile, you know. It's hard to make a go at it. And even the ones that do well don't seem to last very long."

"I know, mom," he answered. "But Bob really knows the business well. He understands the economics of it. He's built up a good rep in the business. And his partner's got lots of contacts with the kind of people who like to have big events where they throw around a lot of money. It could work. It could work really well."

"I hope so," she said. "I hope so. But your only experience is working tables on your weekends home. Surely you can't live on just that."

"Actually I'll be kind of a supervisor," he said. "I've gotten good at working with the staff, organizing who does what, smoothing over rough spots, keeping things moving. That's something Bob's not as good at. He's great at the planning, contracts, purchasing, that kind of thing, but he's already depending on me to make sure everything goes just right at the actual event. And I've been learning a lot about the cooking end too, working with his chef. I think I'm getting pretty good at it."

Molly sighed and looked across the table at her son. She decided it would not be a good idea to express any of her other misgivings. It was clear that his mind was made up. He was an adult who had been living independently for years now. So she just smiled and said, "You know, Marco, I love you, and I'll support you in whatever you do. Tell Marsha I'd love to help with wedding plans in any way that I can."

*   *   *

June, 1977

Marco used his hip to push thru the swinging door into the hotel kitchen, carrying a large box of fresh produce for the evening's banquet. He was surprised to find Clifford there, busy pounding chicken breasts to tenderize them.

"You're off to a very early start today," he said.

293

"That brother of yours decided he wanted baked, stuffed chicken breast on the menu tonight," the chef replied. "If you want to do it right, it can't be done in the last minute."

"Yeah," said Marco, as he put the box down on a counter and began to unpack it, "but it's 8:00 in the morning."

"The filling takes several hours to jell," said Clifford.

"Really?" said Marco, coming over to the chef. "Say, those breasts are sliced awfully thin."

"That's right. Gotta be, so you can roll up the stuffing into them."

"Do you want some help?" asked Marco. "I'd love to learn how you do it."

"That would be fine," Clifford replied, "but you've got to do things exactly like I tell you, or I'd rather not have help at all."

"You've got it," said Marco. "You're the chef."

"Okay," said Clifford, as he slapped the breasts into a large aluminum container and put it into the large refrigerator. "See the pile of onions there? They've all got to be chopped. Small pieces. Almost minced. Then the bags of mushrooms over there. Wash them out in a big colander and then slice them very, very thin."

As Marco got to work on the onions, he noticed that Clifford had begun chopping up a couple of large heads of garlic. He marveled at how quickly and surely the chef wielded a very large, very sharp knife. Most people thought Marco was fast, but he moved at about half of Clifford's speed. Once the garlic was chopped, Clifford found two very large skillets that he put on burners. He poured some olive oil into each one without needing to measure amounts. Then he divided the garlic between them, threw it into the skillets, and began to stir them around with a large wooden spoon. Next he called for Marco's onions.

"Sorry, I'm not quite done with them," said Marco.

Without answering, Clifton turned down the heat slightly on the skillets and went to help Marco finish the onions. His knife was flying.

"Okay," he said, "let's throw them in the skillets."

While Clifford started to saute the onions, he directed Marco to start slicing mushrooms. After a few minutes, the chef once again turned down the heat and went to help Marco with the slicing.
"I'm sorry I can't keep up," said Marco.

"That's okay," Clifford answered. "Actually, you're doing very well. You're chopping and slicing exactly how it's supposed to be done. Speed comes with time and experience. When you've helped me before, I noticed that you seem to know what you're doing. Have you done much cooking before?"

"Well, some," answered Marco. "A fair amount, I suppose. My Aunt Rose was a great cook, and she taught my mother a lot of her Italian recipes. Then my mother passed them on to me. And my mom is German, so she knows a lot of that cuisine as well. I learned a lot from her."

"Alright," said Clifford. "Time for the chicken broth. It's in the right hand refrigerator, top shelf." When Marco brought it, the chef once again added without needing to measure. He also poured in some white wine from a bottle that Marco opened for him. Then he grabbed a large, aluminum shaker, and began shaking spices into the skillets.

"What spices do you have in there, Clifton?" asked Marco.

The chef looked at him, shook his head, and said, "No, no. That's one thing I keep to myself. A good chef develops his own blend that's what he likes, and what helps give his recipes a distinctive flavor. If you want to keep doing this kind of thing, you'll have to find your own blend."

"Well, okay," laughed Marco. "I had no idea."

As the chef stirred in the spices, he gave his next order. "All right, now get two large glasses, and fill them half way with corn starch." When Marco had done so, he added, "Now fill them the rest of the way with cold water. Make sure the water is cold before you pour it in. Then mix it up real good, till it's all dissolved. It should look like milk."

Clifford turned off the burners before adding the corn starch. When he and Marco had mixed that in to the stuffing, they covered the skillets with foil and put them in the refrigerator.

"Now what?" asked Marco.

"Now we let it sit all day," answered Clifford, "so the stuffing can jell. When we come back tonight, we take out the stuffing and roll it up inside the chicken breasts. I might decide to add some chopped up baby spinach to the mix. Maybe some mozzarella. Haven't made up my mind. Then we brown the chicken, and stick it in the oven. Then while it's baking, we prepare a wine and mushroom sauce."

"Sounds delicious," said Marco. While he was speaking, the door swung open and Bob entered.

"Here you two are," said Bob. "I was hoping to talk with you this morning, Clifford. I've got a proposition to make to you. Let's go out to the dining hall and talk about it."

Clifford looked leery, but went along with the two other men to sit at a round table in the banquet hall. After describing in glowing terms the plan to leave their current employer to begin their own catering company, Bob made his pitch to the chef. "Look, as your boss, I know exactly what they pay you here, and it stinks. You're worth twice as much. You're one of the best chefs in St. Louis. I know that, and you know that. It pains me to pay you as little as we do, but I don't have a choice in the matter. My salary is nothing to get rich on either. We've got a golden opportunity here, and with you on board, I know we can make a killing. And you can finally start earning what you're worth. You'd be a key part of the team. Complete control of the kitchen. Anything you need to make it work. What do you say, Clifton? Are you with us?"

Marco could tell that Clifton was intrigued but skeptical. They talked for another half hour, the chef asking many detailed questions about the planned operation. Finally he said, "You know, it sounds like a good plan. I can see how it could work. And I agree that there would be a market for it."

"So what do you say?" asked Bob. "Are you with us?"

Clifford took a deep breath, then finally sighed and shook his head. "No, I just can't see it. If I was a younger man, I'd jump on it in a heartbeat. But I'm sixty one years old. Even though the pay here is crap, I've got some money in my retirement fund here, and that's what I'm going to be depending on. I just don't have the energy for a fresh start. But I'll be cheering for you. I hope you can make it happen."

Bob was badly disappointed. "Oh man, Clifford, you're an important part of the plan. We need you to make it work. I don't know anybody else who could make it work like you could."

"Why not him?" asked Clifford, nodding towards Marco.

"Who? Marco?" Bob was amazed?

"Sure. Why not?" asked Clifford. "He already knows a lot, and he's a quick study."

Bob looked at Marco without saying anything, a shocked look still on his face. Marco was just as amazed himself, too surprised to know how to react.

"I'm serious," Clifford continued. "I've worked with a lot of people over the years, and Marco's probably in the top three of the best of them. He's got a real feel for how things need to be done. He doesn't try to cheat on recipes to make things easier or cheaper. He's already handling the purchasing, so he understands quantity and quality issues. He's very good with German and Italian dishes, and he's learned a lot about more contemporary cuisine. Besides, I'd be happy to stay in touch. You guys have always treated me right, and you can call me anytime you want for ideas or suggestions."

Bob and Marco looked at each other without saying anything. It was very quiet for some time.

July, 1977
Wedding Reception

Marco stood with his friend, Danny, sipping fruit punch. Oak Hill Chapel, the small wedding venue where the wedding ceremony had just been performed, had made this room available for a reception. A group of twenty five people had gathered there to mingle, talk, eat bakery goods and finger sandwiches, and sip on soft drinks and fruit punch. Marco looked into his glass and swirled it around, estimating that the punch was made of Seven-Up and cranberry juice, with scoops of lime sherbet floating in the large bowl to make it more festive and flavorful.

"You really fooled me," said Danny. "I always pictured you having a wedding with twice as many people as my brother Gary's. I figured you'd start out in a big church with a long aisle, six guys in monkey suits up in the front, six women in fancy dresses walking down the aisle, a bride all in white with a veil over her face. Then a huge reception hall with a sit down dinner, a five piece band, lots of dancing, and an open bar. But here we are in this very laid-back, very quaint little spot, with an intimate group of friends and family eating finger sandwiches and sipping sodas. Not that I'm complaining, mind you. I like it. But you sure had me fooled."

"Sorry to disappoint you, Danny," said Marco. "But all of this happened so fast, we were lucky to find this place was still available. And we had to do it on a shoestring."

"Yeah, these wedding venues book up over a year in advance. And YOU, my friend, were a man in a hurry." Danny got a sly look on his face and swiveled his hips suggestively, causing Marco to shake his head in disgust.

"But you mean Marsha's father didn't want to give her a big send off?" asked Danny. "He looks pretty prosperous to me."

"Not as much as you might think. He's got a government job. Works at the Federal Reserve Bank. Besides which, he's not exactly thrilled with his daughter's choice of a husband, he's very frugal, and he doesn't much like the pastor either."

"My, my," said Danny. "Now that you mention it, he doesn't exactly look overjoyed."

"No, he sure doesn't," answered Marco. "But I'm not complaining. He showed up. And he walked her down the aisle. That's all that matters, as far as I'm concerned. Once he sees that I treat Marsha right and that I'm not a deadbeat, I think he'll come around. Listen, Danny, there's another reason we did it on the cheap, but you've got to keep it under your hat."

"What's that?" asked Danny.

"I've committed almost all of my Air Force savings for a business opportunity. My brother, Bob, is leaving his job to start his own catering company, and I want to buy into it. But until we really get that off the ground, money's going to be very, very tight."

"Whoa!" said Danny. That's a surprise. What are you calling it?"

"Bob & Marco's."

"How clever," said Danny.

"I thought so," said Marco.

"And Marsha's okay with this?"

"Yes, she is, amazingly so. She's all for it. Thinks I'll be good at it."

"Wow! said Danny. "You've got yourself a winner there. I think you need to do something a little more special for her than this family gathering, nice as it is."

"Oh, I agree," said Marco. "As soon as we get a chance, we're heading over to the Cheshire Inn. We'll spend a couple of nights there."

"Snazzy," said Danny. "That sounds more like it. But by the way, I hope you remember that I'm the good friend who invited you to my brother's wedding, and that's where you met your beloved.

So I figure you owe me, big time. So who, in this much smaller crowd, might be interesting for me to meet?"

"See the dark haired one over in the corner, talking with her hands to a laughing and appreciative audience?" asked Marco.

"Yeah, I see her," Danny answered.

"That's my cousin Frances," said Marco. "She's really terrific. But you'd better be on your A game if you expect to get anywhere with her."

"Well," said Danny. "That's a challenge if I ever heard one. And you know me. I never back down from a challenge." He glared at Marco, turned on his heels, and headed off towards Frances.

As Danny walked off, Marco's Uncle John came over.

"I told you so, Marco. I told you so," said John, wagging his finger.

"What do you mean, Uncle John?" he asked.

"You owe me 20 bucks, Marco," said John, holding out his hand. "Let's have it."

"What are you talking about? Twenty bucks for what?"

"Don't play dumb with me," said John. "We sat there on my back porch last summer, and I bet you $20 that one of these days you'd find the right woman, and you'd be a goner, just like that."

He snapped his fingers. "And look what happened. Was I right, or was I right? Answer me, Marco. Was I right, or was I right?" He held out his left hand, and stroked it with his right as he said, "Right here, Marco. Twenty bucks, right here."

Marco laughed, "What can I say, Uncle John? I guess you got me."

"You bet I got you," he said. "I had you pegged all along. So where's the twenty? Let's ask your lovely bride." He turned and looked until he saw Marsha talking with some people across the room. Then he called out in a loud voice, "Hey, Mrs. Russo. Mrs. Marco Russo!" When Marsha turned his way, he called, "Come on over here for a minute. We need you to settle something here."

Marsha excused herself and walked over. She gave Marco a puzzled look, but he just shook his head. "What is it, Uncle John?" she asked.

"This husband of yours is trying to weasel out of a bet he made with me last summer. So I need you to set him straight," he said. "Oh really?" she replied. "What bet was that?

"I bet him twenty bucks that when he met the right woman, he would fall like a ton of bricks. And was I right?" he asked.

"Yes, Uncle John," she laughed. "I guess you were right. Marco, you'd better pay him off."

Marco reached in his coat pocket, took out his wallet, and pulled out a ten dollar bill. "I'm afraid that's all I have on me," he said. "I'll have to owe you the rest."

John looked at Marsha and asked, "Do you think I can trust him? Is he good for it?"

"Oh, I'll make sure he makes good on it. In fact, I think that in order to be fair, we should pay you Forty dollars," she said.

"Forty dollars?" asked Marco, incredulous.

"Hey, I like the sound of that," said John. "But why forty dollars?"

Marsha put her arm around Marco's waist, pulled him close, and said, "Because I fell just as hard and fast for Marco as he did for me. And I've been in an even bigger hurry to get married that he has," she replied.

At that, Marco took her in his arms, leaned over, and gave her a big, long kiss, to which everyone in the hall turned and cheered.

*   *   *

September, 1977
Governor's Banquet

"Going great, Marco!" said Bob. "It's going just like we hoped. We're going to get a lot more business from this, I guarantee it. I knew you've got what it takes. The food's coming out right on schedule, and it tastes great. The wait staff is operating like a well-oiled machine. See, I knew you had it in you. You're a natural, Marco.

"Oh, oh, what's that?" he asked, looking at a table across the room where some kind of disturbance seemed to be happening. Several people had rapidly stood up and were stepping back from the table. A waitress was picking things up and seemed to be apologizing to the people as she did so. She looked very upset.

"What in the hell has that dizzy broad done?" asked Bob, and started towards the table.

Marco grabbed him by the arm and said, "Let me take care of it, Bob. It's my job. Besides, I know her, and I know the people. I'll handle it."

"Okay," said Bob. "Okay. But I want her out of here. She's gonna cost us business."

Marco hurried across the room. As he walked, he quickly signaled to two other staff people to get over to the table. They immediately headed that way, and began straightening up the table and speaking to the people. The original waitress hurried towards the kitchen with several plates in her hands.

Marco apologized profusely to two people who had food spilled on them. He assured them that everything would be taken care of, and gave them his business card, promising to pay for any cleaning bills resulting from the accident. In a few moments he had them laughing at the incident, and sitting down calmly as replacement dishes were placed before them. Then he went off to look for the waitress, who had not reappeared after the incident.

He found her in a hallway outside of the kitchen, crying.

"Come on now, Diane," he said, giving her a hug. "It's just a little bit of spilled food. It's happened to every one of us, one time or another. No big deal."

"I'm so sorry," she sobbed. "So sorry, Marco. I just can't do it tonight. I'm so sorry."

"What's the matter?" he asked. "This is not like you. You're usually one of the best servers I've got. What's up?"

"Oh, Marco. I'm sorry. I just can't, I can't . . ."

"You can't what, Diane? What's the problem?"

"I got a notice from my landlord today. I'm behind in my rent, and he's going to evict me if I don't get him full payment tomorrow, and I just don't have it," she said. "I work two jobs, and I still can't make it. I don't know what I'm going to do. What am I gonna tell my kids? Where will we go?"

'How much do you owe?" he asked.

"$600," she said, "and he wants the whole thing, and I just don't have it. What am I gonna do?"

Marco thought about it for a few seconds and said, "Listen, Diane, I tell you what. We'll figure it out. We can't have you out on the street now, can we? Let's do this. Why don't you take the rest of the night off." He reached in his coat pocket for his billfold, took out some bills without counting them, and gave them to her. Then he said, "This is all I've got right now. But I want you to call me first thing in the morning. We'll figure something out. Can you do that, Diane?"

"Oh, Marco, thank you," she said, still crying.

"And don't worry," he said. "We'll work it out. I'll see you first thing in the morning."

When he returned to the hall, everything seemed to be back under control. Right away three of the staff came up to him, wanting to know what was up with Diane. He let them know she was taking the rest of the night off, but that she'd be okay. Two of them went back to work, but the bartender, Jerry, stayed. As the two of them stood looking over the crowd, he spoke to Marco from the side of his mouth. "I hate to tell you this, Marco, but the governor is getting sloshed again tonight."

Marco took a deep breath and exhaled it with a sigh. "So, what else is new?" he asked.

"Wish I could cut him off," said Jerry, "but it's his party. Besides, he's not the one who comes up for the drinks. It's always one of his goons, and they, thankfully, remain stone cold sober all night. He did, however, favor me with his favorite joke again."

"What's that?" asked Marco.

"Well," answered Jerry, "Governor Bale staggers up to the bar, leans over it, and says, 'Just call me Skip.' Then he laughs at how hilarious he is, spews slobber all over the bar and me, and does his best to get back to his table under his own power."

"Skip Bail, huh. So you've heard that one before?"

"Every time, without fail."

Marco just shook his head. "I'm just glad it's not our responsibility to get him home in one piece, " he said.

"You got that right," said Jerry. "That wife of his, though, she's another matter entirely. I'd sure like to give her a run for her money."

"I'm afraid she's a little out of our league," said Marco.

"You're telling me," said Jerry. "I hear her family could buy half the state without taking out a mortgage. Financed the guy's campaign with spare change. Oh, man, speak of the devil. She's headed this way. I'd better get back behind the bar so she doesn't see the way she affects me."

Marco just shook his head as Jerry returned to the bar. But it did indeed look like the state's first lady, Heather Lee Hampton Bale, was headed straight his way. Lots of male heads turned as the tall, curvaceous blonde approached in a tight, shiny blue, low-cut gown. He hoped she was going to compliment him on the quality of his food and service, but was afraid she might instead complain about the incident of the spilled food. She was extremely hard to please.

"Good evening, Ma'am," said Marco as she approached. "I hope that everything is to your liking this evening."

Rather than engaging him in conversation, however, she just said, "You know, Mr. Russo, you really shouldn't be billing us at all for this. The mere honor of serving the governor should be more than enough payment in and of itself." Then she turned and walked off to engage people of more importance in her estimation.

Marco glanced over at Jerry who, with a big grin on his face, signaled with his head towards the governor's table. There he saw that Gov. Stephan Bale was wobbling badly after trying to stand up. One of his body guards had stepped in to support him by slipping in under his left arm, as another moved in on his right. They proceeded to lead him towards an exit, while a third went ahead to clear a pathway and open doors.

When Marco looked back at Jerry, the bartender had made himself busy wiping glasses and was trying his best to hold in his laughter.

Chapter 18
Should I? Can I?
St. Louis, Spring 1978

Marco wiped his hands as he shut the door to the walk-in refrigerator of the small store front that served as the base of operations for Bob & Marco's Catering: *Affairs to Remember*. He went across the kitchen to review - for perhaps the tenth time - the list of parties they would be working this weekend. They had a Friday graduation party, two Saturday wedding receptions, and a Sunday night Golden Anniversary. It was a big weekend, and he wanted to make sure he had the right people lined up to work each event.

So much had happened since last summer, when they made their big move. Their business had been growing slowly but steadily, which is why it made sense for them to rent this facility. It had just enough space to store all of the linens, thermal food containers, chafing dishes, dinnerware, and other innumerable supplies that would be carried by van to each location. They already had two vans, and it looked like they would have to get another one soon. The small kitchen could get extremely hot and crowded when they were cooking for two or three events at the same time, but it was doable. It sure beat the early days, when they had to do everything from their own kitchens.

Bob had been reticent to rent a storefront, but Marco's idea had turned out to be a good one. They were able to open a deli in the front, and it served a dual purpose. The deli business provided regular cash flow (already they were doing 200 to 300 dollars a day in receipts), and it also provided a location to showcase menu items to prospective catering customers. Marco also put to work one of the tricks he had learned from Clifford, by serving items left-over from catering jobs as daily specials at the deli. Due to their very large investment in getting the business started, money was very tight, of course. But things were looking hopeful.

As Marco was thinking about how much and how quickly his life had been changing, he heard a tinkling bell that indicated some-one had entered the store. He stopped to quickly wash and dry his hands, and went thru the door to the deli counter in the front of the store. A middle aged woman with very neatly coifed brown hair stood in front of the deli counter, looking at the salads, meats, cheeses, deserts, and casseroles on display in the counter.

"Good afternoon, ma'am," said Marco. "What can I do for you to-day?"

"Oh, I'm not sure," she answered without looking up. She placed a thumb and forefinger on her chin as she said, "I've never been here before. You must be new in the area."

"Yes, we are. We just opened this location a few months ago, but we've been in the catering business for close to a year, and my partner has been in the food business for a very long time."

"Hmm," she replied. "Would you be willing to let me sample some of your dishes?" she asked.

"Certainly," answered Marco. "What would you like to try?"

"How about some of that potato salad? Just a little bit, please. I only want a sample."

"Happy to let you try anything you'd like," he said. "We're pretty proud of our dishes here."

Marco put a portion on a small paper plate, and handed it to the woman, along with a plastic fork and a napkin. She tasted it slowly and carefully, as though she was trying to determine all of the spices and other ingredients that had been used to prepare it. Then she began to ask for samples of several other items, until Marco began to think that she was just trying to get a free meal under the guise of sampling dishes. He didn't really mind, but he was getting antsy to get back to work.

The woman proved him wrong, however, because eventually she ordered lasagne, spring salad, and two cannoli to go. After she had paid and received her bag of food, she asked for a menu and any information he could give her about their catering services. Marco added those items to her bag of food, and the woman left the store.

He quickly got back to his to-do list of preparing for the weekend. There was a special urgency to his work, because he would be leaving town on Friday morning. It would be his first chance to get away with Marsha since the wonderful two nights they spent at the Cheshire Inn beginning on their wedding night. He and his brother had been working non-stop since then to get their business off the ground. Finally they felt that things were going smoothly enough that they could take a little time off. Bob and his wife were just finishing up ten days in Fort Lauderdale. When they returned on Thursday, Marco would turn things over to his brother, and he and Marsha would head for Missouri's Lake of the Ozarks area.

While he was thrilled to finally have some time to get away with Marsha, Marco was somewhat apprehensive about leaving his brother in charge. Even though Bob had a lot more experience in the business, he had not been directly supervising on location for some time now, didn't know the staff as well, and avoided the kitchen like the plague. "Oh well," he thought, "It's got to happen sometime."

*   *   *

Marco and Marsha laughed as they hurried thru the front door of the Tan-Tar-A Resort in Osage Beach. The boat ride they had been enjoying was rudely interrupted by a sudden downpour. The driver had seen it coming, but they were a long way from the dock, and they had not made it back in time to beat the rain. This early in the year, the rain was cold, but fortunately they were wearing water repelling spring jackets, which kept them from getting totally soaked. They took off their touristy hats and bent over to shake off their wet hair, then removed their jackets and shook them out over the ceramic tiles of the foyer to the resort's entrance. A little rain could not dim their happy mood, however, and they continued to laugh as they shared a warm embrace before going thru the interior door to the main lobby.

Arm in arm they started across the lobby towards the elevator that would take them towards their room, when a young woman at the reception desk called out to Marco. "Oh, Mr. Russo. You are Mr. Russo, aren't you?"

"Yes, that's me," he answered, turning to walk towards her as Marsha continued to the elevator and pressed the button for the third floor.

"I have an urgent message for you, Mr. Russo," she said. "Your brother Bob called looking for you. He said that he needs to speak with you right away.   It's urgent.   He said it's an emergency."

"Thank you," said Marco cordially, or at least as cordially as he could. He was not happy to be disturbed now that he was finally having a great time off with his wife.   After indulging himself in some uncharitable thoughts about his brother — he knew Bob would screw something up without him being there — he took a deep breath, tried to smile at the receptionist, and said, "I'll call him from my room."

Not a word was spoken on the brief elevator ride, nor on the long walk down the hall to their room, nor as Marco took three tries to get his plastic key to open the door, nor as they entered the room and hung up their jackets. Then Marco erupted.

"I knew it! I knew this would happen! Bob is always spouting off about how he put this operation together, what a great idea it was, and how much money we're going to make.   But all of the hands-on stuff is up to me.   And I do mean **ALL** of it. He doesn't have a clue what it takes to run the kitchen.   Not a clue.   And handling the staff! Half of them have probably quit already. He thinks the way you supervise people is to look over their shoulders and yell at them all the time.   I've been looking forward to this time away with you for months, but I was afraid this would happen."

While he was pacing and venting (trying to hold back his volume level for the sake of neighboring rooms), Marsha slowly walked up to him, took his arm, looked up at him, and said gently, "Marco, don't you think it would be a good idea to call your brother and find out what the emergency is before you get so all upset about it?"

Marco looked down at her, took a deep breath, and leaned over to kiss her forehead. Then he smiled and said, "You think?" They both laughed as he went to the phone, got an outside line, and dialed his brother.

When Bob answered, he said, "Marco, thank God it's you. Thank God. Listen, I hate to do this to you, but you've got to get back up here right away. I need you! Things are going nuts back here."

Marco gave Marsha a disgusted look and shook his head as he answered. "Okay, Bob. What did you screw up? I was afraid this would happen."

"No, no, that's not it," said Bob. "We didn't screw anything up. That's the problem. We've got so much business we can't handle it all. The deli took in $1,000 today. Same yesterday. I had to send somebody out for more supplies twice, cause we've run out of stock. We've got six big events coming up this weekend, and I had to turn down three more. Nearly killed me to do it. I've had to call in every warm body we've ever hired, even the ones we didn't like very much. Plus, I tell them to bring their friends, their distant cousins, and their grandparents. It's crazy. You've got to get back here. I need you."

"Whoa!" said Marco. "What happened?"

"Good question. Apparently some woman came in here a while ago and get samples of all our stuff. Do you remember that? I don't."

"Yeah, I remember somebody," said Marco. "Why, what about it?"

"Well apparently that woman was Lorna Green," said Bob. "Do you know who she is?"

"No, afraid I don't," said Marco.

"Well Lorna Green happens to be the food editor of the St. Louis Post-Dispatch. So she loves your cooking, Marco. Gave us a glowing report in the Sunday supplements. Said we've got the best catering business in town. Real gourmet food, not just bland, conventional items."

"Just what we've been going for!" said Marco.

"That's right," said Bob. "Just what we've been going for. And like I've been saying all along, it's just what St. Louis needs and wants. So let's not blow our big chance. Get your butt back here, quick!"

Kansas City, Fall 1979

Long lines had formed all around the four entrances to the new Macy's Department Store in downtown Kansas City. Over each entrance hung a large banner declaring "Grand Opening." The doors would not be opened to admit the general public for another two hours, but the eager crowd was anxious to be among the first to enter the highly publicized event.

The excitement of the waiting crowd, however, was nothing compared to the pandemonium that reigned inside the store. Even though the displays were in place at all of the merchandise counters and the salespeople were mostly ready at their appointed stations, nervous supervisors and administrators were frantically running around, double checking, making small, last minute adjustments, and generally keeping everyone else on edge.

Marco felt some of the same nervous anticipation himself, but he tried to project a sense of calm and confidence to his staff. When he got up in the morning in his hotel room, he almost had to pinch himself to make sure he wasn't dreaming all this. In the past year, their business had grown from nothing to one of the biggest caterers in town. The first year they had taken in about $150,000 gross and almost starved. But now they were on a pace to break a million, and still growing rapidly. They had eighty part-timers on the payroll, mostly young college students.

Several months ago he and Bob had been contacted to do the catering for this major event. Macy's wanted to open with a big splash, and had run a huge ad campaign to hype it. There were to be food stations on all six floors of the department store. They were set up on long folding tables that had been placed near each of the escalators. The menu was to be several varieties of finger foods, along with beverages and sweets.

Marco had hired a staff of fifty people, bringing as many as he could from St. Louis, but needing to scrounge around for almost half of them in the unfamiliar territory of K.C. It made him nervous to depend on people he didn't know for such a big event, but so far everything was going smoothly. Everyone had shown up on time, wearing acceptable black pants, white shirts, and bow ties. Each station had three staff people, so that there could always be at least one person there while one or two others would be going or coming from the fourth floor kitchen with fresh sandwiches.

He saw a young woman hurrying from behind the nearest serving table towards the escalator and called out to her. "Diane. Oh, Diane."

The woman stopped and turned towards him as he came up to her. "How are things going?" he asked. "You look like you're in a big hurry, but there's plenty of time yet."

"Everything seems to be going the way you said it should, Marco," she answered. "I just want to make completely sure that we're ready. There's going to be a big rush when they open those doors."

"I appreciate that," said Marco, "but it's going to be a long day. Why don't you take a breather for a few minutes? I'm really glad you agreed to come out here for this job, Diane. It helps to have some of our regular, dependable staff here, who know how we like to do things. The people we've taken on from the KC area seem to be fine, but I like having some of you here I know I can count on."

"Oh," said Diane, "you know I'd do anything for you, Marco. I don't know what I would have done if you hadn't helped me out last winter. Besides, it's been nice to have a couple of days away from home and staying in a hotel. My mom is taking care of the kids for me. I almost feel like I'm on a vacation."

Marco laughed and said, "I guarantee you won't feel that way come six o'clock tonight. And by 8 o'clock, when we've finally finished clean-up and take-down, you may have a totally different opinion about whether you should have taken this job. That is, I **hope** we'll be finished by 8 o'clock."

"You know me," she said. "I thrive on this. Remember that day last spring we had three big parties back to back? I was really dragging by the end of it, but I loved every minute."

"Well," said Marco, "you're going to need that same attitude today, I guarantee it. So can I count on you to keep your eyes open for all of the stations on this floor? If there are any problems, I'd like you to hustle up to the fourth floor and let me know about it. I'll be somewhere around the kitchen area."

"Sure. Be glad to," she answered. "But isn't Bob going to be making the rounds and checking up on everything?"

"Yes, he is," said Marco, "but just between you and me and the lamppost, I think you will notice things that slip his attention. Let's just say that another pair of eyes is always a good thing."

"You've got it, Marco," she said.

Just then four sets of doors were simultaneously opened on all sides of the building, and hundreds of excited Macy's customers came charging in, heading like a cattle stampede towards the opening day specials that had been advertised in the newspapers, on radio and t.v., and by word of mouth.

*   *   *

It was nearly ten o'clock at night, and Marco was still supervising the loading of catering equipment into the rental trucks that would carry it all back to St. Louis, when he noticed one of his workers sitting on the curb off to the side. He had his head in his hands, elbows propped up on his knees. Marco walked over and sat down next to him. "You okay, Jimmy?" he asked.

The young man gave a deep sigh and lifted his head to look at Marco. He looked totally exhausted. "Yeah, I'm fine," he said.

"Would have fooled me," said Marco.

Jimmy made a weak effort to smile. Then he just shook his head. "I'll be okay in a few minutes. I'm just really beat, and my feet are killing me. And," he said as he looked away, "I'm also embarrassed."

"Embarrassed?" asked Marco. "You've got nothing to be embarrassed about. It's been a long day, and you worked really hard today. I noticed, and I appreciate it. I really do. Nothing to be embarrassed about."

"Thank you," he said. "But I'm embarrassed because you warned me what hard work this is, and I just blew you off. Told you I was used to working hard. And I thought I was. But I had no idea. Thought this would just be a quick way to make some good money. But this has been non-stop for over twelve hours, and on those hard marble floors. My feet ate killing me! I had no idea." Marco just patted him on the back, chuckled and said, "Join the club, Jimmy. Join the club. But you did great today. I mean it. And I'll have a lot more work for you in the future, if you're up for it. In the meantime, you just sit here as long as you need to. The rest of us will finish up."

As Marco spoke, he noticed a short, neatly dressed man standing in front of a nearby display window and watching. The man looked familiar, but Marco couldn't quite place him. But once he looked that way, the man smiled and motioned for him to come over. When Marco approached, the man put out his hand and Marco shook it.

"I'm sorry," said Marco. "You look familiar to me, but I can't quite place you. I don't really know many people here in Kansas City though."

"I'm Nathan Shapiro," the man said. "And I'm not from here. I live in St. Louis. I'm just here on business, and I stopped by Macy's tonight because I heard that you would be catering the grand opening. I don't really expect you to remember me, but we were introduced in passing at an event you catered last spring."

"What event was that?" asked Marco.

"It was a benefit for St. Louis Legal Aid. George Montrose, the president, told me you had given us a really good deal on the event, and he really wanted to talk you up, so to speak, hoping to get you more business."

"I was happy to do it," said Marco. "I believe that justice should be for everybody, not just the wealthy."

"That's what George told me," said Shapiro. "He said you're somebody who genuinely cares about people and is willing to help out."

"Well I think that's what we're all here for," said Marco.

"Yes," said Shapiro. "I agree. And after watching you working here tonight — and by the way, I thought the food was exceptional, especially for this kind of an event . . ."

"Glad you liked it," interrupted Marco.

"I did," he said. "And I was also impressed by how well everything was organized, how efficiently, how smoothly everything ran. And it could not have been easy to do, especially in another city."

"Well, it did have its challenges. But I have a really great staff, and we worked with a local caterer here who was a big help."

"Yes. I could see that. But anyway, observing all of this got me to thinking. Have you ever thought of getting involved in politics?"

"Politics?" said Marco. "No, not really. I mean, I actually don't have a very favorable opinion of most of the politicians I've run into."

Shapiro laughed. "Yes, I agree with you about that. But that's exactly why the rest of us need to get involved. I don't want to interfere any more in your work here, but would you be willing to meet with me sometime back in St. Louis to talk about it? I think that you're a man who could do a lot of good in our city."

"Well, I don't know about that," said Marco. "But sure, I'd be willing to talk with you about it."

*   *   *

Two weeks later Marco sat with Shapiro at a table in the company restaurant. It was in between the lunch and supper crowds, so there was no one else there, but a waiter kept them supplied with water and coffee to wash down their cannoli.

"What exactly did you mean about getting involved in politics?" asked Marco.

"Just that. Getting involved. I'm a lawyer, not a politician. Here's my card."

Marco read from the business card, "O'Neal, Shapiro, and Norton, Attor-neys at Law. What kind of law exactly?"

"Just about anything, actually," he answered. "My specialty is corporate. O'Neal's is criminal. Norton does personal injury. But we have several others on staff who can handle family law, inheritance, taxes, you name it. And one of the things we all agree on is the need for civic involvement. So everyone does a certain number of *pro bono* cases, and the firm is a major supporter of Legal Aid."

"Sounds pretty impressive," said Marco. "But why did you specifically ask about politics?"

"Because I think that our local Democratic Party has been very weak lately. It's been lacking in energy and focus. It needs new leadership. I've been a member for years, but not really personally involved. I'm thinking of getting more active myself, and I'm looking for people who might share some of the same interests and concerns. So have you ever been interested in politics, Mr. Russo?"

"Please, call me Marco," he said. "Actually I have very mixed feelings about politics. I have had an interest since I was young. When I was nine or ten years old I watched both national party conventions, gavel to gavel, on tv. It was 1964. Walter Cronkite was the announcer, and he was very impressive. I was fascinated by the looks and demeanor of the speakers. And I had a lot of fun mimicking the southern accents. I think I got pretty good at it. Made people laugh. Then when I was about 15, my uncle ran for alderman, and I helped him put up signs in the community and a few other things. That was interesting, and even kind of exciting at times."

"So why the mixed feelings?" asked Shapiro.

"Well," said Marco, "the idea of it is a lot more . . . what's the word I'm looking for? . . . worthwhile? . . . meaningful?"

"I'm not sure that I know what you mean," said Shapiro.

Marco squirmed in his chair as he struggled to articulate his feelings. "Well, I really liked being involved in my uncle's campaign. It was exciting. A lot of it was fun. But at the end of the day, the only reason he ran was to be a spoiler and keep somebody else from winning. And the only real issue between the two other candidates was that one was Irish and the other was Italian. Maybe I'm just naive, but I always thought that the reason people ran for office was to do some good for the community. That was just a squabble between two ethnic groups that in my opinion ought to be working together on all the problems we've got in this city."

"You're absolutely right about that," said Shapiro. "That's exactly why we need good people to get involved who really care about our city."

"And since I've gotten in this business," continued Marco, "I've met a lot of politicians — the governor, state legislators, alder-men, committeemen — and frankly, they're mostly a bunch of jerks. They think they're somebody special because they got elected, and it's like you should bow down before them or some-thing. We did this big banquet for the governor, and he got shit-faced drunk. Apparently that's his normal status. Then his wife even had the nerve to tell me that we should have done his big shindig for nothing, just because it's such an honor to be able to serve his majesty. As if I didn't have expenses to pay and my employees didn't have bills to pay at home."

By this time Shapiro was in stitches, and was rocking back and forth, and hitting his hand on the table. "Oh, that's priceless, Marco. Really priceless. I agree with you one hundred percent. But you see," he said, as he leaned forward over the table, "that's exactly why we need people like you to get involved. If we don't, that's the kind of people who continue to run things, and all the rest of us suffer for it. That's why I've decided to get more in-volved myself, and why I'm looking for people like you to join me. I like to think that we Democrats are a little bit better than that, but sometimes you can't tell the difference. For instance, our ward committeeman — do you know him, by the way? Bob Mulvihill?"

"No, I'm afraid I don't."

"Well, Mulvihill started out okay, but he's been in the job for twenty years or so, and now he just goes thru the motions. We need somebody who still cares and knows how to get things done. Bring some life into the party."

"I'm not sure that I'd know how to do that, Mr. Shapiro."

"Nate, Marco. Call me Nate. And you know exactly what you need to do. You know how to organize people. I've seen you do it at several of your big catering functions. And that Macy's event in Kansas City! That was superb, the way you pulled that off so smoothly, and with such class. And I was watching how you interacted with your workers. They love you, do you realize that Marco?"

Marco looked off to the side, embarrassed. "Well, I don't know about that," he said.

"They do. They do," said Shapiro. "They have great respect for you. It was obvious by the way they responded to you, how they paid attention to everything you said, and immediately got to it. They were a team, everybody working together, everybody proud of what they were doing, everybody very attentive to the guests and making sure things were just right. It was very clear to me that you know how to organize people, Marco. You know how to bring people together to make good things happen. And that's just what we need in our local politics right now. And you won't be alone. There are several of us who are thinking along the same lines, and I'd like you to work with us."

"Well, I don't know," said Marco. "I like the idea, but the business is still new, and it takes up so much of my time. My wife is already complaining that she hardly ever sees me anymore."

"I'm not asking you to take on a second job, Marco," said Shapiro. "Just to be a part of things. You could just go to a meeting or two and check us out. Take it from there."

"Well," said Marco. "I'll think about it."

*   *   *

The following week a group of staff from the nearby office of the Textile Workers Union were among a crowd of people who came in the deli to get lunches to go. Since they were regulars, Marco joked with them by name, as he and two employees hurriedly filled orders. The last in line of the group was someone he didn't recognize. After ordering a hot Italian beef sandwich *au jus* with two pepperoncini, he introduced himself as Arthur Denton. The man ahead of him turned back and said, "Yeah, Marco. He's our mouthpiece. You ever need somebody to bail you out of jail, he's the man."

"I'll bet you give him a lot of business then, Paddy," joked Marco.

"I believe in keeping our legal eagles too busy to cause any more mischief than they already do," he replied.

Denton just shook his head and said, "Paddy, sometimes I think you'd be better off just getting a lease on one of the cells over at the local precinct. You'd probably come out ahead on the deal." Then he looked at Marco and said, "Nathan Shapiro mentioned you the other day. Said I should get to know you. Do you have a few minutes to talk?"

"If you don't mind waiting a bit," answered Marco. "The rush will slow down in about ten minutes."

"That'd be fine by me. I'll just find a spot to eat my sandwich here and wait till you've got a few."

Twenty minutes later, Marco finally hung up his apron and joined Denton, who was sitting in a high-backed chair and looking out at the traffic going by outside. Stepping up into the adjacent chair, Marco looked at the empty plate and glass sitting in front of the union lawyer, and turned to call back for a couple of fresh lemonades.

"That was a mighty fine sandwich," said Denton. "I can see why the workers like to come here."

"Why thank you," said Marco. "We do our best. So I guess Nate actually followed up on his threat."

"His threat?" Denton replied, surprised. Realizing that Marco was joking, he just laughed and introduced himself. Then he made his pitch.

"You know, next year's election will be very important for our party and for the country. Unfortunately President Carter has lost the confidence of many people in this country for a number of reasons. But we can't afford to let the Republicans win with their right wing agenda. We need a government that values working people, and wants them treated fairly. So it's important that we nominate a really strong candidate and work hard to bring out as many voters as possible, because when we get our voters to the polls, we win."

"Sounds like you have a different candidate in mind," said Marco. "Who would that be?"

"Most of the unions are going to push for Ted Kennedy," he said. "He's always been a strong advocate for working people. He's got great name recognition all over the country. And a lot of people are still upset that his brother's chance in the White House got cut off short. They think that putting Ted in office will help make up for that, and maybe bring back the good times before the divisions over Vietnam."

Marco thought about it for a bit, then asked, "What exactly would you have in mind for me to do?"

"Do what you're so good at. Talk to the people in your ward. Get them to come out for the caucus in the spring, where we'll elect delegates to the state convention. Once people have actually come out and participated, they usually get more invested in the election. They're more aware of the issues, they're more committed to a candidate, they're more likely to make a contribution and to work in the campaign, they're more likely to talk to their friends about it, and especially they're very likely to actually make it to the polls themselves on election day. So Shapiro says he already told you about our issues with the committeeman in your ward. He's loyal, but he's just been coasting for several years now. That won't be good enough this year. We need somebody who will get out to the voters and get them fired up to vote in the fall. We think you're our man in that ward. You know lots of people, you've got good rapport with the unions, and you know how to work with people."

"I've never been to a caucus," said Marco. "How does that work?"

"It's pure democracy in action," answered Denton. "Every registered Democrat in the ward is invited to attend. They gather in groups around each candidate for office. Each group has somebody who speaks for their candidate, and why that person would be good in office, what their issues are. Then people talk about it, ask questions, debate. They have an opportunity to move around to other groups and hear what other candidates are saying. Then eventually somebody calls for a vote, and people vote with their feet. Your vote goes to the candidate you're standing with at that time. Then the votes from all the caucuses are tallied, and the person with the most votes becomes the official candidate of the Democratic Party of Missouri for that particular office."

"Sounds interesting," said Marco.

"It is," answered Denton. Then he smiled and said, "Some of us even think it's a lot of fun."

Marco laughed and said, "I'll bet it is. I'll think about it."

* * *

Spring, 1980

Marco sat at his desk in the tiny office off of the kitchen behind the deli. He had a telephone cradled between his shoulder and his left ear, as he looked at a piece of paper sitting on the desk before him. "That's right, Mr Phillips," he said. "The caucus will meet at the public library over on Vandeventer . . . That's right, anybody is welcome to come. Bring your wife. Bring your friends . . . No, there's no obligation to vote for the person that the caucus decides on. But this is your chance to tell the party who **you** think we ought to nominate."

As Marco spoke, his brother Bob came into the office, got a disgusted look on his face, and deliberately slammed the door behind himself. Then he sat in the chair at his own desk, but turned it to face Marco, and stared at him expectantly.

Marco looked up briefly at his brother, but continued with his phone conversation. "No, I'm just a citizen like you are. I'm not getting paid. I'm just doing this because I care about our country, Mr. Phillips, and I think that it's our duty to be involved . . . Yes, I did serve in the armed forces . . . Air Force . . . I got your name from the Democratic party. You're a registered Democrat, and we need to make sure that we nominate the best person for president, and that we get all of our people out to vote."

At this point, Bob picked up a large ledger from his desk and dramatically dropped it on the floor in front of Marco, while giving him a very pointed stare. Marco glared right back at him as he finished his conversation.

"Thank you for your time, Mr. Phillips. I hope to see you at the caucus. And feel free to call me if you have any more questions."

As soon as Marco hung up the phone, his brother verbally jumped all over him. "Jesus Christ, Marco. You spend more and more time on that crap every day. We're supposed to be working here. We've got a business to run here, in case you've forgotten. We're up to our necks with catering orders, the restaurant is short of staff, and we're got six events to plan for this weekend, and here you are, talking bullshit to who-knows-who over the phone. We've got a business to run. What the hell are you doing here?"

"I'm very well aware of how much work we have to do," said Marco, "because I do three quarters of it myself. Whenever we're short of staff, or low on supplies, or there's any kind of crisis whatsoever, **I'm** the one who has to deal with it. You're always too busy at your desk working on the books. Or making plans for that McMansion you're building out in Ladue. So apparently we're not doing so badly with business, are we? Actually I'd like to know how you're able to afford that monstrosity anyhow. We're doing well here, but not **that** well."

"Well let me tell **you** something. All your work for the asshole Democrats is sure not going to help matters any," yelled Bob. "Some of our best paying gigs come from the Republicans, and they're starting to notice what you're doing, for your information."

338

"We get plenty of work from the Democrats," said Marco.

"Yeah," said Bob, "and you always give them a big discount."

"Look," said Marco, "All of the political jobs are ones that I bring in. Both parties. And I'm the one who makes them work. And for your information, we make plenty of profit from the Dems, even with a discount."

"We could make a lot more," said Bob.

"Well, I tell you what," said Marco, "How about you start bringing some of them in yourself. Then you can charge whatever you think you can make them pay, and you'll make more money to go for your McMansion."

After Bob got up and stormed out of the office, Marco picked up his phone again, found his place on the printout of Democratic voters, and dialed the next number.

*   *   *

The small conference room at the library was full, and people were still coming in. Ward Committeeman Mulvihill greeted them as they signed in at a table in the hallway just outside the door. Marco, Nathan Shapiro, and Arthur Denton stood in the center of the room, where a Teddy Kennedy sign was taped to the wall. Three other people stood with them. A sign at the far end said

"Uncommitted." Eight people or so stood there, while the largest group by far stood nearest the entry door by a sign that said "President Carter." A few people wandered from one group to another, listening to what people were saying.

"Looks like more people than four years ago," said Shapiro.

"A few, maybe," answered Denton. "But the Carter folks are way ahead. We may not have enough to get any Kennedy delegates to state."

A state representative was speaking to the Carter group, mostly answering questions about the oil shortages and the Iranian hostage crisis. He assured them that President Carter fully understood and shared their concerns, that he was working hard on both issues, and that a Democratic administration had the best hope of solving them without going to war.

In the meantime, Shapiro had wandered over to the uncommitted corner, where no one seemed to be taking the lead. The people there were mostly complaining about the same issues, but without having any clear solutions in mind. They were unhappy with Carter, but not sure that there was a realistic alternative.

Shapiro returned to the Kennedy group with a suggestion. "Listen, I think we should all join the uncommitted group. They're looking for change, but don't see how to do it."

"I thought we wanted to be Kennedy delegates," said Marco.

"We do," said Shapiro. "But the way things are going, we don't have enough people to get any delegates. But if we make it to the convention as uncommitted, we can still vote for Kennedy once we get there."

The Kennedy group then moved together to the uncommitted area, and began introducing themselves to the people there. Marco was surprised to find that three of them were there because of his phone calls. They thanked him for calling, because they had not been aware of how the process worked. They were glad they had come.

Soon afterward, Committeeman Mulvihill called the group to order and announced that everyone had five minutes to make a final decision and stand with the group that indicated their presidential preference. The count turned out to be 34 for Carter, 17 uncommitted. He explained that their ward was entitled to send three delegates to the statewide nominating convention. According to the voting results, the Carter group would be allowed to choose two delegates; the uncommitted group one.

When the uncommitted group began their discussion, Arthur Denton assumed leadership, but stated that he did not wish to be a delegate himself. He would be busy lobbying all of the delegates on behalf of the Textile Workers Union. Someone immediately nominated Shapiro. Then came some big surprises. First of all, one of the original uncommitted delegates nominated Marco. Then, after a few minutes discussion, Shapiro turned to Marco and said, "Listen. Why don't you go? I don't really have time for it anyway, and you'll make a good delegate. I'll run for alderman instead." The whole group seemed happy with that solution, and that was what was reported to the whole group.

After all three groups had reported, Committeeman Mulvihill adjourned the caucus. As Marco was leaving the room, still in shock over what had happened, the committeeman stopped him at the door.

"I'm glad you came tonight," said Mulvihill, extending his hand to Marco, who shook it. "I've been wondering who this Marco Russo was, who is running against me for committeeman. I want you to know that I'm not angry with you for opposing me. I haven't had any opposition in years, and that's not a good thing for the party. Or for me, for that matter. It says that people are getting apathetic. Not good. But from what I hear, you've been working the ward pretty hard, and are getting people more interested in the election. That's a good thing for all of us Democrats. So I hope that whoever wins the election, we'll be able to work together for the good of our party."

"Thanks a lot," replied Marco. "I appreciate that. And I've always been somebody who believes in working together for the good of everybody."

*　　*　　*

The Hearnes Center in Columbia, Missouri was the largest auditorium at the University of Missouri. When the Missou Tigers basketball team is having a good season, more than 13,000 cram their way into the arena. As Marco parked his car in the huge lot outside the arena, he wondered for the umpteenth time why this venue was chosen for the Democratic Party convention. With just one thousand delegates — even though there would probably be five times as many family members, press, and other observers milling around — he suspected they would feel dwarfed by the huge space. He hoped that didn't bode ill for the difficult election that lay ahead of them. Oh, well. No one had asked his opinion.

Getting out of his car, he headed towards a huge banner that read,

"MISSOURI DEMOCRATIC PARTY."

As he got closer to a line waiting to enter the arena, he was surprised to see a woman waving to him as she approached from the other side. She looked vaguely familiar, but he couldn't quite place her.

"Hello," the woman said, as she put out her hand. "I'm sorry that I don't remember your name, but we met at Danny's wedding. My name is Nancy Price, and I don't know anybody else here, so I was glad to at least see a familiar face. I've never been to one of these before. Have you?"

"No," answered Marco. "It's all new to me too. My name is Marco, by the way."

"That's right," she said. "Now I remember. I was very impressed with what you told us about your military experience."

As they joined a line entering the building, Nancy suggested that if they sat together, they could help each other figure things out. Marco agreed that was a good idea. After entering the building, they noted that several tables were set up across a wide foyer, and people were directed to tables according to their last names. Nancy headed towards O,P,Q; Marco towards R,S. They each showed their credentials and received a badge and a packet of information. Then they met up again on the other side of the registration tables and helped each other with their badges.

As he was helping Nancy pin her badge on her lapel, Marco noted that she had put a button on her other lapel. He stepped back to look at it. "My Body/My Choice," he read. "Is there something coming up about abortion here?"

"You bet. An initiative on the right to choose. Are you behind it, Marco?"

"Yes, definitely. But you didn't have that button on before."

"No, I just picked it up at that booth over there," she said, pointing to a long row of tables off to the side. The two of them headed in that direction towards vendors who were giving out buttons for all of the candidates, trade unions, interest groups, and a wide variety of issues that various groups were promoting. Most of the people walking by who took one or more of the buttons, but then never put them on. They simply threw them into the first trash container they passed. Marco decided not to take any of them.

As they followed another line, this one going up a set of stairs, Marco said, "Apparently we're supposed to sit in the section designated for our candidate. So I'll be looking for the uncommitted delegate area. How about you?"

Nancy turned to him with a shocked look on her face. "You mean you're not supporting President Carter?" she asked.

"Well, I'll vote for him if he's the one we nominate, but I really would prefer Teddy Kennedy."

"Oh, Marco," she said. "I'm so disappointed to hear that. I just love President Carter. I think it's terrible how he's getting blamed for things that are not his fault. That oil embargo. And those Iranians taking over our embassy. He couldn't do anything about those things. But look how he got Egypt and Israel to sign a peace treaty. Do you realize how historic that was? It's the first time any of the Arab countries has ever recognized Israel's right to exist. It's the first step towards peace in that part of the world we've ever seen! Nobody else could have made that happen. Nobody but Carter. And I think that he's the most sincere Christian president we've ever had. Besides, we Democrats have to stick together and support him. He's our president."

"All that may be true," he answered. "but I'm afraid most Americans vote with their pocketbooks. Inflation is out of hand, the economy is stagnant, and he doesn't seem to know what to do about it any more than he's been able to get our hostages home. Besides, I'm mostly here as a pro union voter, and the unions are solidly behind Kennedy."

They emerged on a catwalk overlooking the seating area above what was usually a basketball court, and stopped to look around. Marco noted that a large stage had been constructed at one end of the basketball court. The delegates were to be seated on folding chairs that had been set up on the gym floor, facing the improvised stage. Large signs indicated sections of seats that were designated either for Carter or uncommitted delegates.

Nancy turned to him and said, "Well, I guess this is where we part company. But I hope we get a chance to talk some more. I'm not

346

giving up on you yet." Then she started down the stairs towards the Carter delegates' area.

Before heading down to a seat, Marco took a moment to scan the crowd for familiar faces. He recognized James Conway, the current mayor of St. Louis, wandering around the delegation and glad-handing everyone he could. He noted Congressman Dick Gephardt standing on the stage, talking to several others. He thought he recognized former St. Louis Mayor Cervantes finding a seat. Finally he saw a sign for uncommitted delegates off to the far right, and he headed in that direction.

Gephart's speech was the major one of the convention. He was considered a strong union backer — his father was a Teamster — but he came out very forcefully for Carter. Gephardt was noticeably unhappy about the tepid response he received for praising Carter. And when some people in the uncommitted sections of delegates even booed a few of his comments, he gave them an angry glare.

When the vote was tallied, it was determined that Missouri would send 61 Carter delegates to the national convention. The 20 uncommitted delegates selected were clearly for Senator Kennedy. The lack of unanimous support in his own party for a sitting U.S. president did not bode well for Carter's chances in the fall.

Marco looked for Nancy on his way out of the stadium, but didn't see her. A sea of people carried him along, as the delegates poured out to their cars to begin their journeys home to all corners of Missouri.

*   *   *

"So, what did you think of the state convention?" asked Shapiro.

"It was interesting," answered Marco. The two men were seated at a table in the corner of his restaurant. He was about to elaborate when he noticed Arthur Denton coming thru the door, so he stopped to wave Denton over to their table.

As Denton sat down, Shapiro said, "So Art, I just asked Marco for his impression of the convention. What do you think he said?"

Without missing a beat, Denton replied, "He said that it was the most significant and inspiring event of his entire life."

All three had a good laugh. Then Shapiro said, "Don't we wish. Don't we wish. No, he said that it was — get this — interesting. Interesting. Do you think he's already becoming a politician?"

After another laugh, Denton replied, "Oh God, I hope not. I truly hope not. If he does, all our work is in vain. But seriously Marco, we really would like to hear your impressions of it. Without us steering it in any way. Was it helpful? Did you learn anything? Did you make any good connections?"

"Actually I have some mixed feelings about it," said Marco. "There were some good things. For one thing, It gave me a better feel for the many different parts of the state, and the different perspectives those delegates have about things. I talked to a farmer from the Bootheel who was outraged over gas prices. Another one from the north central part of the state doesn't think we're doing nearly enough to support exports. So that part was good. The speeches were . . ." (Here Marco waved a hand back and forth and assumed a facial expression that indicated he was less than im-pressed.)

"But I had no idea of all the business we had to take care of, " he continued. "Elections, budgets, committee reports, focus groups. They were herding us around like cattle all day. No wonder you were so willing to have me be the delegate instead of you, Nate."

After chuckling and shaking his head, Shapiro replied, "No, no, Marco. You've got me all wrong. I would have been happy to go, but I'm going to the national, remember? It's only fair that you got to go to state. Besides, Art and I have big things in mind for you, and you needed to know firsthand how the whole process works. Not to change the subject, but we're both very anxious to hear about how your 'Russo for Committeeman' campaign is going. I'm sorry that I haven't been much help to you so far. Too busy with my own campaign. But we're going to have to start coordi-nating very closely from here on out. Has your team come to-gether as well as you hoped?"

"Now that's something I'm feeling a lot more positive about," said Marco. "We had our first meeting about a month ago, and I think it went pretty well."

Chapter 19
Campaigning

"Thanks for coming, everybody," said Marco, smiling at the small group that was sitting in chairs around his living room. "I really appreciate it, more than you know. More than you know. I think this is a critical time in our country, and our Democratic Party . . ."

"Just a minute, please, Marco," interrupted Marsha. "I'm sorry to interrupt, but I want to make sure that everybody has something to drink before we get started. We have beer, lemonade, iced tea, coffee, juice, water. Does anybody need anything? Anybody need a refill?"

After Marsha took care of a refill and two new orders, Marco resumed speaking. "As I was saying, this will be a very important election year, and our party is going to have to be very strong to keep our country moving forward. As you know, I'm very passionate about making our country and our government work for everybody, not just the wealthy and the well-connected. But there are powerful forces working hard to turn back all of the progress we've been making under Democratic leadership. So it's very important that our party not only stays strong, but gets even stronger.

"And that strength always begins at the local level. The state and national parties can only be as strong as their local branches let them be. But unfortunately, here in St. Louis, Ward 16, we have a ward committeeman who has been in charge for over twenty years, and has just been coasting on his laurels. He's not engaging younger voters. He's not raising up new leadership. He's not getting out to hear what the people are saying, beyond what he gets from a few old cronies. And I'm afraid that also means that he won't do a good job of getting out the vote this fall. That's why I have decided to run for the position. I feel that I have the passion and the commitment to do all the things that my opponent has been neglecting."

After receiving some emphatic nods, some positive affirmations, and even a bit of applause from the small group, Marco continued. "But it won't be easy unseating somebody who is so well known in the ward. That is why I need all of your help to get out the word of my candidacy. So once again, thank you for being here tonight, so we can start making plans to run a very strong campaign. We'll look for ways that everyone can help. And to that end, I'll turn our meeting over to my cousin, Frances, who has agreed to be my campaign manager. Frances . . ."

As people looked at her and followed Marco's lead by clapping, the young woman raised both her hands and shook her head in disclaimer. "Please, Marco," she said. "Please don't call me that. I can't be your long-distance campaign manager from Chicago. I told you that I'll do everything I can to help, starting with this meeting tonight. I'll get down here as much as I can, and I can give you some long weekends in the summer, but I see myself as more of a consultant than a campaign manager. I'm afraid that's all I can do."

"Well," said Marco, "that's a whole lot, and I'm grateful for it. We can talk about titles later. In the meantime, why don't you get us started?"

"I'd be happy to. Since some of us have never met before tonight, I think it would be a good idea if we introduce ourselves once again, and say just a little bit about why we're here tonight. So to be fair, I'll go first."

Looking first at Marco, then at the others she continued. "Some of the reason I'm here is personal. As you all know by now, I am Marco's cousin — I like to say, his favorite cousin — and we have been close friends as well as relatives for most of my life."

Looking then at Marco, she continued. "Over the years, Marco, I have continued to grow in my respect and appreciation for you as a person. You are honest, dependable, and — unlike most of the politicians I have met, I'm sorry to say — you genuinely care about other people. You must have the biggest heart of anybody I know. Do you remember when we were at Grandma Rose's funeral last year, Marco? And all those people stepped up and told stories of how many times she had helped them out when they were in a tough spot? Do you remember, Marco?"

"Yeah, I remember," he replied.

"And do you remember how emotional some of them got when they told their stories? Some of them got so choked up they could barely talk about it. Do you remember?"

Marco nodded. "I remember," he said.

"Well I remember looking at you when those people were telling their stories," Frances continued, "and I could tell that their stories affected you deeply. You were almost in tears yourself when you heard their hard luck stories."

Marco looked to the side as she spoke and said, "Now you're embarrassing me."

"No, Marco, I'm not embarrassing you, I'm bringing out into the open the reason that people love you so much. That's right, Marco. We do, whether that embarrasses you or not." Marco squirmed and blushed as the others laughed and affirmed what Frances was saying.

"This is what we need in public life today," she went on. "We need to put people in office who are not in it for themselves, but because they care about their neighbors, especially the ones who need some help. And that's exactly who Marco is. That's what's so great about him."

Heads nodded as she spoke. Then she went on.

"But there's something else that's needed to be successful when you're running for public office. You need to be strong, and tough, and hard working, and tenacious all at the same time. Because it's hard to get elected. And if you do get elected, it's hard to make meaningful change. You see a way to do something that will be a great benefit to your constituents, and it looks like a no-brainer to you. But as soon as you try to implement it — surprise, surprise. All of a sudden this wall of resistance rises up in front of you, often from people you would never have suspected would be opposed. And even if a big majority of your constituents are in favor of whatever it is, most of them won't actually **do** something to make it happen, other than maybe put a check mark on a questionnaire, while the people who are opposed will work overtime and spend some of their own money — and lots of money that comes from who-knows-where — to make you fail. So you've got to be tough as well.

"Surprisingly enough, our tender-hearted Marco is also one super tough dude. Who here ever saw Marco play football?" Only two hands raised. "Well let me tell you, you missed something. The way he mowed down opposing linemen was truly awesome. And look at how well he's done in business. The catering business is really cut-throat, and Marco has built his business from scratch in a phenomenally short time. So is Marco tough? Strong? Persistent? Savvy? You bet. He's just the kind of person we need in public office, so I'm going to do whatever I can to help. So that's why I'm here tonight. How about you? What brings you here?"

A woman in her late 20's spoke up first. "Hi, everybody, I'm Diane," she said. "First off, I want to agree with Frances that Marco genuinely cares for other people. I've been working for him for two years now, and I've seen first hand how true that is. His company has really grown, but he knows every one of us, and he treats every one of us almost as if we were family. I've been trying to raise my two kids on my own, and sometimes it gets real hard . . ." (As Diane started to tear up, a comforting arm came up over her shoulder.). "Anyway, I don't know how I would have made it without you, Marco, and I want to help you any way I can. I don't know what I can do, but I'll sure try."

"Thanks, Diane," said Frances. "And don't you worry. There will be plenty of things you can do to help. You can count on it. Who's next?"

"I'm Danny, and Marco's been my best bud for as long as I can remember. He's a guy you want to have on your side if you ever get into a barroom brawl, believe me." This statement got a lot of laughs, but Marco just rolled his eyes and shook his head. "I don't usually pay much attention to politics, but if Marco is crazy enough to get into it, I guess I'm crazy enough to go along for the ride. I can certainly vouch for what a stand-up guy he has always been. And you can always count on him to do what is right. That's enough for me."

Two union men spoke up next. As they were speaking, Marsha reentered the room carrying a tray of cookies, which she passed around to the group. Then she added her own comments. "There's no way I'm going to do any knocking on doors or calling up strangers on the phone," she said. "But I've told Marco that I'd be willing to be the campaign treasurer, and to file the reports with the Election Commissioners. Those are jobs that are more up my alley."

"And they are very essential," said Frances. "So thank you, Marsha. And my thanks to all of you. By being involved personally in an election at the grass roots level, you are helping to make the process work the way it is supposed to work. This is where it all starts — at the local level, with citizens coming together to make our country work for everybody. So lets give ourselves a hand here."

After some self-conscious clapping, Frances continued. "What I have in mind for the rest of the evening is to first familiarize ourselves with the voter information that we have from the Democratic Party and how it can be used effectively. Then we can make some plans for phone calling and door-to-door canvassing.

Marco knocked three times on the front door of a modest home in south St. Louis. Then he stepped back two steps that led to the small landing in front of the door, letting the storm door slowly close behind him. After a short moment, the door opened cautiously. Seeing that Marco had retreated a safe distance from her door, a middle-aged woman wearing a green house coat re-opened the storm door enough to poke her head out. "Can I help you?" she asked.

Marco stood with one foot on the stoop, the other one step down. He smiled and said, "Good morning, Maam. My name is Marco Russo, and I am a candidate for Committeeman of the 16th Ward Democratic Party. I am going around introducing myself to the voters, and encouraging everyone to remember to vote on April 4. May I give you one of my flyers?" he asked, as he took one step onto the stoop and reached out his hand in her direction.

The woman watched as he stopped, still well back from the door, then reached out her hand around the storm door to take the flyer. The top line read, "Beat the Machine! Vote Russo!"

As she began to read, Marco asked, "You are a Democrat, is that correct?"

"Yes," she answered. "But how did you know that?"

"The Democratic Party makes the information available to all legitimate candidates. We think it's very important to get all of our voters to the polls, so that we can have our best possible candidates on the ballot next fall. What do you think are the biggest issues we have here in our 16th Ward?"

The woman sighed, as she continued to read the flyer. Then she said, "Oh, I don't know. I'm really more concerned about what's happening in Washington," she said. "That Reagan guy really scares me."

"You and a lot of other people," said Marco. "But that makes our local efforts all the more important. We have to make sure that we get all of our Democratic voters out to the polls, and that's part of the job of the ward committeeman. I don't think our current committeeman has worked hard enough to register new voters and to get our people out to the polls. But we're going to need every vote we can get this fall. So I promise you I will work harder than anyone else to make that happen. Can I count on your vote on April 4, maam?"

The woman looked up at him, smiled, and said, "I'll think about it. Thank you for coming by." Then she quickly closed her door.

Marco stepped down from the stoop and back to the sidewalk, where he stopped to make marks on a list of voters that was fastened to a clipboard. He checked the box that indicated the woman was a 'maybe.' Then he moved down the list to the next name, and looked up to see that the house was three houses further along the street. He had to make a quick move to keep from dropping his stack of flyers, as he began walking to the next address. Since no one answered at that door, he stuck one of his flyers into some grating on the storm door, marked 'not at home' on his list, and moved on to the next house.

Another middle-aged woman answered, wearing a light jacket and carrying keys in her hands. She smiled and listened politely as Marco began his pitch, but he could see that she was anxious to be going. As he got into his talk, the woman got a concerned look on her face and interrupted.

"You mean you're running against Mr. Mulvihill?" she asked.

"Yes," he answered.

"Oh no," she said, shaking her head. "I'm afraid we just couldn't do that, Mr . . . Mr. Russo, did you say? I always admire people who are willing to give of their time to run for office, but the Mulvihills are such wonderful, faithful members of our parish, St. Philomena. They have dedicated themselves to this community for so long, I'm afraid that we could never vote against them. But I thank you," she continued, while turning to lock her front door, "for taking the time to visit. Now if you'll excuse me, I have to be going."

Marco followed the woman down the steps, and said, "Thank you for your time, maam," as she stepped into the street, got into her car, and drove off.

After several more not-at-homes', Marco spoke to a man named Nunzio. "You've got my vote," he said. "I always will vote for an Italian."

A union man in his fifties asked how he could be sure Marco backed his issues. "I have the endorsement of the Progressive Democrats," Marco said. "Also, Together for Community Progess supports me."

"TCP supports you? asked the man. "Then you've got my support too."

A woman in her sixties didn't take that endorsement as well, however. "I'm afraid you may be a little too liberal for my taste, young man," she said.

It was well past what should have been lunch time, when Marco rang the doorbell of a small, but neat looking home. Since this house was lower to the ground than others in the area, the walkway went directly to the door, without steps or a stoop. Still, he stepped back from the door, to make sure he would not look intimidating to whoever answered.

A woman who might have been in her late thirties opened the door, which had no storm door in front of it. Her reddish-brown hair looked damp, and she was holding a towel in front of herself. She might have just emerged from a shower, and Marco noted that her legs and feet were bare below the towel. He tried not to sound nervous as he introduced himself and reached out to hand the woman a flyer. She did some adjusting so that she could hold the towel steady with one hand, while she reached out with the other to take the flyer. As she took it, she gave Marco a big smile, pushed the door further open with her foot, and said, "Come on in, so we can talk about it."

He replied hastily, "Oh no, that won't be necessary. I just want to introduce myself to all the voters, and make sure you remember to vote in November."

The woman gave him a mischievous smile and asked, "You're not afraid of me, are you?"

"Oh no, maam," he quickly answered. "It's just that I have a lot more homes to get to yet today. But thank you for your time. I'm sorry if I interrupted anything."

Then he turned and walked back down the street, noting from his peripheral vision without turning to look, that the woman watched him for a moment before closing the door behind her. He was surprised to note that his hands were shaking, and he had to make a conscious effort to keep from dropping his flyers. He decided that he had done enough canvassing for the day.

*   *   *

Marco stood on the stage of a large auditorium. It was full of people, who were all standing and cheering for him. Or were they jeering? He wasn't quite sure which, and that made him very uncomfortable. He looked out at the crowd to try to determine which it was, but that didn't seem to help. Sometimes it looked like they were cheering, but as soon as he smiled in return, the cheers seemed to turn into jeers. He saw a podium with a microphone in the front and center of the stage, and knew that he was expected to go there and speak to the crowd, but somehow he couldn't seem to move. After what seemed to be a long time, he finally began to walk towards the podium, but each step was astoundingly difficult. He had to concentrate on moving one foot at a time, and each step took all the strength he had. What was going to happen? Why couldn't he move? He had to make it to the podium. He had to speak to the people. But what was wrong wlth hls legs?

"Marco! Marco! Wake up," said Marsha as she shook him.

He suddenly jerked awake, momentarily disoriented.

Marsha, who was sitting up in bed next to him, put a hand on his shoulder and asked, "Are you all right, Marco? You must have been having a nightmare."

Marco shook his head, opened and shut his eyes, and looked around the bedroom, slowly coming back to the land of the living.

"Whoo," he said, and shook his head to help clear it. Then he propped up his pillow against the wall, pushed himself up into a sitting position, and rubbed his eyes open. "Sorry if I woke you up," he said. "Was I making a lot of noise?"

"Mostly groaning," she said, laughing. "You sounded like you were trying to push a semi-trailer or something. And your legs were moving. You kneed me in the back."

"Oh, gee," he said. "I'm so sorry. It was a really weird dream. I was trying to walk, but just couldn't move. It was like trying to walk thru mud up to my waist. It was crazy. I don't know what that was all about."

"Oh, really? Well, I know what it's all about. I can't wait until this stupid campaign is over. It's driving you nuts. Which means, it's driving me nuts too."

"Well, it won't be much longer now."

"Praise the Lord!" she laughed, holding her hands up in the air. "Now please, let's go back to sleep," she said, as she poked him playfully in the chest. "Mr. big-shot politician."

Marco grabbed for her hands and they began a rolling scuffle that quickly turned into something very different. Eventually they did get into a deep sleep, with bodies locked together and smiles on their faces.

*   *   *

The party faithful had gathered for their election night celebration in the back room of McGurk's Pub. Marco's campaign workers had joined those of Nathan Shapiro's aldermanic campaign. Arthur Denton had made the arrangements, and was clearly - though informally - presiding over the gathering. His wife, Karen, stayed close to his side, regularly shaking the ice in the cocktail glass in her hand. It was common knowledge that Denton was prepping her to run for state rep. Marco liked her.

Drinking, schmoozing, and munching on appetizers had been going on for hours as they anxiously waited for election results to come in. Several t.v.'s on the walls had been broadcasting the latest updates. Unfortunately, the mood had been trending steadily downward, along with the returns.

Everyone seemed to be in shock as they struggled to come to terms with what looked to be a sure victory for Ronald Reagan in the presidential race. Just as bad, if not worse, it looked like Reagan's victory would also help to propel Republican Skip Bale to a win over Joe Teasdale for governor.

Local returns were coming in more slowly, as usual. However, as poll workers came into the gathering, and phone calls steadily arrived, the party had a pretty accurate idea of where things stood long before the television announcers did. It looked like Shapiro might squeek out a victory in the aldermanic race, but Marco was clearly behind in his own run for ward committeeman.

"I can't believe that Missouri voters were dumb enough to elect that bozo as governor again," said one of the garment workers to Marco. "They were smart enough to turn him out of office after the fiasco of his first term."

"I'm afraid we just didn't get enough of our people out to vote this time," he replied. "People were just not fired up enough to come out for Carter. That's why I thought we would have had a better chance with Kennedy."

Marco was getting tired of having the same conversations over and over again, sometimes with the same people.

Denton came over and put an arm around Marco's shoulder. "Congratulations, Marco," he said. "You ran a great campaign, especially for a first timer."

"The results sure don't look like it," he said.

"Oh, I beg to differ with you," said Denton. "You went up against a guy who had virtual 100% name recognition, a guy who's been doing favors for people in the ward for almost 20 years, and you made him run for his life. Looks like you'll come in with around 30% of the vote. That's quite an achievement."

"Well, thank you, but it doesn't feel like it."

"Believe me, Marco it was. Look what you accomplished. How many voters did you talk to?"

"Oh, I don't know. I knocked on every registered Democrat's door at least once. My team also got to a lot of them. Then we went a couple of rounds with phone calls."

"That's really great!" said Denton. "You really don't realize how big that was, but it was, believe me."

"I'm not sure how," Marco answered.

"Look," said Denton. "First of all, you got a lot of people to the polls who probably wouldn't have made it. And now those folks know who you are. They know you're somebody who cares a lot and is willing to work hard for them. That's something you can build on. Secondly, you undoubtedly helped Shapiro win his race for alderman. Since your campaigns were linked, the people you did get out would have more likely voted for Nate. Third, you helped drum up more interest in voting by our people. We could have lost even bigger than we have tonight, believe me. This has turned out to be one of these wave elections, unfortunately, and I'm afraid we Democrats are going to have it rough for awhile. But we ain't going to quit, that's for sure. Fourth, you forced Mulvihill to finally get off his ass and get to work for a change. That guy has just been coasting so long he almost stood still, and it's been bad for the party. But he had his hands full this time, and he knows it. Hopefully he'll start to actually do his job again.

"And one more thing, Marco. You're just getting started. Next time you won't be starting from scratch. You've got a base to work from in the ward, and a lot of people have been taking notice. — party people, donors. We're looking for big things from you in the future Marco."

"Well, thanks, Art. But I don't know if there'll be a next time. All this can so easily suck up all of your time, and I've got a growing business to run. My brother has really been on my case lately, and I'm not sure that I blame him."

"I hear you, Marco. I know what it's like, believe me. But tonight's not the time to make any decisions. Let's get together in a few weeks, when we can think about it more clearly. Tonight I just want to shake your hand and drink a toast in your honor. You ran a great campaign."

* * *

Late the next morning, Marco was eating a big breakfast at the local IHOP with his cousin, Fran. "Marsha isn't joining us this morning?" she asked.

"Afraid not," he answered. "She had to be back at work. Don't think she got more than a couple of hours sleep. I didn't really get any. Just dozed a little, here and there."

"So how do you feel about your first foray into politics? I thought you did great. I was really proud to be working with you, Marco."

"Thanks a lot. I appreciate it. Art Denton tried to perk me up last night too. I don't know. Maybe I'll feel better about it after awhile. Right now I'm just really tired. And disappointed. But I really appreciate your help. I wouldn't have had a clue without your organization skills."

"Oh yes, you would have," she said. "This was your campaign all the way. I just helped to smooth things out a little to help you get started."

"More than a little," he said. "You have no idea."

"Well, next time you want to go again, I'm in. I really meant the things I said to your team, Marco. I think you could go someplace in politics and really make a difference."

"Thanks for saying it, but I don't know. I just don't know."

"Understood," she said. "I don't blame you. Like I've said so many times, real change is hard. It doesn't come quick, and it doesn't come easy. At least a dozen times a week I look at myself in the mirror, and I ask myself, 'What are you doing, Frances? Why don't you use your education to get into something that will pay you a real salary?'" She shook her head and laughed. "But you know, I really like shaking things up a little, and I really like thinking that maybe the things I do make a little bit of a difference, and I really love the weird, kooky people I work with. So . . . " (she shrugged), "I keep doing it. Maybe I'm just too lazy to change. But what about you, Marco? What motivated you to put so much of yourself into this campaign, when you were already up to your ears in your business start-up?"

Marco finished chewing and swallowing a large bite of sausage and pancake, washed it down with a swig of coffee, and looked across the table at his cousin before finally answering. "I have been wondering that myself for some time now. My wonderful wife, who has supported me thru all of this, has frequently asked me if I'm sure of what I'm doing. And my brother and business partner has been on my case about it to the point that we can hardly speak to each other these days. So I ask myself too, why? Wouldn't my life be a lot easier if I just did my job and went home to my wife? And it would be easier. It would."

"So? Any answers?"

"Maybe," he said. "You know, ever since I got out of the service, I've been kind of obsessed with learning about our family history, my father's struggles, that kind of thing."

"I'm well aware of that," she said. "If you remember, I've even taken part in some if it."

"Right," he nodded. "And it seems to me that all of it has been about more than just survival. It's been about trying to make a life, a community, a world that's a little better for everybody. Like our grandparents coming here from Italy, and struggling with building something here, and finding community, and I don't know, helping your neighbors. Like I said, maybe making the world a little bit better place for everybody. As corny as that sounds."

He looked down at his plate, picked up another mouthful, and paused just before he put it in his mouth to look across at his cousin. "But it seems like such a struggle. You know, I could see myself staying very involved. I could eventually win an election or two. But then you're in a system where it's hard to accomplish much more than keep getting elected. What's the point? What keeps you going, Fran?"

She looked off in the distance for a moment, took a deep breath, and turned back to Marco. "I don't know if I can really pin it down that clearly, but this is what occurs to me. As you know, my folks — against my will — sent me to that Catholic high school. At least it was co-ed, thank God. But we had to take a religion class every year. I was not thrilled. I always tried to pick the class that sounded the least religious of the religion classes. So my senior year I took this course called social ethics. It was taught by this good looking young priest who everybody called Father Rich. He was all into the radical social action priests, like the Berrigan brothers. You've heard of them, haven't you, Marco?"

"I think so. Weren't they involved in the anti-war movement?"

"Anti-war, anti-nuclear bombs, civil rights, you name it. They're still around, by the way. Anyhow, one of the books Fa. Rich had us read was by this Protestant theologian named Niebuhr, who was also an activist. And one of the things he wrote has always stuck with me. He said — and I'm just approximating here, I don't know how accurate this is, it's just the way I remember it — he said something like this, 'Nothing that is worth doing can be achieved in a lifetime; therefore we must be saved by hope. None of our plans and strategies ever make perfect sense in the situation we are in; therefore we must be saved by faith. And nothing important can be accomplished alone; therefore we must be saved by love.' Something like that. Anyhow, that has always stuck with me. It helps me to go easy on myself, and hopefully on other people. It helps me keep my sense of humor about things, and appreciate the little victories. And to stay hopeful, even when a step forward is inevitably followed by two steps back. I don't know if that's helpful, Marco, but it's all I've got."

*   *   *

Finally arriving at his deli around two in the afternoon, Marco paused across the street to look up at the sign above the door,

BOB & MARCO'S DELI
Affairs to Remember Catering

It looked like there was a pretty good lunch crowd still there, and a few more people went in as several left. He knew that he had a

good crew working today. They were good at what they were doing and would be handling things fine without him. But he also
knew that as soon as he walked in the door, his brother would be
on his case, complaining about how Marco had not been holding
up his end of the business, and probably saying how glad he was
that Marco had lost the election so that he could get back to his
real job.

Marco took a deep breath and stood a moment longer. Faith,
hope, and love, he thought. Maybe that's it after all. Then he
looked both ways on the street, walked across, and went back to
work.

AFTERWARD

As my subtitle suggests, this novel was inspired by actual events, both in the life of the author and friends. The events occurring in 1919 and 1920 have been presented essentially as reported in the Chicago Tribune at that time. Sergeant Byrne and Father Bastioni (with name shortened) were real people, as was St. Philip Benizi Church. St. Matthew's Methodist is still on the corner of Oak and Orleans, though in a newer building. Richard J. Daley, the legendary long-time mayor of Chicago, was actually president of the Hamburg Athletic Club at the time of the 1919 race riots. Many witnesses claimed that the club was a major instigator of the awful events. Trinity College is fictional, though several real institutions bear that name. Most other names in the novel are the author's fabrications, including that of Marco Russo.

The author wishes to express deep thanks and gratitude to several people who shared ideas and suggestions, especially Mark Cutelli, Ed Zeidman, Susan Asher, and of course the two most important people in his life, Kendra and Eric.

Listen to Jerry Lee Lewis sing

"Looking for a City":

youtube.com/watch?v=VMHSxuNZHVWQ

RUSSO FAMILY
(Major characters in bold print)

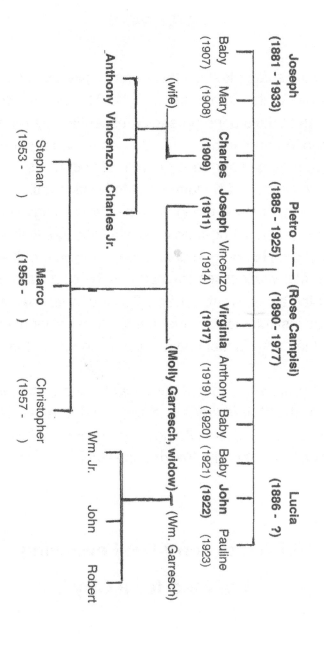

Joseph
(1881 - 1933)

Pietro — — — (Rose Campisi)
(1885 - 1925)   **(1890 - 1977)**

Lucia
(1886 - ?)

Baby (1907)

Mary (1908)

Charles (1909)

Joseph (1911)

Vincenzo (1914)

Virginia (1917)

Anthony (1919)

Baby (1920)

Baby (1921)

John (1922)

Pauline (1923)

(wife)

Anthony Vincenzo.   Charles Jr.

Stephan (1953 -   )

Marco **(1955 -   )**

Christopher (1957 -   )

(Molly Garresch, widow)   (Wm. Garresch)

Wm. Jr.

John

Robert

Made in the USA
Monee, IL
09 August 2023

40755226R00207